"THIS IS MUTINY!

I ran toward the camp. Up ahead I heard musket shots. As I ran, I almost stumbled over a body on the ground moaning, "Help me, help me."

He grabbed the hem of my petticoat, and as I peered down at him, I could see he'd been shot. I could smell the blood pouring down his face. And in that instant, while I pondered whether to run on and leave him or stay and assist, he loosed his grip, and his arm fell to the ground. He was dead.

I ran on. I leaped forward, wanting the darkness to swallow me up. But the night was lit by the belching musket fire, like fireflies all around. I beat my way through bushes and past tree branches, following the familiar path I'd taken to camp so many times.

My heart was a burning thing inside my chest. My breath came in spurts of pain. And then the path fell away, and I stopped and looked around.

I was in the middle of everything.

A RIDE
INTO
MORNING

The Story of Tempe Wick

ANN RINALDI

Gulliver Books • Harcourt, Inc.

ORLANDO   AUSTIN   NEW YORK
SAN DIEGO   TORONTO   LONDON

Requests for permission to make copies of any part of
the work should be mailed to the following address:
Permissions Department, Harcourt, Inc.,
6277 Sea Harbor Drive, Orlando, Florida 32887-6777.

www.HarcourtBooks.com

First Gulliver Books paperback edition 1995
Gulliver Books is a trademark of Harcourt, Inc., registered in
the United States of America and/or other jurisdictions.

Library of Congress Cataloging-in-Publication Data
Rinaldi, Ann.
A ride into morning: the story of Tempe Wick/Ann Rinaldi.
p. cm.
Originally published: San Diego: Harcourt Brace, 1991.
Summary: When unrest spreads at the Revolutionary War
camp in Morristown, New Jersey, under the command of
General Anthony Wayne, a young woman cleverly hides her
horse from the mutinous soldiers who have need of it.
1. United States—History—Revolution, 1775–1783—Juvenile
fiction. 2. Wayne, Anthony, 1745–1796—Juvenile fiction.
[1. United States—History—Revolution, 1775–1783—Fiction.
2. New Jersey—History—Revolution, 1775–1783—Fiction.
2. Wayne, Anthony, 1745–1796—Fiction.] I. Title.
PZ7.R459Ri 2003
[Fic]—dc21 2002027502
ISBN 0-15-204683-6

Text set in New Baskerville

Designed by Martha Roach
Printed in the United States of America
C E G H F D B

To Joanna,
who deserves the title of friend
as well as agent.
And without whose urging
I would not have written this.

Acknowledgments

This book could not have been written without the support and encouragement of many good people.

For their constant and invaluable advice and assistance, I wish to thank the staff of Morristown National Historical Park in New Jersey, most especially James Kochen, supervisory curator, and Eric Olsen, Michael Puzio, Mark Gieser, and Joe Craig, from the division of interpretation.

Appreciation goes to Joseph Kleiner of the Academy Street branch of the Trenton Public Library, Trenton, New Jersey, for lending me a copy of Carl Van Doren's *Mutiny in January* when no other library would.

Although she thought she had not given me information enough to earn her credit, Joanne J. Brooks of the Suffolk County Historical Society in Riverhead, New York, helped me more than she realized. The few papers she sent on the Cooper family proved extremely enlightening.

Claire Kissil, reference librarian at the Local History and Genealogy Department of The Joint Free Public Library of Morristown and Morris Township, also deserves my gratitude for her patience in directing me to the books and papers I needed to further track down the Cooper family

I am eternally appreciative for the work done by the men and women who wrote the factual books I referred to, as well as to those who assembled and documented the evidence I needed. These historical scholars, as well as the museum curators and librarians who keep such material over the years, never get the credit they so richly deserve.

No historical novel of mine could have been written, of course, had not my son, Ron, "turned me on" to history in the first place, years ago. I owe Ron a special debt for that. As well as for allowing me free use of his extensive library on American history and U.S. military history. And for always being able to answer my questions.

My husband, Ron, deserves thanks for putting up with me while I did the writing, which was done evenings and weekends. The same goes for my daughter, Marcella. Although she deserves a different kind of thank-you—for bringing over a new grandson to visit and play with, so I was refreshed and given new perspective.

Credit for the idea for this book goes deservedly to Bonnie Ingber of the Children's Book Division at Harcourt Brace & Company. Having grown up in Basking Ridge, Bonnie, too, apparently heard of the myth of Tempe Wick and wanted such a book for Harcourt Brace's Great Episodes series. I am appreciative also to Karen Grove, my editor at Harcourt Brace, for her unswerving enthusiasm that greeted every mailing of chapters to California.

Finally, although I never really thanked her in person, my eternal gratitude goes to Joanna Cole, my agent. I never would have undertaken the writing of this manuscript had she not urged me to do so. Every week, when the two chapters I had written and sent were received by her, she would call and highlight something wonderful I had done. A writer could ask for no better agent or friend.

Ann Rinaldi
May 23, 1990

1

Toward four in the afternoon, on the twenty-sixth of December to be exact, I had an appointment to meet my friends David Hamilton Morris and Jeremiah Levering in the orchard, near the magazine.

The magazine is where the army, which is camped all around this farm, keeps its ammunition and six fieldpieces. Although the day was bright and mild, as sometimes happens in the colony of New Jersey in midwinter, I knew they'd be cold, waiting for me. And hungry. They were always hungry, and I'd promised to bring food.

In my blue-and-white striped haversack, I had two chicken legs wrapped in napkins, this morning's bread generously spread with freshly churned butter, and two large pieces of gingerbread.

I'd just reached for my cloak, which was hanging on a wall peg, when my cousin Tempe came into the room.

"And where do you think *you're* going?" she said.

Her presence was startling to me. And disturbing. I never can look at her in that bright red cloak she wears without seeing anew how pretty she is. Her rich dark hair tumbled all about her shoulders. There was an energy about her that always diminished my own. And I knew, without hearing the words, that she was going to stop me.

"Out," I said. "I'm going out."

"Have you finished your chores?"

"Yes." I had my cloak on and was fastening it in front. "I swept the kitchen, put clean linen on Aunt Mary's bed, and gave her pottage and sweet-potato biscuits for her noon meal. She's napping now. But first I read to her before she fell asleep."

"Well, you can't leave now. Someone's got to stay with her. And you know this is my time of day to ride Colonel."

But my friends are waiting for me, I wanted to say. *Oh, the injustice of it! They're hungry, and I promised I'd be there.* But I didn't say it. For it would only make things worse than they are between us. And things are not good. The fault is mine, I am sure of it. For I failed with my own family, was sent away, and now it is not working out here either. And I like it here. I do not want to be sent packing again.

"You promised I could go out after I finished

my chores," I said. I'm not a ninny. I'm not wishy-washy. It isn't in me to be that way, so I looked her right in the eyes and reminded her of her promise.

"Well, I didn't know you'd be finished so late. I'm sorry, but you'll just have to wait. This is the time I ride Colonel every day. I told you how he waits for me. He knows the time."

"He's only a horse. He doesn't know time," I said. I know I shouldn't have said it. She's daft over Colonel. He is white and clearly one of the most beautiful horses I have ever beheld. Seeing him reminds one that there is still a God, even though we are in the middle of this dismal war. Watching Tempe ride him, in that red cloak, makes one remember poetry.

"Only a horse, is he?" She threw her gloves down on the kitchen table. "I'll remember that the next time you beg me to ride him, Mary Cooper!"

"I'm sorry, Tempe. I didn't mean . . ."

"You never do. But you always manage to provoke me, don't you?"

I offered no excuse, for there was nothing that would mend the moment.

"It wasn't my intention to provoke."

"What was it your intention to do then?"

I shook my head dismally and sighed. "I have a headache."

3

She picked up her gloves and came toward me, searching my face with her eyes. "It's my mama, isn't it? Was she asking for my father again?"

Her father, my Uncle Henry, died a few days ago of the pleurisy. We buried him yesterday, down to Mendham at the Presbyterian Church. Aunt Mary doesn't comprehend yet that the man she married back in 1735, the man she birthed five children for, is gone.

"She talked about him a lot," I said.

"What did she say?"

"She speaks as if he's out in the orchard and will be in for supper, driving his team and the wagon with Oliver Cromwell lollygagging along."

Oliver Cromwell is the dog.

"She's been under a spell since he died. Even at the funeral she couldn't accept it. Well"— Tempe sighed and picked up her riding crop— "perhaps it's God's mercy she doesn't realize he's gone yet. I don't know how she'll bear it when she finds out."

She brushed by me, going toward the door. "Take off your cloak. I'll be back in less than an hour. Then you can go out."

"I think you ought to tell her he's dead, Tempe. I think you ought to say it plain to her."

I held my breath, waiting. She stopped at the door, her hand on the latch.

"You were not sent here to tell me what to do, Mary Cooper," she said. "You were sent here, a fortnight ago, to help me with my parents."

"Every day that goes by with her expecting Uncle Henry to come through that door will only make it worse, Tempe."

"You were also sent here," she said coldly, "because you provoked your own family so, with your Patriot leanings, that they just wanted you out of the way. Must I remind you of that?"

"No. But this is a Patriot household. My leanings shouldn't provoke anyone here."

"Your tongue does. So learn to hold it, Mary Cooper."

"You told her *Henry* is dead. So why not tell her about your father, too?"

Her eyes flashed with anger. It seems to come and go like the winter sun these days. She took a step toward me. "I never told her Henry was dead."

"Yes you did. I heard you. And he isn't. You told her James is dead. And you don't know if *he* is. Yet you allow her to babble about your father returning from the orchard. What's the sense of that?"

She fidgeted with her gloves. "The sense of

5

anything is where I find it these days. We haven't heard from James in years. Why keep her hopes alive about him? As for Henry, he might as well be dead." Her face was all tight when she spoke of her older brothers. And not pretty the way it used to be before the war, before there was an army camped on her father's farm, "Poorly clothed, badly fed, and worse paid," as General Wayne puts it. But I dare not quote the dashing general. For Tempe hates him.

"Now you listen to me, Mary Cooper, and you listen good," she said. "I'll not have you talking to my mama about either James or Henry. And the less mention there is of my father right now, the better she'll be."

"She wants to speak of them, Tempe."

"Well, change the subject. Get her talking of other things. Ask her about the time she pulled your father out of the well when she was a girl living on Long Island. She saved his life."

"She told me that story six times already."

"Well ask her to tell it again. If she wakes before I come back, talk about *anything* but James and Henry and my father!" She strode to the door.

"What if Ebenezer Drake comes by?"

"He's her old friend. Let him in. Tell him the hired man he sent around quit. And while there's nothing to be done now but care for the

6

animals and keep the wood stacked, I still need someone. Ask him if he can get that fellow who helps out at the Guerins.' "

"Suppose Ebenezer Drake tells her he's seen Henry in the area?"

She had the door half-open. Now she slapped the riding crop against her booted foot. "Ebenezer Drake will not tell her such a thing! I've asked him not to. And if you, Mary Cooper, tell her Henry is running around out there, I'll box your ears first, then ship you back to your family. If I have to take you to Elizabeth Point and put you on a British ship myself!"

Her voice crackled like the hiss of the fire in the hearth. Her blue eyes were as cold as the ice that had dripped, like tears for us all, from the windows of this house before the thaw. I said no more. For the last place I want to go right now is back to my family. They are not to be borne. With the exception of my brother Abraham, my family is evil. It has nothing to do with their being Tories. Most of Long Island is Tory, just like half the Jerseys. No, being Tory is only a conveyance for my family's evil. I believe they would enter into deals with the devil himself if it meant they could accumulate more money.

Not Abraham, no, he's off with another part of the Continental Army, and the only Patriot besides me in the family.

No, I won't go back there. And Tempe knows how I feel. She holds the threat over me like a sword, though. Oh, if she sends me back, I'll jump that British ship and run off to find Abraham. He's in New Windsor, up in the colony of New York, with Washington. I'll ask General Wayne how to get there when he comes to supper tonight.

"You're in a fine fettle today," I called after her bravely as she went out the door. "I feel sorry for General Wayne tonight. All his courtly manners will turn to ashes with you."

She tossed her head. "If any women or children from camp come round begging, you're not to give them any of our supper."

"What shall I give them, then?"

"A bit of those sweet-potato muffins and a slice or two of bacon. Don't worry your head about General Wayne. If war hasn't already killed his courtly manners, I'll not be able to either."

Then she was gone. For the better part of an hour no one came to the door, not even Ebenezer Drake. That meant there'd be no hired hand sent around today, and I'd have to help Tempe feed the animals again tonight.

I had water boiling for tea when Tempe returned. She was grateful for the tea. She almost smiled at me, but then she checked herself. Her face was flushed from her ride and her hair completely undone by the exertion. I am grateful to Colonel, since her daily rides are the only things that keep her sweet-tempered. If that is how one can describe those sudden sunbursts of decency in her disposition.

"Tea." That was all she said. She warmed her hands on her cup as she sat on a stool in front of the hearth. "Come sit and have tea with me, Mary."

I had hoped now to be permitted to leave. I had started to reach for my cloak. Would my friends David and Jeremiah still be waiting for me? Did they think I wasn't coming? I was fairly jumping with impatience to be on my way. She patted a nearby stool. "Come, I must needs chat a while."

Oh, she must needs chat *now*. It was all fine and dandy for her to lash out at me whenever she chose, but when she wanted me at her beck and call, I was to be there! I felt a retort come to my lips but bit it back.

"Just a few minutes," she said.

A few minutes would pacify her. I took tea and sat.

"This is British tea," she said immediately.

Yes, it was. And a far cry, too, from that pathetic mixture of sassafras, sage, and strawberries the Patriots have been brewing in this

9

colony. "It was sent over by Doctor Leddell," I told her.

She scowled at the name, for which I cannot fault her. Leddell is married to her older sister, Phoebe. Poor Phoebe lost two children already, which I suppose he cannot be blamed for. They have little Henry, who is five, and two-year-old Tempe. And now Phoebe is with child again.

But Leddell can be faulted for plenty else, I hear. They have a farm nearby, and we constantly hear gossip about his running afoul of the law. He had an unauthorized mint in his house for a while before the authorities got wind of it. And Tempe suspects he is importing rum without a license.

"I ponder on if he's got my brother Henry running British tea in for him now as well," she said.

"I thought we weren't supposed to talk of Henry."

"Don't sass me, Mary, I mean it. Can't you ever be sweet-tempered?"

She was one to ask such a question! "You don't know that Henry is running rum."

"He'll take part in any madness Leddell suggests. He's a plague to us and always was. Sometimes I wish he'd just go off to fight Indians in the wilderness like James."

James, if he is alive at all, is forty now to

Henry's forty-four. Her sister Mary, who is married to Doctor Blachley, indeed seems to be the only sane one amongst my Jersey cousins. I like Phoebe, but she seems driven out of her senses by Leddell sometimes.

"I shouldn't drink this tea if it's contraband run in by Henry," Tempe said.

"It was sent by Phoebe for Aunt Mary. I'm sure even General Wayne wouldn't consider you unpatriotic for drinking it."

She sniffed. "I don't care a shilling for what the gallant Wayne says. I've had my fill of this war, Mary. Of that miserable army camped out there, of their wretched women coming to our door begging for scraps of food, and of their wretched children. But I do care that Henry's back in the area and involved in one of Leddell's lunatic schemes."

I fidgeted on the stool. "I must needs leave, Tempe," I said.

"And why? Are you meeting someone out there?"

"I need some fresh air."

"You can't spare a moment to talk with me?"

All right, I'd talk. "You're a Patriot as much as I am," I said. "Your whole family is Patriot. Your father allowed Washington's army to camp on his land for two winters now."

"Don't remind me of last winter," she said.

"It was horrible. It was the most bitter winter I recollect in years. There was not one day in January that the thermometer went above freezing. Snowfall came upon snowfall. And we had to share this house with General St. Clair. He was genteel enough, but I never liked him. The soldiers in camp were doing nothing but coughing their lungs out and dying. Those who survived told me it was worse than the winter at Valley Forge."

I said nothing, sensing her need to talk.

"I couldn't stop my father from giving away our food. He couldn't bear seeing the starvation, the condition of the soldiers. It wore him down. It broke his heart. I think that finally killed him as much as the pleurisy. I'm a Patriot, you say? You're an incurable romantic, Mary. My father let the army camp here so they could clear his land."

"Did he take payment for the land?"

"No."

"My father would have. Then he'd charge the army rent for the huts."

"I live in fear that Henry will be caught rum-running," she confided. "And bring disgrace upon us. It would break Mama's heart."

"Henry slips in and out of camp like a fox." Too late I realized what I'd said. She looked up quickly.

"You've been in camp? I've *told* you to stay away from there!"

I covered my tracks. "It's what I've heard from David Hamilton Morris of the 3rd Regiment and his friend Jeremiah Levering."

"Are you lying to me? If I find out you are . . ."

"No, Tempe." I was, of course.

"Your friends are children," she said disdainfully.

She was right. David has been in the army for a year now, though he's only twelve, two years younger than I. His widowed mother, who lives near here, put him in under the charge of Captain James Crystie. Which should give a body some idea of the times we're living in.

Jeremiah is fifteen. He's been in the artillery for three years. I was walking in camp with them one day when they pointed out Henry to me. Although Henry is of an age when he should be seeing to his widowed mother and younger sister, he appeared as if he couldn't even see to himself, poor soul. The look of him is gentle enough. He reminds me of a big old dog. His clothes beggar all description, which doesn't make him any different from most of the soldiers. The day I saw him he was stuffing shillings from the soldiers into his haversack.

"When did they see Henry in camp?" Tempe demanded.

"On the tenth of the month."

"What say they of him?"

"That he is gentle and decent, and they welcome him and any rum or tobacco he sells. And he doesn't cheat them. The troops had no spiritous liquor for sixty days, except half a gill of rum per man two weeks before Henry came."

"Better they should have none."

"General Wayne says rum is an article as necessary in the eye of a soldier as provisions or clothing."

"Wayne *would* say such a thing. He's a roué. That's what Washington calls him."

My face flamed. For I was smitten with Wayne and she knew it. Ever since the first day I'd seen him in camp, with his dark, snapping eyes, his tall, muscular build, his energy, the way he is so alive and friendly yet takes no sass, he has had my heart.

"Why do you talk so of Wayne? Why do you dislike him?"

"I have my reasons."

I got up. It was all well and good for me to sit and chat with her, but I saw no reason to let her run down Wayne in my presence. "I know you blame him for the wretched condition of the Pennsylvania Line. They and their women

and children suffer every privation But Wayne
has been writing all month to Philadelphia, begging for provisions. The men like him. They
hated General St. Clair. What does he care for
the sufferings of the men? He's on leave in Philadelphia!"

"Those are not my reasons for disliking
Wayne."

I took my cloak from the peg and put it on.
"I'm leaving now," I told her.

"I'd better not hear that you've been traipsing
through camp with those friends of yours."

I said nothing.

"We sup at six-thirty. General Wayne is coming, as you know. I'd advise you to rein in your
adulation and not languish over him at the table.
It's unseemly behavior for one your age. He's a
married man, old enough to be your father, and
he has a sweetheart, in case you haven't heard
about the lovely Mary Vining."

Oh, the cruelty! Tears came to my eyes. I
could not look at her. I can take her sharp
tongue and her bitter remarks. Lord knows, I
took enough from my own family. But I cannot
take the realization that things are not working
between us.

For I came here remembering a different
Tempe. Growing up, she was always my favorite girl cousin. She has twenty-two years to my

fourteen, is tall where I am dumpy, well-formed where I am not, wise where I am a fool, and saucy where I am tongue-tied. Always, I wanted nothing more than to be like her, to be as sophisticated as she is, to toss off men's admiring glances with disdain, to keep my own good counsel instead of babbling like an idiot as I tend to do.

But the war has changed her. I found that out soon after I got here. She is no longer the sweet, generous Tempe I recollect.

"Did you hear me?" she asked.

"I heard."

"What's wrong with you?"

"You're not a nice person anymore, Tempe Wick."

"This war makes me vile."

"Well, you needn't make me suffer for it."

"I'm only trying to help. You'll heed my advice about simpering over Wayne, if you know what's good for you. I'm only trying to keep you from making a fool of yourself."

"Why did you invite him for supper if you hate him so?"

"He cheers Mama. She says he reminds her of my father when he was that age. Why do you stay here if you think me so unpleasant?"

I turned at the door to face her. "Because

my family sent me. They've had enough of what they call my Patriot nonsense. When I was staying with my brother Nathan, after I disgraced Mother and Father by taking part in ceremonies at a Liberty Pole last summer, I embarrassed Nathan in front of his rich Tory friends. I told him he was wrong for doing business with Tories."

"He's a merchant. It's what merchants do."

"Not in wartime."

"More so in wartime."

"I can't help it. I despise their Tory sympathies. Even my brother Samuel, who is studying for the ministry at Yale, has them. He says he takes no sides in this fight we find ourselves in. But to me, taking no sides is an evil in itself."

"The biggest lesson we must learn in this life, Mary, is compromise."

"Not me. I won't. Not ever. That's all my family does. My sister Martha is so busy with her marriage and social life, she can't bother with any leanings. Henry's only fifteen, but being apprenticed to Nathan, he's anxious to please. And Elizabeth is a prig already at seven. Only Abraham understands me, and he's with the army up north."

"At your age, all young girls feel the way you do about their families," she said knowingly.

"My father is too busy counting his earnings to know I exist! There are times I wish your mama hadn't pulled him out of that well!"

Tempe got up and set her teacup down on the table. "Since you feel so strongly about not going home, I'd advise you then to heed my words. And mind when I speak. I'm responsible for you now that my father is dead and Mama's head is addled. Your behavior, so far, has not recommended you. I happen to know you've been in camp. You've been seen there by certain people. Which means you've lied to me. I'll not tolerate lies, Mary. I have enough to do keeping this place going and worrying over Mama without you disgracing yourself and adding to my woes."

Her face was very white and set. I trembled at her words.

"Keep out of camp. I mean it. There are enough loose women in camp."

Tears tumbled from my eyes. "I'm *not* a loose woman! I have no intention of being one!"

Her voice softened. "I never said that. But this is a military encampment. Behavior can be misconstrued. I must think of that. I'll not have you running wild, Mary. If you do, I'll ship you home, I swear it."

I wiped the tears from my face hastily. In my haversack was the chicken and bread and gingerbread for my friends, who were probably still waiting for me. I would not abandon them, I would not!

"We understand each other better now, I hope." Her voice was smooth, brooking no argument.

"We understand each other perfectly, yes," I said. Then I opened the door and went out into the winter afternoon.

2

Oliver Cromwell aroused himself from a patch of sunlight outside the door and thumped his tail at me. I smiled because his appearance alone invites smiles. He has lots of black hair that grows at cross purposes on his face, and you cannot see his eyes. If it weren't for the thumping tail, you wouldn't be able to tell which end is which.

The first thing he did was sniff at the food in my haversack. I picked up a stick and threw it to distract him. Just in case Tempe was watching out the window. I couldn't have her suspect I had food, or she'd know I was meeting my friends.

"Come along, Oliver, good boy." He followed, for we were staunch companions. Since I'd come to stay here, we'd had many a fine adventure together, exploring the Wick farm. He slept at the foot of my bed at night, a practice Tempe did her best to discourage. But when I reminded her that Caesar and Cleopatra, her two lazy cats, slept at the foot of hers, she ran out of argument. And she did confess that last winter when General St. Clair occupied one room of the house, Oliver slept at the foot of his bed. I'll wager she never scolded the general for it.

We headed through the orchard toward the magazine. It was guarded by sentries, but they were accustomed to seeing me. They waved. But my friends were nowhere in sight. They'd gotten tired of waiting, and I couldn't blame them. I hurried to Foot Hill Road and came into camp by Colonel Proctor's artillery. I walked on the snow-encrusted road with my head down, for to look around invited trouble. There were so many huts, so many soldiers, so much activity all around, with women stringing clothing and airing bedding and throwing out slops, and children running in all directions.

In November past, Washington had divided the army for winter quarters. He assigned only the "bad clothed men of Pennsylvania" to Morristown. They came here, David and Jeremiah had told me, on the twenty-ninth of November and pitched their tents in the woods. They found many of the huts from last year's encampment demolished and in early December started repairing what they could and building new ones.

I heard that General Wayne had been right out there working with them, in the cold.

Last year General Washington hadn't allowed women in the camp. But there are about a hundred women and children this year. They are allowed half rations. Such as the rations are these days. The men have brought the women because they have no other homes for their families. And General Washington knows they will desert if their families are not provided for. David and Jeremiah say the women are a plague, always throwing soapsuds or refuse on the parade. They must be reminded to use the necessary houses, too. My friends say the officers will tolerate no messes in camp.

The December days are short, and this time of evening smoke rises from the huts' chimneys as the women do their best to assemble an evening meal out of scant provisions. Which is why I hurried along. They know me as Tempe Wick's cousin, and the women send their little ones to beg for food. The faces of the children are pinched and drawn. They are dressed in every castoff one could conjure. Many of them have deep, hacking coughs.

It distresses me to see them. When I first came here, I was giving away all Tempe's food when they came to our door. She had to stop me. There is no end to it, she says. And if I encourage them, we'll all soon starve.

Far up ahead on the road, I saw my two friends approaching. Neither one carries a musket. The soldiers say Jeremiah Levering is too small to even beat the drum or blow the fife. He was a waif they picked up and enlisted so they could feed and clothe him. David Hamilton Morris, though younger, is sturdier in build.

We became friends the very day I came here. They were at Tempe's door, asking to do chores for food, but she suspects it was just to meet me, since they'd heard a girl near their age was visiting. She objected from the first, saying they were not a good influence and insisting I don't run about with them but that we visit only when they come to the house. Which makes no sense whatsoever, because she discourages them from coming around. So I sneak out to see them.

They give me information about the army. I have learned so much since I've been here! For my mind has been seized by the excitement of this war from the very beginning.

Freedom. The word is so simple and direct. It is as stark and bold as the clean brass and wood lines of the soldiers' muskets. And as appealing as the blue-and-buff uniform of General Wayne himself.

I decided, a long time ago, that there must be something dreadfully ailing in me that makes me harken so to the sound of the word. But if it's ailing in me, it's ailing in a lot of others, too. Perhaps it's because my family suffocates me so.

They tried to suffocate the spirit of my brother Abraham, also. Abraham always considered himself the black sheep until the war came. Then he found a kindred feeling in the sentiments of the Patriots, the same as I.

Our family laughed at us and called the American army rabid dogs in need of shooting. I envy Abraham, old enough to go off with a musket and fight. As a girl, there is little enough I can do except make friends with Jeremiah and David, smuggle some food to them, and try to keep up with what's going on with the inner workings of the army.

I'm here, at least, in the middle of everything. And who knows, before this war is over, perhaps I will be called on to do something.

In bed at night I ponder on it, when I am not crying for the hungry and cold soldiers. What keeps them here? Tempe tells me that last winter they were five or six days without bread and meat. At one time, she says, the soldiers ate every kind of horse food but hay.

Last year they stayed for Washington. Do they stay now for Wayne? Or for something that goes beyond any man and serves some hunger inside them that no bread or meat will satisfy?

Yes, that must be it. They, too, are ailing for something. The British have treated them like my family treats me. And they do not wish to be treated like children forever. They wish to act and think for themselves.

"What did you bring us, Mary?" David asked as they got closer.

"Hush." Jeremiah poked him.

I opened my haversack. I thought David's eyes would pop.

"Chicken!" he said.

But Jeremiah placed a restraining arm on his friend. "Not here." Being older, he is more cautious. "Let's go into the orchard."

We returned to where we were supposed to meet, to a spot near the magazine.

"We waited and waited," Jeremiah said. "Then we pondered that Tempe wasn't going to allow you out. So we left."

I explained to them what happened. They know Tempe doesn't like them. They don't hold it against her, however. They are beyond childish grudges. The army has made them old beyond their years.

After we sat down, I gave them a few moments to fill their stomachs before plying them with questions. Jeremiah remembered to ask about Uncle Henry's funeral.

"Did Tempe's brother Henry show up?" David asked.

"I don't think he knows his father died," I said.

"He knows," David advised.

"Well, thank heaven he didn't come to the church. Tempe had enough to occupy her mind."

"She'll have more to occupy it with when Henry appears at the house," Jeremiah said. "He said he wants to find out what his father left him in the will."

"I didn't think Henry had the presence of mind to know about a will," I said.

"When it comes to money," Jeremiah put in, "you'd be surprised at the presence of mind even a lunatic can have."

"I think the will is just an excuse," David said. "I think Henry really wants to see his mama."

"Tempe won't let him near the house," I told them. "She doesn't want anything to do with Henry. And she'll never let him see Aunt Mary."

"Do you think that's fair?" Jeremiah asked.

"No. But Tempe is unfair about a lot of things these days. The war has changed her. She's not the same Tempe I remember as a little girl. We aren't getting along at all. She fusses at me constantly."

"The war does that to some people," David said solemnly. "Tell you what I think." He wiped his mouth with a ragged coat sleeve. "I don't think Henry's really a lunatic."

We just stared at him.

"What ails him then?" I asked.

"Whatever it is that ails a man when he can't stand to live with himself anymore," David said sadly. And he fastened his blue eyes on us with all the wisdom of a lad of twelve who's been living in the army for a year and heard all the talk that goes on between soldiers at night in huts.

"Well"—Jeremiah poked him—"tell us then. What is it?"

"He was with Washington and Braddock and the Provincial Army in the French and Indian War in '55," David said. "I heard him talk of it one night around the fire. There was a terrible battle. Washington had his horse shot from under him. Braddock was mortally wounded. Many men ran. Henry was one of them. And I think he's never forgiven himself for running. That's what I think."

We pondered on that for a moment. "That may be, but I still think he's lunatic," I told them. "My father always said that old John Wick, Tempe's grandfather, was lunatic. And he was evil. My father said that back in Long Island he owned a tavern. And he killed peddlers and others who stayed the night. Then he stole their money and goods and buried them in the well."

I had their attention now, and flushed with the headiness of it, I went on. "My father says that old John Wick even buried a servant of his in the well. And that he was accused of having supernatural powers. It's been said that some men of Bridgehampton, who were fishing off the coast at the exact time of his death, saw the devil carrying his black soul out to sea."

I finished, breathless. They stared at me.

"I thought you didn't like your father," David accused.

"I don't."

"But you believe this?"

"Yes."

"Why?"

"Because when I asked Tempe about it, she wouldn't answer. But she didn't deny it, either. And because Aunt Mary says all the Wicks are crazy."

"Tempe." Jeremiah scoffed. "She's a secretive one, all right. Why don't you ask her about her friendship with Billy Bowzar?"

Now I perked my ears up. "Bowzar?"

He nodded. "From the 10th Regiment. Lounges around with Dan Connell of the 11th and the likes of George Goznall and that fellow who calls himself Macaroni Jack. Troublemakers, all of them, General Wayne says."

"In what way?" I felt a mixture of alarm and interest. My perfect cousin, Tempe? Mixing with troublemakers? I had to know more about this!

"In what way is she friends with Bowzar?" I insisted. "Why, she's practically betrothed to Captain Will Tuttle who was stationed here with the 3rd New Jersey last winter. She gets letters from him from up in New Windsor."

"She may be betrothed to Tuttle, but she meets with Bowzar for talks when she goes on her rides," Jeremiah said. "And General Wayne doesn't like it. I heard him say he's going to talk to her about it when he goes to your house to supper tonight."

My head felt dizzy. I looked up at the sky where an evening star was hung over our house in the distance. I saw smoke rising out of the chimney. *I should be getting back soon*, I thought. *Tempe will need me to help with supper.*

"Why should General Wayne be concerned about Tempe meeting with Bowzar?" I persisted. There was something here they weren't telling me about, I was sure of it.

Jeremiah bit into a piece of gingerbread. "I told you. Wayne thinks Bowzar and his cohorts are trouble."

"What *kind* of trouble?" My heart was pounding. I sensed something sinister in the winter twilight.

Jeremiah shrugged and regarded his gingerbread in the most provoking way. "I can't say any more."

I hit his arm, knocking the gingerbread from his hand. "You'd best say, Jeremiah Levering, if you want any more handouts from me."

Calmly, he retrieved the gingerbread from the ground and recommenced eating. "Your tongue is sharp as a knife, Mary Cooper."

"So is your appetite."

He smiled. "If you weren't so pretty, I'd be insulted."

"You mean, if you weren't so *hungry* all the time."

We grinned at each other. "Tell me," I begged. "Tempe's always lecturing me about this and that, saying I'm not proper enough. She won't even allow me in *camp* for fear my presence there will be misconstrued and I'll be taken as a loose woman. If she's up to some mischief, I must needs know."

"Oh, and why?" David asked.

"So she can use it on Tempe, why do you think," Jeremiah said.

So he told me then. "I saw a letter Wayne wrote to his old school friend Francis Johnston, who's a colonel in the 5th Regiment. 'I sincerely wish,' he wrote, 'that the Ides of January was come and past. I am not superstitious but can't help cherishing disagreeable thoughts about this period.' "

"What does *that* mean?" I asked.

30

Jeremiah shrugged. "Wayne thinks the troops' minds and tempers are soured by neglect. He thinks there's more bad blood among the men than the officers are generally aware of."

"Bad blood?" I echoed.

But he just kept chewing his gingerbread in a way that drove me to distraction. I fastened my gaze on David, who was eyeing me knowingly.

"Wayne's afraid of mutiny," David said. He said it plain.

"Mutiny?" I was starting to sound like the village idiot.

Jeremiah studied what was left of his big piece of gingerbread. David nodded. "The threat of mutiny," David explained, "has been hanging over the Continental Army for two years now. Last January about a hundred Massachusetts men from the garrison at West Point started to march off and had to be brought back."

"Is this true?" I whispered to Jeremiah. Mutiny? These Patriots? These dear, starving, dedicated soldiers?

"It's true about the men at West Point last year," Jeremiah said. "And last June, thirty-one men of the 1st New York at Fort Schuyler left to go to the British on the St. Lawrence. The Americans went after them with a party of friendly Oneida Indians and brought them back. And you know what happened here last May."

"No, I don't. Tell me."

"The Connecticut Line was five months without pay and had no meat for over a week," Jeremiah recited sadly. "Two of the regiments got under arms, started to beat drums and assemble on the parade ground, and prepared to leave camp to search for provisions. They were stopped. But Wayne now has all this on his mind, I'll wager."

I sat stunned. For I had heard of none of this before. "And this Bowzar fellow? Wayne suspects him of plotting mutiny?"

"Wayne sees him as trouble. And Wayne knows we've all read the handbills the British have planted in camp, promising all kinds of things if our soldiers will desert."

"These men won't desert," I said angrily. "They're Patriots!"

"They can't live on patriotism," Jeremiah said. "They can't eat it. They can't feed it to their wives and children."

I felt sick. It was getting dark now. The sky in the west was streaked with red and purple, and the trees in the orchard were stark silhouettes. I got up from the ground. I wanted to go home, and yet I couldn't pull away. I stood rooted to the spot, like the trees. I stared at my friends. They'd gotten to their feet, too. Jeremiah was blowing on his hands.

"Don't say anything," he begged. "I'll get in trouble with Wayne, and he won't want me around anymore. I've said more than I should have."

"You haven't said anything," I snapped. "Not to me."

My friends smiled, and we stood wrapped in the misery of the possibilities we had discussed. "Wayne can abide with it," Jeremiah insisted.

"I know," I said.

"He has the hearts of the soldiers," David put in.

"Yes," I said numbly. He would have. Perhaps he had their hearts as he had mine. Perhaps what I felt for him was simply the adulation people feel for a man who can lead, a man one can look up to. *No*, I thought miserably, then. *I'm sure what I feel for him is more than that*. Oh, how ashamed I was about it! For, as Tempe had said, he was a married man!

"Keep your eyes and ears open at supper tonight," Jeremiah advised. "If Wayne says something to your cousin about Bowzar, listen. And watch how she responds."

I nodded. And we moved apart, promising to meet tomorrow. I walked toward the house, but my heart was heavy now. Oliver Cromwell brought a stick, begging me to throw it. I did, with all my might. He raced ahead joyously to fetch it back. But it wasn't the same as before, as when I'd started out this afternoon. Something had changed, in the sky, in the lay of the land, in the outline of the house. Everything had changed in a few short hours.

Mutiny. The word sat like a stone inside me, dragging me down. But I had to hurry home. I was late.

3

The first person I saw as I hurried through the orchard toward the house was Lieutenant Enos Reeves of the 10th Regiment. He was coming down the path from the stable. He stopped by the well to greet me.

"Evening, Mary." He gave a formal bow.

I was glad to see him, more than I realized I would be. He'd started to come around a lot when the hired man quit right after I got here. He cares for the livestock for Tempe. In his twenties, tall and amiable, I minded his good looks the first time we met. For I am not blind. My problem seems to be that my eyesight has gotten better than ever in that department lately. My sister Martha, who along with brother Nathan was always trying "to make something of me," would say I was behaving like a doxy. Which is another word for a loose woman.

When Enos was a guest at our table on Christmas Day, I noticed how smitten he'd seemed. It came to me then that he is languishing over Tempe.

It pleasured me now to see him bow. For, in spite of the fraying cuffs on his regimental coat, the elegance of his manners was not lost on me. Oh, I suppose sister Martha would be right about me! I can't help the way I feel in General Wayne's presence. And I'm not exactly a pillar of salt when Enos bows to me, either. Of all the people I've met here, he's the only one who treats me like a grown woman.

I think Tempe treats him shamefully, sweet-talking him sufficiently to keep him coming around to help, yet keeping him at arm's length.

He brushed the hay from his coat. "You look like the cat that stole the cream off the top of the milk, Mary. Where have you been?"

"Walking."

His blue eyes twinkled in his eager, open face. "With your friends, David and Jeremiah? Don't look so worried. I won't tell. I know Tempe frowns on them. But you must promise not to let out that I help Tempe with the livestock. My superior officers wouldn't look kindly on that."

"I won't breathe a word."

He smiled at me in the deepening dusk, and something sweet in the moment worked favorably for us.

"Are you here for supper?" I asked.

"Do you want me to be?"

"Well, I do think Tempe should invite you after you've done the chores."

"Is that the only reason you'd like me to be invited?"

Was he provoking me? "I don't think Tempe should treat you so shabbily," I blurted out.

"Well, thank you for caring, Mary. But I'm not invited. Only General Wayne has been asked tonight."

"Why *do* you let her treat you so?" I asked again.

His smile only deepened. And got sadder. "Why do you constantly make cow eyes at General Wayne when you know that half the women within fifty miles of Philadelphia are smitten with him?"

I felt tears come to my eyes. The lanky young lieutenant recognized misery when he saw it.

"I've angered you," he said.

"No. What you've done is remind me of my brother Abraham. He would say such a thing to me."

"And what would you say in return?"

"That I was glad he bothered to pay heed. So I could speak of it to someone."

"Where is Abraham?"

"With the rest of Washington's army. In New Windsor."

"How old is he?"

37

"Nineteen. And we're the only Patriots in a family of Tories. After the war I'll go and live with him if I don't marry."

"Is there someone you wish to marry someday, Mary?"

I blushed. "I don't know." I looked at the stones at my feet. "I've pledged my heart to no one, if that's what you're asking. I suppose you think I'm despicable for being smitten with General Wayne."

"All the women fancy him. He's a dashing, romantic figure, and he represents our Cause to them."

"Am I no different than those frivolous women in Philadelphia, then? We've all heard about Philadelphia. And how the civilians there live in luxury in well-appointed houses with all sorts of good food and merriment."

He sighed. "I'm afraid that what you say about the citizens of Philadelphia is true. But you are different, Mary. And I'm sure your thoughts about General Wayne are all wrapped up in your notions about the war."

"I still feel guilty over such feelings."

"Why?"

"No self-respecting Christian girl should entertain such sentiments about a man who is married."

"How old are you, Mary?"

"Fourteen."

"Well, in the first place, you're not a girl any longer. You're a proper woman."

I blushed, thanking him.

"I don't flatter you. In wartime, especially in this camp, there are no children. And in the second place, we can no more help our feelings than we can stop the sun from going down as it's just now done. So don't waste your energies with guilt."

"Thank you, Lieutenant."

"Enos," he corrected.

I nodded. "Can you answer a question for me?"

"I can try, Mary."

"Is it true that General Wayne seldom, if ever, sees his wife, the lovely Polly Penrose of Waynesborough?"

"Yes, it's true."

"Why?"

"There's word she's dealing with the British. Selling to them from the family farm and tannery."

"Oh," I murmured sadly.

"It pains Wayne. He's written to her, instructing her to stop. But she won't. He's given his life to our army, to Washington."

"My brother Nathan is a merchant, and he's dealing with the British, too."

He nodded sympathetically.

"And what of Mary Vining of Delaware?" I asked.

"What of her?"

"They say she is beautiful. And the love of General Wayne's life. They say the plume he wears in his hat was given to him by Mary."

He sighed. "The beautiful Miss Vining gave him that plume, yes. She has captured the hearts of many, including Lafayette and Washington. As a cousin of Caesar Rodney, signer of the Declaration of Independence, she is very popular. She has many suitors, though she doesn't marry."

I pondered all this in silence.

"Don't look so unhappy, Mary. I can see your feelings for the general are on the finest level. So satisfy yourself by knowing that no one has ever questioned his bravery or loyalty. And that his letters to his wife are dutiful and affectionate."

"Is it true that Washington says he's a roué?"

"Washington depends on him, Mary. Don't trouble your head about gossip."

I smiled. "You've helped me, Enos. Thank you. It's good to be able to speak freely with someone who can understand."

"I'd take it kindly if we could be friends, Mary Cooper."

"Yes. Oh, yes. If there's ever anything I can do for you, Enos . . ."

"There is. You can talk to Tempe about her friendship with Billy Bowzar from my regiment."

My heart fell all the way to the stones at my feet. Another warning. Two now within the last hour. I raised my troubled eyes to his face, not bothering to conceal my distress. I felt a stab of jealousy. More people worried about Tempe's well-being than ever gave a thought to mine. And here was one person in love with her to boot.

"I've heard about her friendship with Billy Bowzar. My friends have told me."

"What have they said?" he asked.

"That Bowzar is trouble." No, I could not repeat the mutiny talk. For it was a bile within me that would bring up my innards once I acknowledged it. And talking with Reeves, I'd almost forgotten. Now it came back, with all the rudeness of a bucket of cold water in the face. For now it was not just camp talk from my young friends anymore. Reeves's mention of it confirmed our suspicions.

He knew of the rumored mutiny. I could see in his eyes that he knew of it. His gaze held mine for an instant, and he looked past me to the orchard where the dark outline of the trees, petrified now in winter, seemed a proper reflection of my own feelings.

He was waiting for me to say more. But I kept my own counsel. For I am not the kind of person to betray one friend to keep another.

"I must go." He started to move away. "I've said enough. Tell Tempe I've fed and watered the livestock."

"Good night then," I said. "And thank you."

"Take care, Mary Cooper. You know where to find me if you need a friend. And oh, yes. One matter you may want to be made aware of. General Wayne celebrates his birthday on January 1. You may want to wish him well this evening."

I felt a rush of gratitude. "Thank you, Enos. How old is he?"

"He'll be thirty-six."

"Have you told Tempe?"

"I forgot."

"Don't, please."

I could see his bemused appreciation. "Wayne has been invited to dine with Lucas Beverholt at his home in Whippany, five miles north. But he's declined. I know he's asked some of his favorite officers to sup with him in his quarters."

"I wish I had something to give him," I said

impulsively. "If I'd known in time, I could have sewn him a shirt. I made many shirts for the army with my friend Sarah when I was back home."

"I'm sure he wouldn't think lightly of a meat pie. Like the one you made when I was invited to dine at your house on Christmas."

"It wasn't much of a Christmas this year," I said dismally. I minded the Christmases I'd had in my father's commodious two-story brick home on Long Island, with a grand feast at the table and relatives of all ages gathered around. It had always been my job to festoon the mantel in the dining room with fresh fruit and evergreens.

"It was the finest Christmas that I recollect in a long while," Reeves said. "You helped brighten the day considerably, Mary. If not for you, it would have been intolerable."

"Me?" I laughed. "You needn't flatter me, sir. I'm not the kind of girl who needs flattery. Good friends can do without it."

He sobered. "Then we are friends, Mary?"

"Yes. And I just may make that meat pie for General Wayne. You don't think he'd consider it unseemly, do you?"

"I think he'd be most gratified."

"Then I'll do it. Oh, thank you, Enos! You have been the best of friends to me."

Did he bow again? It was too dark now to see. But I did not have to. For I knew that this night we had become kindred spirits. And it had nothing whatsoever to do with his elegant manners. Or with my acting like a doxy.

4

"Oh my, General, I do like a man who cuts a dashing figure. How do you manage to keep the ruffles on your shirt so white?"

No sooner had the man come through the front door than Aunt Mary said this, looking up from her handiwork to smile at him.

The fire was lit in the dining room, the table laid with Aunt Mary's best pewter. The two lazy cats snuggled at her feet by the hearth. Fresh from her nap, Aunt Mary was saucy and bright in her lace cap and best shawl. From behind Tempe I could see the lines on the general's face soften as he beheld the warmth of the scene.

"There's always a soldier's wife in camp anxious to make an extra shilling for keeping a general's linen clean," said General Wayne. "And I confess, I have a weakness for spotless clothes. Everything you've heard about me being vain is true, I'm afraid."

He handed his tricorn hat and blue cape to Tempe and strode across the room to bend over Aunt Mary and kiss her hand.

I thought I would melt into the floorboards, watching him.

Everything about him was so wonderful. From his dark hair tied behind his neck in a queue and his blue-and-buff regimental coat, open in front to reveal the whitest of shirts and vests and a crimson officer's sash, to the tassel on the handle of his sword.

I thought I would swoon.

"Vain?" Aunt Mary laughed. "Yes, I hear that about you. But I also hear it is the vanity of a performer and not a cloak of incompetence."

Oh, how I wish I were sixty-two years old like Aunt Mary so I could say such things out plain. Instead, I am fourteen and tongue-tied.

"You flatter me, dear lady." Wayne straightened up to his full height. His posture was so erect, his presence so commanding. Yet he exuded a ready charm. "Please accept my condolences for your recent loss. Our army will always be indebted to your late husband for allowing us the use of his land."

"Late! Ha! Exactly!" And Aunt Mary brought her frail hand down hard on the arm of her chair. "I keep telling them around here he's late. Lollygagging with his old friends from the Morristown militia most likely, while we wait supper for him! Well, we'll not wait a moment longer.

Tempe! I say let's eat now. We're all hungry. What say you, General?"

Wayne could say nothing for a moment, momentarily taken aback by Aunt Mary's statement. But then, in an instant, his soldier's sensibilities took over, and he arranged his clear-cut features in as normal an expression as possible. Over Aunt Mary's head, Tempe was motioning to him, shaking her own head and pointing to her temple. Never indicating that anything was amiss, Wayne inclined his head only slightly and smiled again at Aunt Mary.

"May I have the honor of escorting you to the table, Mrs. Wick?"

"You may."

"Mary, come along. I need you in the kitchen," Tempe directed.

General Wayne looked in my direction then, where I was standing in the shadows of the room, outside the circle of candlelight. "Why, Mary Cooper, I didn't see you there, child."

I winced at the word "child," yet gave a graceful curtsy.

"Come here where I can see you."

I went forward to stand before him. I was trembling, it seemed, all over.

"Ah, Mary," he said kindly. "You should wear blue all the time. It goes with your eyes."

I was wearing my blue short gown over a striped petticoat. I could think of no adequate reply. My throat constricted.

"My Margaretta has eyes the color of yours," he continued. "She's eleven now. Growing into quite the young lady. Seeing you reminds me of her . . . Are you enjoying your stay?"

"Yes, sir," I croaked. *Oh, the agony of it! I reminded him of his daughter. A little girl!*

He was helping Aunt Mary to her feet, guiding her across the room.

"Now you sit at that end of the table, General," she ordered, after he'd pulled out the chair she'd pointed to. It was to the right of the head place of the table. "This is my Henry's chair. His place is always set for when he comes in."

It was, indeed. I'd set it myself, at Tempe's bidding, carefully arranging his napkin and pewter plate and goblet, angry with Tempe for keeping up the pretense.

General Wayne did as she bade him. He sat at the opposite end of the table. He unfolded his linen napkin and poured wine for them both. They were getting on like two old tent mates when I left the room. Tempe and I brought in the food, bowls of chicken stew and buttered turnips from our root cellar, scarlet runner beans, freshly baked bread, cheese, and boiled pudding. A feast. I could not help thinking of

Jeremiah and David and what they would say at the sight of our table.

"Will you say grace, General Wayne?" Aunt Mary asked. "My Henry usually does."

Wayne set down his wine goblet and thought for a moment, then spoke.

"Lord, we thank Thee for this food. We ask Your blessing upon this house and these good people, on our soldiers, and General Washington. You know, Lord, that I don't wish to complain, but our soldiers have only a mended coat, a bad shirt, a worse pair of trousers apiece, and scarcely what can be called shoes. And two men share a blanket between them. I've written to the Supreme Executive Council of Pennsylvania, asking that they adequately serve our men. Food would be good, Lord, and clothing. But they must give these soldiers a landed property and make their interest and the interest of America reciprocal. Move them to accomplish this, Lord, and I will answer for the men bleeding to death, drop by drop, to establish the independency of this country. Amen."

We all whispered amen and commenced eating. But a silence fell over us at Wayne's prayer. A silence we feared to break with even the clinking of a spoon on a plate.

For a while we just spooned the stew into our mouths. Then Aunt Mary spoke.

"That was a proper Episcopalian prayer, General Wayne."

"Thank you, Mrs. Wick."

"Right to the point. You don't believe in shilly-shallying with the Lord, I see."

"I don't believe in shilly-shallying with anybody, ma'am."

"I like that in a man. No nonsense. Tell me, General, in your considered opinion, is this as bad as the winter at Valley Forge?"

"Yes. But we endured there, and we'll endure here."

"They say you conducted a cattle drive out of south Jersey, bringing a whole herd into the camp at Valley Forge."

Wayne smiled. "I was detached by Washington for an incursion into New Jersey, yes, to collect supplies. There was no forage around Philadelphia. The British had taken everything."

"You can't do that now?" Aunt Mary asked.

"I dare not leave my command here, and I can't spare any of my officers. There's been word of activity in the waters around New York, and reports are so contradictory we give little credit to what we hear. Nevertheless, we must maintain the security of the camp. There's no telling what the British are up to."

"I've heard that the British intend a landing

in New Jersey and may advance as far as Morristown," Tempe said.

Carefully, Wayne sipped his wine and set down his goblet. "Where did you hear that, Temperance?"

My cousin's face went momentarily red. For she had given herself away, if what David and Jeremiah said about her was true. *Where had she heard it indeed*, I wondered. *From Bowzar?* No doubt Wayne was wondering this, also.

"Everyone calls me Tempe, General," she said.

"I prefer Temperance. I like what the name stands for."

Well, you didn't have to be as blind as Ebenezer Drake's mule to see that these two were going to be at each other's throats within minutes.

"You forget, General, that I'm about the countryside on my horse every day. I hear things."

"I hardly forget, Temperance. Not a day passes that one of my officers doesn't mention seeing you on the roads in your red cape. Which reminds me that a bit more caution exercised on your part might be in order."

"I can take care of myself," Tempe said. "Colonel flies like the wind. We can outrun anybody."

"It isn't you I am concerned with," Wayne said. "It's the horse. My officers all have their eyes on him."

Tempe's nostrils dilated, and she raised her pert chin. I saw the effect of Wayne's words immediately, for tears came into her eyes. She was accustomed to admiring glances, my cousin. Even to flattery. She expected it from men.

She did not expect, however, to hear that the men first admired her horse.

Wayne smiled wryly. "You didn't answer my question, Temperance," he said quietly. "Where did you hear about the British?"

"I have friends in camp."

"In the 11th Regiment, no doubt."

"And what of it, General?"

Wayne lowered his eyes. "From what I've heard, Temperance, your friends are trouble. You are ill-advised to keep seeing them."

"This is still my father's farm, General Wayne. I'll go where I please and see whom I please."

"And I'm sure your father would be the first to suggest that there are certain places and certain people a young girl should avoid," he replied.

Their eyes locked across the table. And held. And for a moment it was as if they were the only two people in the room.

But I had discounted Aunt Mary, who, if there were only two people left on the face of the earth, would find some way to worm her way into their conversation to set them straight.

"What's this? What's going on here that I don't know about? Are you two fussing at each other? I won't have it. I won't have any conversations in my house that I'm not a part of. Especially if there's a good argument going."

"We're not fussing, Mama," Tempe said. "General Wayne was saying how his men admire Colonel."

"Well, they should. He's the finest bit of horseflesh in Morris County. I'll wager you haven't got anything like him in Pennsylvania, General."

"You're most likely correct, Mrs. Wick." General Wayne smiled.

"I hear tell that the British are circulating printed matter in your camp, General," Aunt Mary said, "to entice your men to desert."

"You're quite right, ma'am. The British are using our present dolorous situation to say they will receive any deserters with open arms and kind forgiveness."

"How have the men responded?"

"My men are using the circulars to light their fires," Wayne said.

"That's the spirit!" Aunt Mary slapped her

hand down on the table. "The men are with you. As they were with Washington when he was here last year. They know you have stood for hours, exposed to the wind and weather, while they built their huts. They remember that."

"It will take more than spirit," Tempe put in softly. "Your soldiers are not devoid of reasoning, General. Although many of them can't read, they've now served their country for near five years and have not seen a paper dollar in the way of pay for near twelve months."

Wayne said nothing for a moment, but even I could see he was composing himself. "Even if the bankrupts in the capital did send money to the paupers in camp, there is little enough for them to purchase with it," he said carefully. "We need clothing. The ten thousand suits expected from France this year have not come. The ladies of Philadelphia subscribed money to buy shirts, but they are still being made." Then he turned to Aunt Mary.

"It is my considered opinion, ma'am, that you should never have named her Temperance. The name does not suit her."

Aunt Mary nodded her head vigorously, her lace cap bobbing as she chewed. I could see she was exhilarated, to say the least. Her eyes were bright, her cheeks flushed. "We never could do anything with our youngest daughter, General.

Her father spoiled her. My two oldest girls are proper and amiable wives and mothers. My oldest son was lunatic, you know, before he died. My other son is off fighting the Indians or possibly dead, too. Tempe is all I have right now, and I'm afraid that running the place in my husband's absence has made her a bit bold and cantankerous."

"The war has taken its toll on us all," Wayne said.

Aunt Mary nodded. "When my husband returns, things will settle down around here. Tempe, mind your manners. Don't take any sass from her, General. If she can give, she can take. Mary, pass me some of that boiled pudding."

It was time to clear away the plates. I got up to do so, but Tempe admonished me to sit, and she brought the dishes into the kitchen herself. I fetched bowls from the sideboard for the pudding, feeling General Wayne's eyes on me.

"We've ignored you, Mary," he said. "Tell me, what do you hear from your family on Long Island?"

I finished spooning out the pudding and sat back down, doing my best not to tremble because he had spoken to me—wishing he hadn't, yet gratified that he had. And trying to form my words so I would not sound like an idiot.

"Nothing. They don't write. I think they are glad to be rid of me."

He looked at me solicitously. "I doubt that, Mary. You must consider that it's difficult for mail to get through."

"Perhaps. But I'm a Patriot, General. And my family is Tory. I've been sent here for that reason. I've angered them with my Patriot activities. They were at their wits' end with me, you know."

He smiled kindly. "And pray, what were those subversive activities?"

My face burned as I studied my pudding. "I was always at my friend Sarah's house, sewing shirts for the American army. But what really angered them was when I took part in ceremonies at our Liberty Pole last summer on the fourth anniversary of the Declaration of Independence. After that, I was sent to stay with my brother Nathan and his wife. But I angered him, also."

Wayne nodded, his eyes kindly. "Do I dare ask what you did to brother Nathan?"

I raised my eyes to meet his. "He's a merchant. And he's dealing with Tories."

Wayne swiftly lowered his own eyes. I saw his determined mouth turn even more determined, and a muscle in his face twitched. I know he was thinking of his wife, who was engaged in the same process.

"And what did you tell brother Nathan?" he asked.

"I told him it was incumbent on him to review the facts. And to remember that our soldiers were dying while he was dealing with the British. I told him he and his merchant friends were so busy making money that they didn't realize a new country was being formed."

Wayne nodded gravely. "And what did brother Nathan say to that?"

I shrugged, trying not to remember Nathan's outrage—the way he'd sent me from the table, locked me upstairs in my room, and kept me there until a servant packed my bags and a carriage was sent around to take me to the docks on Long Island, where a British ship awaited. Without seeing my parents or home again—yet with their written permission—I was put aboard the ship with a black servant and brought to Elizabeth Point, where Aunt Mary's friend and adviser, Ebenezer Drake, met me with a carriage.

My voice constricted, remembering. But I met General Wayne's gaze unswervingly. "He sent me here," I said simply. "My parents agreed to it."

"I see," Wayne said. And apparently he did. For he accepted the cup of coffee Tempe set down before him and nodded solemnly into it. And when he again looked at me, I saw that he no longer viewed me as a child.

"You've made your choice, Mary. We've all

had to, in this war. And no matter what side we've chosen, we all pay for it."

"Yes, sir," I said.

"I would pray my own Margaretta would have such courage if the choice was put to her."

"I don't mind being here," I said cheerfully. "I like it. I only mind that my brother Abraham, who's with Washington in New Windsor, doesn't know where I am. So he can't write to me."

Wayne nodded. "Why don't you write to him, Mary. When you've done so, bring the letter to my headquarters at Peter Kemble's house. And I'll see it gets in the right post."

"Thank you, sir." I proceeded to eat my pudding, warmed by his words. They formed something solid inside me.

"Your host, Peter Kemble, is a Loyalist of the firmest principles, isn't he, General Wayne?" Tempe asked. "I understand he used to be a member of the Royal Council of New Jersey."

Wayne nodded, sipping his coffee. He seemed weary suddenly. I think my story about my family had touched a raw nerve in him. He just nodded.

"And isn't Kemble's son a lieutenant colonel in the British army?" Tempe persisted.

Wayne nodded again.

"And his daughter married to Thomas Gage,

who was commander of the British when the war broke out?"

"You have done your research, I see, Temperance." Wayne did not bother looking at her as he spoke.

"What do your men think of your accepting his hospitality?"

"As far as I know, he is considerately treated by all Americans. As he has treated us. When Peter Kemble dines with us, which isn't often, we never discuss politics."

"Your men are starving, General," Tempe said sweetly, "and you call it politics?"

Now Wayne's eyes flashed. Quickly I looked at Aunt Mary, who, mercifully, was dozing in her chair. We hadn't noticed that she'd fallen asleep, but now she even snored. It filled the silence.

"You object to the company I keep, Temperance?"

She was startled at the tone of voice, which, although lowered to a whisper, had about it the manner of a man not accustomed to having his decisions questioned.

"I do," she said. But she hesitated, wavered. *Good heavens*, I thought, *if the general looked at me like that, I'd not only waver, I'd faint dead away in my chair.*

"Then the field is open for me to say again that I object to the company you've been keeping these days."

"What company is that, General?" And she seemed to diminish as she said it.

"You know full well. However, I'll not leave it to interpretation. I speak of Billy Bowzar. You've been seen on several occasions, meeting with him."

Again Aunt Mary snored. We all waited.

"Are you insinuating," Tempe asked, "that there is something improper going on between me and Sergeant Bowzar?"

"I'm insinuating nothing," Wayne said. "My concern isn't for your morals. I'm saying he's a bad egg. That he's filling your head with his erroneous ideas. I'm saying he's a malcontent who is destined for trouble, and you do not understand the gravity of encouraging, or even giving credence to, his words."

"The men are resentful, General. They have grievances."

"Of which I am not unaware, Temperance. And which I am doing my utmost to gratify. I'll thank you to stay out of it. And if you persist, I'll have to restrict your movements in camp."

The color returned to my cousin's face, which had gone quite white by now under Wayne's withering words. She rallied.

"I cannot stay out of it, General. The women and children from camp are at our door constantly seeking food. I am involved in it. More than I ever wanted to be. What would you have me do?"

Wayne's voice got gentler. "I'm sorry about that, Temperance. All I can suggest is that you do what my cousin Sarah Walker did, when I stayed in her house while at Valley Forge. Do you have a sufficient supply of salt pork?"

"Of course," Tempe answered.

"And greens?"

"We have an abundance of greens in our root cellar."

"If you can spare any, boil them with salt pork. Make a pot every day. It goes far and serves many. When they come to the door, distribute some. It's nourishing, will fill their stomachs, and absolve your conscience. I'll issue an order that they stay away from your door. It won't work, but you'll be less bothered."

"Thank you, General," Tempe said. "Now if you will excuse me, I must get Mama to bed."

The supper was over. General Wayne stood up.

"See General Wayne to the door, Mary," my cousin directed. She was helping Aunt Mary to her feet. I fetched Wayne's cloak and tricorn. When I came back, he was bowing to Aunt Mary and thanking her for her hospitality, with those courtly manners of his.

"Do come again, General," Aunt Mary said. "I do miss having a man around here. Your visit was delightful."

In the entranceway he took his cloak from me and put it on. I handed the tricorn to him, and he held it in his hands, considering it as if he'd never laid eyes on it before. "Delightful," he said. "Yes. Good evening, Temperance."

But she only tossed her head at him as she led Aunt Mary from the room.

"Mary, you seem to be a sensible young woman," he said to me.

I glowed at the praise. "After a manner of speaking, I suppose, General."

"Will you grant me a favor?"

"Oh yes, sir! Anything!"

He smiled dourly. "Keep an eye on your cousin. She's pigheaded. And beautiful. 'Tis an unfortunate mixture. And one that brews trouble."

My heart fell. Was that all he wanted from me, then? To look after Tempe? Always Tempe! When she was around, men went out of their way to make fools of themselves. And she treated them all despicably, with never a twinge of conscience. It wasn't fair!

"Try to discourage her from seeing this Bowzar fellow."

"How can I do that, General? Tempe doesn't hold with anything I say."

He sighed and pondered for a moment. "Isn't she betrothed? Somebody from the 3rd New Jersey?"

I nodded. "Captain Will Tuttle. But it's only after a fashion."

"One is either betrothed or one isn't, Mary. Which is it?"

"She's inordinately fond of him, Aunt Mary says. But they're waiting until the war is over."

"Well, then remind her of her inordinate fondness for him whenever you can. Will you do that for me, Mary?"

"Yes, sir, I will."

He seemed about to turn to the door and leave. Then he hesitated. "Your aunt thinks her son is dead. Certainly both you and Temperance know he's been in and out of camp."

"Yes, sir. But Tempe believes it better if her mother doesn't know. Henry has always broken Aunt Mary's heart."

He nodded. "Yet she thinks her husband is alive."

"Tempe believes it best that she doesn't know the truth about that yet, either."

He sighed and clamped his hat on his head. "I've been away from the company of women too long," he said. "The ways of war are less confounding. Write to your brother, Mary, and bring the letter to me."

And then he was gone in a swirl of blue cloak. I watched him go across our lawn to where his horse was tethered to our rail fence in front. I stood watching as he untied the reins, mounted, and rode off.

Long after I couldn't see him anymore, I heard his horse's hooves beating a cadence on the road. There was something solid and comforting about the sound. I went back to clear the table, thinking that I had made two good friends in one night. But it was General Wayne's voice and presence and face that I held close as I did my last chores of the day.

5

At home in Southampton I was noted for my cooking. I do pride myself on being able to concoct a tasty clam pie or commonsense biscuit. My biscuits are my special accomplishment. The secret to them is that you have to exercise judgment with regard to the amount of lard used. If you use too much or too little, the results can be disastrous.

I learned this from Linsey, our nigra cook. She never minded my milling around the kitchen, and I think I persisted in the pastime because once the final product was on the table, it was the only real way I could earn a compliment from my father. He puts great store in good cooking.

"Mehitable," he would say to my mother, "if the child never has another redeeming quality, she can at least cook." It was a compliment that came in the back door, as my brother Abraham would say. But a compliment, nevertheless.

Father has a special weakness for my clam pie, made out of clams that Abraham and I used to catch in Long Island Sound. My Muster Day gingerbread is quite respectable, too, if I have to say so myself. When the Southampton militia drilled—twice a month in those anxious days before the war actually started—I'd be up at first light with Linsey. I was only nine then. But under her supervision I soon learned to mix a proper batch and get it in the beehive oven so Abraham would have a goodly supply in his haversack when he went off to muster on the town green with the other Patriots, to drill all day. He could starve himself, for all the rest of the family cared. Abraham often told me my gingerbread was the best of any brought along for the occasion.

I'm not a bad hand at fried oysters, either. As a matter of fact, it's the fresh fish I miss here in Morristown—if I miss anything besides Abraham.

I lay awake a long time that night after General Wayne left, thinking and wishing I had some clams for a pie. I'd have to make do with chicken pie. I'd put some diced ham in it and some light cream. We've plenty of cream from Daisy, the cow. It came to me then that I'd make the pie tomorrow, not wait until New Year's Day. I'd tell Tempe it was in return for General Wayne's favor of dispatching my letter to Abraham. That way she wouldn't know it was Wayne's birthday. I wanted that to be my secret, something I could do without Tempe outshining me.

Only one fly was in the ointment. I'd have to write the letter to Abraham tonight. Tempe had said when we cleaned up the supper dishes that I was to help with the salt pork and greenery soup we'd make tomorrow. And hand it out to the camp followers and their children, as General Wayne had suggested.

Oh, how I dreaded getting out of my warm bed! But I wrapped my quilt around me and lit the candle from the hearth fire. Then I sat down at my small table and commenced to write, struggling in the cold with my quill pen.

Dear Abraham,

Since you must think, by now, that I have disappeared off the end of the earth, I write to tell you I am not only in such good health that it is almost scandalous but enjoying a fine stay in New Jersey with Aunt Mary and cousin Tempe.

The last you heard from me I was at brother Nathan's house. Well, I couldn't abide that. And neither could he. Nathan and I argued constantly. I just couldn't hold with his philosophy or with his selling to the British. So in no time at all we were at each other's throats. Nathan said I was too sassy for his liking and my Patriot sentiments were making me a shrew and no man worth his salt would want me if I continued to be such a scold.

Well, considering that a bushel of salt is now thirty-five dollars in hard Continental dollars here in Morristown, that puts a premium on the opinion of men, I suppose. But I told Nathan I didn't care, that I'd rather be a scold for my country than a prig like his wife. As you can imagine, things deteriorated from that point on. Since he is thirty-one now, Nathan savors all the fruits of middle age, and one of them is lording it over his siblings. He always was a plague to me, as you know, and to make short of a dreary story, he bundled me off for a week in my room to ponder on my sins. All the while he was getting written permission from Mother and Father and having my clothes packed and making arrangements to have me shipped here.

However, I am having a most agreeable stay, although it is my sad duty to report to you that poor Uncle Henry died right before Christmas of the pleurisy. And the army camped on this land is in a most sorry state as I have ever seen people to be in and still

68

be people. But General Wayne has the confidence of the men and holds the soldiers' interest uppermost in his mind and heart.

He is most dashing and capable, Abraham, and I am smitten with him. It is causing me much misery. Do you remember how I felt about Jonathan Hatfield at home? Well, this is considerably worse, and I ache to talk to you about it. But I have friends here, not the least of whom is General Wayne. He was here to sup tonight, and when he'd heard I longed to correspond with you, he immediately offered to have the letter dispatched. Tomorrow I am baking him a chicken pie. I can't write more now because it is late and I am tired. I miss you. I miss Southampton and the fish we were able to catch and eat there. Although I do not wish to place you on the same level as the fish. Please respond to my letter if you can. I hope you are well and warm and have enough to eat.

> Your affectionate sister,
> Mary

When I stumbled into the kitchen the next morning, I was disappointed to find Tempe already up and about. I'd hoped to have the place to myself to start my pie crust. But she was chopping vegetables on the old oak table. The wood box was full and a pot already bubbling on the swinging crane in the hearth.

"You're up early." She was seated at the table, sipping coffee as she worked. She's not much for cooking. To her it's a duty, not a joy.

"I've written to Abraham." I stood in the kitchen, the warmest room in the house and pleasant enough, with Aunt Mary's hutch to one side filled with pewter and all the dried herbs from the garden hung overhead on beams, providing color in the winter.

She nodded, and realizing this announcement was some sort of preamble, she waited.

"I'd like to take it to General Wayne's headquarters today. So I thought I'd make him a chicken pie in return for the favor."

"That's rather pushy, Mary," she said.

"I don't see anything pushy about it. And I'm sure General Wayne won't either. Back home I often made a present of a meat pie for someone who was ailing or sad."

"Oh, and have you noticed that the general is ailing or sad? Well, perhaps if he is, he's pining for Mary Vining. Have you considered that?"

I shifted my weight from one foot to the other. Abraham had always told me that in a respectable argument you should attack your opponent. So I gave her the equivalent of a good round of bird shot. "I have considered that he is far from home and has a lot on his mind. And that January first is his birthday. I wasn't going to tell you because I didn't want to give you the chance to give him something before I did. But now I don't care if you know. Because I mind that you dislike him so. And you probably won't be giving him anything. I mind, too, that if he is sad, it's because he misses his children."

She smiled at me sweetly. "Do you know what I think, Mary?"

"No. But I suspect you are going to tell me something unpleasant. So say it plain."

"I think Wayne looks upon you as he looks upon his daughter."

She knew that would undo me, I'm sure of it. But before I could recover from *that*, she came at me again. "And I think you consider Wayne a safe object for your affections. He's married, older, and too grand for you."

I stumbled to the hearth and filled my mug with coffee, turning from her so she couldn't see the tears in my eyes. She was most likely right. But oh, *why* did she have to be so right?

Recovering, I turned around. "Then surely you can have no objections to my bringing him the pie. As a dutiful daughter would."

She stared at me, pushed a wisp of hair from under her mobcap, and sighed. "You do see things so plain, Mary. I suppose it's the New England influence you Long Islanders have been under for so long now. Bring him the pie if it pleases you. After observing Wayne last night, I'm sure he regards you as a child."

I had won, but my victory seemed empty. Surely she would not allow me to go if she perceived that Wayne looked upon me as anything but a child. I did not want that. What did I want? Why was I bringing him the pie? Did Wayne consider me to be a silly, simpering girl? Just one more flirtatious female? I didn't want *that* either! Oh, the misery!

"Stop standing there like Ebenezer Drake's mule and sit down," she ordered. "You must needs eat."

I sat and watched her as she fetched a plate and spooned some eggs and bits of bacon onto it from the pan in the hearth and piled it high with fresh biscuits. Her pretty face was flushed with exertion, her hands chapped from hard work, and her lovely face pinched with worry. In the next moment it was as if someone had put a pair of Benjamin Franklin's bifocals over my eyes, and I saw her as she would be in a year or two if she kept on like this.

I saw her as old. As some women get when they toil all day over hearth and loom. And then it came to me as I watched her fill her own plate with food, shove aside the bowl of chopped vegetables, and sit down.

Tempe missed her Will Tuttle. She was lonely!

We ate in silence. "Have you heard from your Will lately?" I asked.

She shrugged, not looking at me. "He writes that he is fair to middling. Their lot is not much better than that of the soldiers here."

"Do you miss him?"

"I miss him so much sometimes, I want to die." She said it plain, her voice flat, yet so certain that it startled me.

Then why are you meeting with Billy Bowzar? I wanted to scream it at her, but I said nothing. I looked at her instead. I saw her, pale and lovely and sad, and I despised myself because I did not understand her sadness. If I could understand it, perhaps, we would not be at each other's throats as we were.

"Perhaps Washington could give him permission to come home and see you," I suggested.

She raised her beautiful blue eyes to meet mine. "I don't want to see him," she said. "He'll only ask me to marry him again. And I don't wish to."

"But why? If you miss him so?"

She pushed her food around on the pewter plate. "He asked me to wed last spring. I said

73

no then. I couldn't bear to start out married life with a husband who could possibly be killed. I won't do that to myself. I won't pledge myself to a man who could die by a British bullet in this foul war. It would impoverish my spirit and kill me."

"It's already impoverished your spirit," I said.

"Not the way it would if Will were my husband."

"Does your heart make the distinction whether he's your husband or not?" I said.

She got up to put another piece of wood on the hearth. "I saw what happened to my father last winter. He couldn't hold himself aloof from what was going on out there. He tore himself in two trying to feed those people and us. It killed him. I told you, it killed him as much as the pleurisy."

"And so you're going to hold yourself aloof," I said.

"Yes."

"And that's why you refused to marry Will?"

"Yes."

"And that's why you want to compromise."

"Yes, and you'd best learn, too. It'll mean less wear and tear later on."

"Well, I'm sorry, Tempe," I said. "But I just don't believe all that. If it were the case, our soldiers would be starving and shivering out there right now all for naught."

She stood, hands on her slim hips, pewter ladle in one hand, staring into the fire. "The sooner they all learn how to compromise out there, the better off they'll be," she said bitterly.

What was she saying? Was she talking about the Americans and the British? Or the officers and men of the line? I dared not ask.

"How do you intend to get to Peter Kemble's house this afternoon?" she asked then.

"Peter Kemble's house?"

"It's where Wayne is quartered."

"I was going to ask you if I could ride Buckwheat."

"He needs shoeing. One more reason I'm waiting for a new hired man."

My spirits fell. Then I had a thought. "I could take Colonel. You know I ride well. And I'd walk him at a proper pace, not canter. I could wear your red cloak. Then people would think it was you, and no one would dare bother me. They all respect you in camp, Tempe."

"Your hair is light. Mine is dark."

"I could wear the hood of your cloak. Nobody could tell from a distance that I'm not you."

"You're a plague to me, Mary." She poured water from a bucket into a pot on the crane and dropped in some greens. "Don't you realize that

75

every officer within five miles has his eye on Colonel?"

"I thought it was me you were worried about. And now I find it's the horse," I said. I meant to lighten the mood, but she wouldn't comply.

"For that I should send you to your room for the day." She set the wooden bowl down hard on the table.

"You should, but you won't. Because you need my help today. You don't want to spend the whole of your time tending that salt pork and greenery stew. Or parceling it out to the camp followers who come to the door. If you let me take Colonel later on this afternoon, I'll sit here and watch the pot for you. I'll even dice up the pork."

"You wear me out, Mary. And whether you like it or not, you've just attempted to compromise."

I was dumbstruck. But I suppose she was right. She went to the pantry off the kitchen and secured a piece of salt pork. She set it down in front of me at the table, then handed me a knife. "Don't cut yourself," she admonished.

I commenced to work. We worked in silence for a while, she slicing the remainder of the greens. Then Aunt Mary called out from the other side of the house, and Tempe sighed and wiped her hands on her apron.

"I'll get Mama up and dressed. Finish cutting the pork. As far as I'm concerned, this soup is pig slops. But it'll keep everybody happy. More compromise."

She walked to the door that led into the parlor. "You may have Colonel *and* my red cloak this afternoon, if you milk Daisy when you're finished there. The hired man hasn't come again."

I sat stone-still. I've known how to milk a cow since I was seven. Though we had plenty of hired help at home, Abraham taught me. And Daisy is just about as amiable as a cow can be. But I knew Tempe was ramming this compromise business down my throat to prove her point. And I knew, too, that it would sit in my innards worse than yesterday's biscuits.

"Well?" she asked.

"I'll milk Daisy. But I feel sorry for you, Tempe."

"Don't," she said.

My problems that morning were just commencing, I soon discovered. The milking was no problem. But just as I set the foaming bucket of milk aside and stood up, feeling happy again because the sun was plentiful and it promised to be a nice day, I turned to see my next problem.

He was standing there in one of the empty

stalls with a week's growth of beard on his face, his clothing loose and looking as though it was made for somebody else. He held a battered old hat in his hands.

Henry. Tempe's idiot brother. Old lunatic Henry in the flesh. Oliver Cromwell, who was standing next to me, growled. I put a hand on his head.

"What do you want?" I said.

It was a safe guess to say Henry had slept in the stall. The hay bore the imprint of his body. He stood there bowing his head.

"See Tempe," he said.

"No." I shook my head. "You can't. You'd better be off. She doesn't want to see you."

He bobbed his head up and down vigorously. "See Tempe, yes," he persisted. His blue eyes had about them the look of a fool, but he seemed harmless enough. "Just once. See Tempe."

"Why?"

"Must needs see her."

"She won't see you, Henry."

He lowered his gaze again. Then, as if a sudden thought had come to him, he said my name, softly. "Mary?"

Or was it his mother's name he was saying? Oliver growled again. And then a very surprising thing happened. Henry squatted down and held a hand out to Oliver. And with a thump of his tail, the dog went to him and allowed himself to be fondled.

Oliver Cromwell knew him! Henry rubbed the dog's ears and caressed his neck and face in the way a man does when he is accustomed to being around dogs. With a final pat, Henry stood up.

"Mary," he said again. "Little cousin."

The way he said that made me recollect what David Hamilton Morris had speculated yesterday about Henry. That he didn't think Henry was lunatic.

"Yes, I'm your cousin," I allowed. "I'm staying with Tempe. I've just milked the cow, and now I must get back to the house." How did he remember me?

"Must needs see Tempe," he said again.

I'd had about enough of this, I decided. "If Tempe sees you, you're in trouble, Henry. Don't you understand?" Then I was seized by a brilliant thought.

"She'll tell General Wayne you're a nuisance. And he'll throw you out of camp. Then how will you sell rum?"

"Camp," he repeated.

"Yes."

"Tempe is in trouble. British in camp."

"No, there are no British in camp, Henry. You needn't worry your head about that."

He became agitated then. "British." And he shook his head. "Tell Tempe to stay away from British. Trouble."

"All right." I humored him. "I'll tell her."

He nodded, smiling. Then just as suddenly the smile disappeared. "You have food?"

"Are you hungry, Henry?"

"Henry is hungry."

Here might be the answer. "Well, look here. I'll go back to the house with this milk. Tempe's waiting for it. I'll tell her I left something out here, and I'll be back with some bread and cheese as soon as I can. But only if you promise not to lollygag around after you eat. You must leave."

He nodded in agreement, his eyes never leaving my face.

I took off my blanket coat and laid it down on the straw. "I'll tell Tempe I forgot it. She'll scold that I'm running around in the cold." I picked up the bucket and called to Oliver Cromwell. Henry stood watching us leave the barn. He was still nodding and smiling.

I walked, head down, very fast. *Dear God*, I thought, *I believe that what I have just negotiated is what Tempe would refer to as a compromise.*

It was a good hour before I could escape the house and get back to the barn. And I was on pins and needles the whole time. But finally Tempe left to ride Colonel to her sister Phoebe's, chiding me not to leave until she returned. I promised. Then I left Aunt Mary in front of the fire in the kitchen, telling her I was going to the barn to fetch my blanket coat that I'd forgotten earlier.

Henry was waiting for me. He seized the bread and cheese like a man who hadn't eaten in a fortnight. It pained me to observe his hunger.

"How do you know I'm your cousin?" I asked.

He had the breeding, no doubt left over from his days at home, to swallow before speaking. "Your friends told me."

David and Jeremiah. "Well, I'm happy to make your acquaintance, Henry," I said. "But I really must be getting back to the house now. Remember, you promised that if I fed you, you'd leave and not come back."

He nodded. I moved away.

"Remember your promise, too," he said in the same singsong tone I'd used on him.

That he would mimic me, I found startling. "What promise, Henry?"

"Keep Tempe from British in camp! Trouble there!"

"Of course I will, Henry. Good-bye now."

He nodded, chewing and swallowing. He was

seated on the barn floor with his legs out straight in front of him, his lank, unkempt hair straggling around his ears. I felt a surge of pity. I went out the barn door.

"No lollygagging," I heard him say to himself. "Henry made promise."

6

My head was spinning when I got back to the house. I scarcely remember making my piecrust. Usually cooking soothes me, calms me, but my brain was so addled from seeing Henry and from what I'd learned yesterday about a possible mutiny that I thought it would burst.

So I made two pies, one for us and one for General Wayne. I put a goodly supply of cream in them and some of Aunt Mary's sherry.

Aunt Mary sat and watched me, which made matters even worse. She chatted away, and I was obliged to answer, or at least to follow her line of thought. The conversation was inane. All I could think of was how I'd just sent her son away and how she would never speak to me again if she knew of it.

Oh, I was so confused. I was getting a headache. And to add to my distraction, three times before noon there were knocks on our back door. With my hands covered with flour, I answered the first knock to see a disheveled camp follower standing there. Her hair straggled out from under her mobcap, over which she wore a black tricorn fitted with a corncob pipe in the brim. Her red-and-white striped stockings sagged about her ankles. Her apron no longer bore any semblance of its original whiteness. It looked as if she'd both cleaned her husband's musket with it and wiped his cut finger.

"They told me you had soup," she said. And she held out a wooden bowl. An undersized child, rumpled and pitiable, clung to her leg.

I did not invite her in, but she stepped over the threshold just the same. Once inside the door, she cast an envious eye around our kitchen and over my appearance.

"I heard Miss Wick had her fancy cousin from Long Island staying."

I handed the bowl of soup to her. I'd filled it to the brim. "I'm not fancy," I said.

"I heard they wuz Tories in Long Island."

"Some are." I wiped my hands on my own spotless apron.

"And where's the high and mighty Miss Wick? Out on her horse, prancing about the countryside like a fine lady, I suppose?"

From her chair by the hearth, Aunt Mary was listening intently, though she appeared to doze.

"She was up before light to make the soup," I said.

"I heard the handsome General Wayne dined here last evenin'."

"He did," Aunt Mary snapped. "At my invitation. You hear an awful lot, it seems to me."

The woman shook her head, taken aback. "We hear things, in camp," she said. "I didn't see you there, Goody Wick."

"It was always my belief that the Good Lord gave us five senses," Aunt Mary said. "Perhaps you'd best learn to use the other four. And some common sense. General Wayne is doing his utmost to procure food and clothing for his soldiers. And you'd best hear, too, that if anyone badmouths him in my presence, they'll get none of my soup! Which *he* instructed us, when he was here last night, to give you in the first place!"

"I ain't badmouthin' him, Goody Wick," the woman said meekly.

"Then take your soup and go."

She went. "You were wonderful, Aunt Mary," I said. But I feared for her, for she was agitated. So I made her some tea and helped her into the parlor, where she liked to sit in the sun with Cleopatra on her lap.

"You take no sass from them," she instructed me. "And remember, I'm right here."

I kissed her and went back to my pie-making. Twice more the knock came on the door. The next two transactions went smoothly enough, and I got the pies in the oven. Then a knock brought a woman who, Lord forgive me, looked like a water rat. For some reason she had gotten the bottom of her layers of skirts wet, and over the arrangement of rags on the top half of her she wore her husband's regimental coat.

"You have any spirits?" she asked. She was smoking a corncob pipe. She was of indeterminate age—young, I think, although the ravages of war made her look old.

"No," I said.

"I need spirits. This cough."

"The soldiers have rum in camp," I said.

"And wouldn't you know about that," she sneered. "We see you sneakin' around with them young fellers. I'll wager you know more about what's in camp than you let on, don't you, Missy?"

"I don't sneak," I said.

She leered at me as she took the soup. "I hear you Long Island lassies ain't as cold as you look."

"If you'd stop smoking that pipe, it might lessen your cough," I said.

She left indignant. But she left. It was all I wanted.

I decided, then and there, that if Tempe did not return soon, I would cry. It gave me no sense of gratification, handing out the soup. My head was pounding. I needed fresh air. These women were blaming me for their plight. Me and Tempe. Not Congress, not the Executive Council of Pennsylvania, and certainly not the civilians in Pennsylvania who were eating sumptuous food and wearing fine clothes while the colony's soldiers starved.

I was having a cup of tea and some buttered bread by the fire when there was a timid rapping on the door. Wearily I got up to open it.

A woman stood there with a child of about three in her arms. He was wrapped in a blanket, and she herself had a tattered but adequate shawl around her shoulders. Her mobcap was clean, her face calm.

But she said nothing as I opened the door. Just stared, scarcely blinking at me. A sense of calm came over me. "You want soup?" I asked.

"I'd be grateful," she murmured, "for a clean shirt."

For a moment I did not comprehend. "Ma'am?" I asked. For I could see in an instant that she deserved respect, though I know not why.

"A clean shirt, please. And a bit of soap. And candles. I could use two candles."

"We . . ." I half turned away, gesturing to the table behind me, then looked back at her. "We can spare soap. And candles, yes. But . . ."

"A man's shirt," she elaborated carefully. "I'd

heard the man of this house died. Would there be a shirt about you can spare me?"

"Yes. I'm sure we have one of Uncle Henry's shirts. Is it for your husband?"

"It's for my babe. To bury him in." She said it plain and quiet, looking down at him briefly.

I went hot and then cold and felt prickly feelings in back of my neck. For a moment I thought I would faint dead away. But the pale, unwavering, calm eyes of the woman fastened upon me, held me up. "Please wait. I'll get the shirt," I said. "Please step in."

"I'll wait out here, thank you."

I closed the door and leaned against it, feeling nauseated. *Her child was dead!* Oh dear God, where was Tempe? Aunt Mary, that was it. I'd tell her. She'd know what to do, what to say.

No. I couldn't upset Aunt Mary. I must attend to this myself. I took a moment to close my eyes and take some deep breaths. I could hear my own heart beating like a drum in my ears, it seemed. Then, thinking of that poor woman waiting on the other side of the door, I went through the parlor and the entryway to the other side of the house, to Aunt Mary's room.

In a small cupboard I found Uncle Henry's shirts, neatly folded. I took one, shaping it into as small a bundle as I could and slipping it under my apron as I walked back through the parlor.

She was standing there, outside the door, just as I'd left her. I gave her the shirt. "Many thanks," she said.

"The soap and candles. Wait!" And I secured them from a drawer in the kitchen hutch.

"Just put them in my haversack," she directed.

I did so. Then I straightened up to look at her. I ran my tongue along my lips. "I'm sorry," I said.

"Thank you."

"Do you need anything else?"

"No."

"If you do, come back, please . . ."

"You've been most kind."

And with that she turned and walked down our stone path and around the house. I shut the door and bolted it from the inside. No more, I decided, there will be no more soup given out today.

I went into the parlor and smoothed the comforter over Aunt Mary's lap.

"I heard the door." She looked up at me. "Was that my husband?"

"No. Another camp follower, Aunt Mary."

"Every time I hear a knock, I think it's him. But why would he knock? It's his own house. You're a dear little soul to care for those poor women. General Wayne's idea about the salt pork soup was most convenient. Clever man, that Wayne. I do miss a man around the house."

"Will you nap now, Aunt Mary? Can I help you to bed?"

"No. I'll just sit here and doze. Go back to your baking, child. That pie for the general. Did you put an extra measure of sherry in it?"

"I did, Aunt Mary."

"Good, good. Your hands are cold, child. Go warm them by the fire."

I was weak with anger and helplessness and torn with guilt. There was not a quiet place left in my soul. I went back into the kitchen and sat down at the table to finish my cold tea. *As soon as Tempe returns, I'm leaving for General Wayne's*, I told myself. This part of the war has nothing to do with the word *freedom*, or how I harken to the sound of it. This part of the war has nothing to do with anything I can harken to at all.

7

I sat, with Tempe's red cloak around me, on a bench in the center hall of Peter Kemble's commodious house. In my lap, wrapped in a linen napkin, was my chicken pie.

All the doors to the inner rooms were closed, and in front of one of them stood a sentry. I tried not to pay notice to him, but I saw him casting wary looks in my direction.

I had been completely unprepared for the reception I got as I approached the two-and-a-half-story house at the fork of the main road east of camp. I was too enamored with Colonel, for riding him had been like nothing I had ever done before. I felt like a queen on his back. He held his head high and proud as we rode, and when I spoke to him, I could swear that he understood.

"You're the finest creature God ever made, 'tis true. I can see the muscles rippling under your skin, yet you lift your hooves dainty as a swan. I mind why Tempe loves you so."

He tossed his mane and whinnied, and I felt

such pride I thought my heart would burst. Then two sentries sighted me coming and rushed toward me, demanding to know who I was and what I was about.

They thought I was Tempe. Nothing I said could convince them otherwise. They recognized Colonel and the red cloak, and since they'd never met her face to face, they did not stop to realize that I was considerably younger. They made me dismount and yield Colonel to them. Then they ushered me into the house. I was anxious about Colonel, and I told them so as I watched him being led around the back of the house.

I'd been sitting on the hall bench for about half an hour when the door behind the sentry opened and a young officer stepped out.

"Miss Wick?"

I told him I wasn't Miss Wick.

"Would you please come in, anyway?"

I got to my feet, clutching my pie, and walked, eyes downcast, across the wooden floors that were, to give them credit, well polished. The whole house looked less like a military headquarters than anything I had ever seen—although, if pressed to explain what a military quarters should look like, I'd be hard put to say.

It was richly furnished, with good carpets

and fine old portraits above the wainscoting. It reminded me of my brother Nathan's house. A Tory house, Tempe had called this place. The room I was led into had a cheery fire in the hearth, red draperies, a Persian carpet, and Chippendale furniture. I was told to sit. The officer peered down at me.

"Allow me to introduce myself, Miss Wick."

"You can introduce yourself all you want. I'm not Tempe."

"Who are you then?"

"Who are you?"

"I am General Wayne's aide, Major Benjamin Fishbourne."

"You do have a bit of the look of a fish about you, now that you mention it."

My father had always said I had Aunt Mary's sharp tongue. It held me in good stead now, for I was getting more apprehensive by the minute. General Wayne was nowhere in sight, there was no telling what they'd done with Colonel by now, and they did not believe me when I told them I wasn't Tempe.

"Insolence will get you nowhere, Miss. What did you say your name is?"

"I didn't. But it's Mary Cooper. And I'll thank you to see that my cousin's horse isn't confiscated by your men."

"The horse is tethered out back. I'll see to him myself as soon as you do me the honor of answering my questions."

I looked up at him. He reminded me of Nathan. Imperious. And he had the better of the situation. Although, to give him credit, he didn't gloat as Nathan would have done.

"What do you wish to know?"

"What are you doing here?"

"I came to see General Wayne."

"What for?"

I saw no need to tell him about my letter to my brother. Abraham has always told me that the less you let an adversary know about you, the better off you'll be. And something told me Benjamin Fishbourne was an adversary.

"I just came to see the general. My goodness, you people are suspicious."

"We have reasons to be, Miss. There are spies in and out of camp."

"Well, do I look like a spy to you?"

He sighed. "What do you have under that napkin?"

"A pie. For General Wayne. I baked it myself this morning."

"May I see it?"

"Well, heavens, haven't you ever seen a pie before?"

"Uncover it, please."

I did so. He leaned over to scrutinize it. He sniffed. Then he straightened up. "I'll have to look into your haversack now, Miss."

"What for?"

"I told you. There are a lot of spies around. We're at war."

"Well, you would have a difficult time convincing me of that."

I had gotten rid of my headache on the ride over here. But now it was coming back. I knew General Wayne was beyond that nicely carved door. I wanted to see him desperately. I was sure he would put a stop to this nonsense in a minute. And I had no intention of allowing this rude fish-person to rustle through my haversack.

I was just about to tell him so when a voice from the hallway hailed me. "Mary!"

We both looked up. And there stood Lieutenant Reeves. He came into the room smiling. "I didn't know you were coming this morning. I'd have escorted you. Is something wrong? Is Aunt Mary all right? And Tempe? Does the general know you're here?"

I wanted to jump out of my chair and kiss him. But I had the presence of mind to maintain my dignity.

"Hello, Enos. They're both fine. Nothing's wrong. Except they've taken Colonel, and I'm worried about him. And this fish-person now wants to look through my haversack. I'm not a British spy, Enos. Won't you tell him so?"

"You know this young woman, Lieutenant?" the major asked.

Enos saluted. "Yes, sir. I've been to dine at the Wick house many times. She's Tempe's cousin from Long Island."

"You will vouch for her then?"

Enos's eyes were smiling, but he kept a straight face. "With my reputation. And may I suggest, Major, that the horse in question is most valuable. And is owned by the young lady whose father allowed us to use his land. I think it would upset the general considerably if anything happened to him. He holds the family in high esteem."

The major nodded. "Thank you, Lieutenant. Will you see to the horse, then?"

"Yes, sir."

I could see that the major was relieved. "I have pressing matters to attend to. After you've seen to the horse, come back and wait with Miss Cooper. Jemy the Rover is with the general now. Major General Thomas Church of the 4th has an appointment, also. He should be here presently. If you're back by then, usher him right in. Miss Cooper can wait. She is your responsibility until she is given back the horse and rides off the plantation."

Enos saluted again. *Poor man*, I thought, *all he ever does is salute. Doesn't anybody ever salute him?*

The fish-person strode out of the room. "Just sit quietly," Enos directed. "I'll be back in a few moments."

He left, and I waited alone in the Chippendale chair just to the left of the beautifully carved door. In a moment it opened a bit, and I heard General Wayne's voice. "You're sure, now."

"Have I ever misled you, Anthony? A sloop of war, lying in the mouth of the Raritan, with several vessels, including barges. None of your other spies have given you that information, now, have they?"

My ears perked up immediately. I held my breath.

"The British have gold and silver to give them, Jemy," came the reply. "We've only depreciated paper currency."

"Ah, but Jemy the Rover don't care 'bout that. Jemy works for the love of you, Anthony."

Wayne laughed. "You scoundrel. All right. I'm convinced, whether in your hours of sanity or insanity, you'd cheerfully lay down your life for me. But if I find you double-dealing, I'll have your hide roasted on a spit. I can bear it when other spies double-deal. I come out the wiser, even with their lies. But not you, Jemy, not you." And the general's voice went hoarse.

"Anthony." The man's voice got petulant. "Haven't I served you well? Do you forget Valley Forge?"

"I'll never forget Valley Forge. And yes, you have served me well. But stay off the rum, Jemy. A person in your occupation can't afford what it does to the senses. And one more thing. Don't leave without seeing Fishbourne. I've instructed him to extend you every hospitality."

"Bless you, Anthony."

There was a shuffling, then the man came out of the room and walked toward the doorway, away from me—not seeing me, thank heaven. He was just about as nondescript as a man could be. I couldn't see his face, but he had an uneven gait and a manner of mumbling to himself as he went.

Just as he went out of the room, another man came in. I assumed it was General Church, for he was smartly attired in a full dress uniform, right down to the sword at his side. The door was open wide now, and I was hidden on the other side of it. But I heard Wayne greet him.

"Thomas, come on in."

The door closed firmly again, and I sat clutching my pie and shivering, not from cold but from the knowledge that I'd been privy to a private conversation between General Wayne and one of his spies.

I heard murmurs of conversation from within, but this time I could not make out the words. After about five minutes Enos came back in, smiling.

"Colonel's fine. Hasn't the general seen you yet?"

"General Church is in there."

"Oh." He sat down, and we waited in silence. Then I spoke. "Enos, I saw Jemy the Rover."

He said nothing, waiting.

"He's a spy, isn't he?"

Enos scowled. "Did you hear anything?"

"No," I lied. "But I heard General Wayne mention his name. My friends in camp told me about him."

"You must forget you ever saw him, Mary, or it could endanger his life."

"Why does he call the general by his Christian name?"

"The general is uncommonly fond of him and permits it. Jemy flits in and out of camp as he pleases. Nobody can keep track of his wandering habits and long absences. He enjoys special privileges. But you mustn't repeat a word of this, even though it's known in camp."

"I did hear something, Enos."

"I shouldn't have left you unattended. I knew it."

"It was only a remark the general made. He

said he hoped he'd never catch Jemy the Rover double-dealing. What does that mean?"

"Can't you get your heart set on another line of questioning, Mary?" he begged.

"I'm afraid I can't, Enos. If you'll just tell me that, I won't bother you about it anymore."

Again he sighed. "Very well then. Spies constantly cross lines. They pretend loyalty, give deceiving news, and take back whatever information they can get to the other side. It doesn't matter who they spy for. Both sides have spies like that. Since we know that, we can give deceiving news."

"Heavens, what's the purpose?"

"It's an intricate game of secret military chess. It leads to a mass of tangled uncertainties. But even if spies are double-dealing, we can get enough information out of them to profit. Now, Mary, I've kept my part of the bargain. I'll speak of it no more."

He was so adamant, I fell silent and we waited again. Several moments later Major General Church and Wayne both came out. Again, the door shielded us from them.

"I can't thank you enough, Anthony," the older man said. "An officer's pay is less than the wages of an unskilled laborer in regular life. Without your help, my retirement leaves me without a farthing."

"You've earned whatever I can do for you, Thomas. I wish it could be more. See Fishbourne. He's been instructed to supply you with army rations until spring."

They shook hands, and the older man left. Then Wayne stepped out into the room, turned, saw us, and frowned. Instantly Enos was on his feet again, saluting.

"Sir, Miss Cooper wishes to see you. I've been instructed by Major Fishbourne to wait with her."

Wayne was scowling for a moment, and I trembled. I had heard he had a scathing temper when roused, and I hoped we were not going to be fortunate enough to witness it.

But then his countenance cleared and he bowed. "If I knew the young lady was here, I wouldn't have kept her waiting," he said carefully.

"I haven't been waiting but a few minutes, General," I lied.

Enos said nothing, thinking my remark mere politeness. But it was sufficient to inform the general that I had just arrived and had heard nothing.

"You've brought the letter for your brother then, Mary?"

I stood up. "Yes, sir. But I've also brought something else." And I held out the pie.

He suppressed a smile. "Are you out to bribe me then, Mary? What is it you need?"

"Nothing, sir. I made it for you. For your birthday. I heard it was on the first of January."

This touched him. For a moment he was taken aback and the courtly manners did not serve him at all. He accepted the pie and ushered me into his inner room.

Feeling borne upon wings, I followed. The sense of him, his presence towering over me, was enough to make me swoon.

"So you've made me a pie, Mary."

"Yes, sir. Chicken. I thought you might like it. My father always put great store in my cooking. I think it was the one thing he liked about me. I wanted to make you a clam pie, but we've no clams hereabouts. So you'll have to do with chicken."

I fell silent, realizing I was babbling. He was smiling at me quizzically. "I'm sure, Mary, that if you were my daughter, I'd be most proud of you. And not just for baking clam pies."

There it was again. He considered me as a daughter. Still, the words warmed me.

I do not remember very much of what transpired, exactly, between myself and General Wayne in that meeting. It comes back to me in bright patches of memory, like the makings of a quilt, which I stitch up in my mind in quiet moments.

He accepted my pie graciously. He ordered tea, which was brought, and it warmed me considerably. There were even some small cakes. Although I think he must have been most pressed with more important business, he gave me his full attention and seemed to enjoy chatting.

He told me of his children, Margaretta and Isaac, and how he was concerned they should receive a proper education. He told me how, when a boy at home in Pennsylvania, he attended a school run by his uncle.

"I was the despair of both him and my father," he said. "I organized the other boys into marching with hickory sticks and playing Long Knives and Indians. My uncle was so distracted he wrote to my father saying I'd never make a scholar. But perhaps I'd make a soldier."

We both laughed. "So you see, Mary," he said, "I didn't please my father, either."

And then—in a moment, it seemed—the meeting was over. He was on his feet, taking my hand and kissing it. The room was moving, and he loomed over me, larger than life. It seemed as if all of it was happening to someone else, not me. Everything in the room was in bright colors and seemed out of proportion. Yet I was filled with promise and good feeling.

He ushered me out to a waiting Enos and bade him see me off safely. He took my letter to Abraham and promised a speedy delivery for it.

Then I was mounted on Colonel again, nodding in agreement to what Enos was saying to me, though I cannot recollect for the life of me what it was that he said.

I was riding, lost in my own concerns, in a labyrinth of thoughts that led nowhere in particular. My world was inhabited by the gentle voice and dark eyes of General Wayne, when someone dashed out into the road in front of me. It was completely unexpected, and I had to rein in Colonel severely. The sudden jolt almost tumbled me from the saddle.

A bedraggled creature in some semblance of uniform danced up and down in front of me in the cold.

"Tempe? Absalom Evans of the 2nd," he said.

He thought I was my cousin.

"I've a message from Bowzar."

"Yes," I said quickly.

"Tonight. A wake for little Button McCormick. Molly and Adam McCormick's child. Died early this morning. Come to their hut at eight. He's from the 10th."

"I'll be there," I said.

Then he disappeared, leaving me stunned and rudely pulled out of my dream world into reality. I looked around me to the doings in camp, the sharp, dreary outline of the little huts against what was left of the trees, the ragged children playing about, the camp followers taking in frozen wash from haphazard lines, emptying slops, gathering wood for fires.

It was getting on to dusk. I should be home. My head pounded as I continued my ride. Tempe. A wake tonight. The child I'd given Uncle Henry's shirt for had a name now and parents who would mourn him. Be there, Evans had said. I vowed I would be.

8

The hut of Molly and Adam McCormick was like all the others, from what I'd been told. I'd never set foot inside any of them since I'd been here.

David and Jeremiah had once said they were all the same as those the army had built at Valley Forge. This hut was about sixteen feet long and fourteen feet wide. Though the log walls were made tight with clay or mud, the wind still whistled in at certain places.

The door faced the company street. At one end was the fireplace. The one window was just a hole sawed through the side wall and covered with oiled paper. The floor was packed dirt.

The beds were bunks with straw and blankets for bedding. And on one bunk now lay little Button McCormick. My Uncle Henry's shirt reached down to his feet, and from somewhere had been secured a pair of gray woolen stockings.

Tempe and I got there twenty minutes past the designated hour to see a stream of soldiers and their women moving in and out, paying their respects. About ten people were crowded in the hut, and Tempe suggested we wait until some came out.

I said nothing. I was still too stunned by the fact that she had allowed me to accompany her. But a configuration of events conspired to make that happen, not the least of which was her gratitude that I'd furnished Molly McCormick with one of her father's shirts. Another factor was the fortunate appearance of Ebenezer Drake, who'd come by to visit Aunt Mary.

Tempe had said nothing when I told her Absalom Evans had mistaken me for her. She changed the subject, leading me to believe that whatever connections she had made with soldiers in camp was a matter she did not want questioned.

As the soldiers and their women filed out of the hut, the women hugging their tattered shawls or blankets around them and the men holding their tin or wooden lanterns, I was surprised to see them nod silently to Tempe. She knew them all then. And they knew her. What was she keeping from me?

Just before we went into the hut, David and Jeremiah came up to us out of the darkness. They murmured polite hellos.

"Does General Wayne know the McCormick lad died?" Tempe asked Jeremiah.

"He sends his condolences," Jeremiah answered.

"You'd think he'd bring them in person."

"He knows his presence would only put a damper on the gathering," Jeremiah said wisely.

"As if a gathering could be any more somber," Tempe said.

We went inside. My friends, witnessing Tempe's surliness, shook their heads at me.

Inside there were about eight people now. Immediately Molly McCormick came over to kiss Tempe and thank her for the shirt. "If I'd known, I would have given a better one," Tempe said. Then, to my surprise, she reached into the large basket she carried on her arm and brought out a folded sheet, two loaves of bread, and a slab of bacon.

She was a secretive one, my cousin. I'd sensed there was bread in the basket. But the bacon and sheet surprised me.

"To wind him in for the ground," she told Molly.

I saw tears come into the elder woman's eyes as she clutched the sheet close to her. Then immediately she handed the bacon to another woman, who set about slicing it and putting it into a pan over the hearth. The two loaves of bread were put on the table, where there sat a jug, some apples, a slab of cheese, and a crock of what looked like squirrel stew. Everyone who came must have brought something from their slender larder. I thought of the chicken pie I'd given General Wayne this morning and how much more needed it was here.

I'm starting to think like Tempe, I told myself. *Is that why she brought me?*

People were settling in all around, some on the hearth, some on the floor, a man and woman even huddled on the top bunk above Button. They sat around the table, too. You could scarcely move once you found a place. People were finding places as if waiting for something to happen. Across the room I saw Absalom Evans, who had given me the message this afternoon. Except for him, and Molly, and Jeremiah and David, I didn't know anyone here. A medium-sized man with a beard, a corncob pipe clenched between his teeth, and the remnants of a red Liberty cap that had seen better days stood up, one foot on the table bench, and rested his arms on his knee.

"Are we all here then?" he asked.

"We are and some extra, Billy," a man next to the door said.

Billy nodded as if giving a signal, and the man near the door closed it. It made a solid, ominous sound.

"Then I'll tell all assembled, as I've been telling all night. 'Tis a sad thing we have to do while the body of little Button lies here. But we do it as much for him as for ourselves. I can think of no fitter tribute. Tomorrow we bury him. Today we gave birth to our Committee of Sergeants. For whatever reason, supposedly because I can read and write, they've elected me secretary. We've been talking and arguing and thrashing things out all afternoon. And we figured, with everyone coming to pay their respects tonight, it was time to say what we've done."

"What have you done, Billy Bowzar?" came a voice from a dark corner.

"Formed a Committee of Sergeants."

"For what reason?"

"You need ask? When the gratuity of 1779 was paid, it was a free gift to the veterans. It didn't commit them to any added obligation. You've forgotten how some of the officers took advantage of the ones who couldn't read and made them sign new enlistments? You've forgotten we haven't been paid in near a year? That the only rum we have is run in to us by Henry Wick with the addled mind, who brings it from the British? You've forgotten those of us who wasted away with sickness and famine and nakedness? You are neither clothed, fed, nor paid. You've forgotten James Coleman of the 11th, who had to hear ten names read off, and not one of them his, and who was hanged right here in May?"

"Coleman was a deserter," someone said.

"So were ten others with him. They were pardoned. He hung." He went on.

"You've forgotten Lieutenant John Bigham of the 5th, who was sent by the council in Philadelphia with money to pay bounties and spent it instead? Claiming it was better spent the way he saw fit? What do we fight in this war?"

"The British who have enslaved us," came a voice from a corner.

"And, in taking the money and saying we didn't deserve it, was not Bigham the gentry? Are not the officers who have bullied and despised you the same as the British gentry? Do you forget Captain Theophilus Parke who defrauded his men of their pay and bounty?"

It was then that a small, quavering, but brave voice spoke out from behind me.

"Captain Parke was convicted. And sentenced to be cashiered with infamy. His sword was broken over his head on the public parade in front of his regiment. By Wayne's orders. I was there."

I was so proud of Jeremiah!

Silence in the room. The man called Billy

Bowzar nodded. "Wayne is high-minded. So are Butler and Stewart. But it isn't enough. We have no argument with Wayne. But he can't do for us what needs to be done."

"What needs to be done?" Jeremiah asked.

"Our grievances settled. And we're about to do that."

"How?" Jeremiah asked again.

"That is for the Committee of Sergeants to decide. And it isn't for open discussion. Those who are with us know who's on the committee and will be told what's to be done. You, Levering's the name, isn't it? You serve Wayne?"

"Yes," Jeremiah said.

"And your friend there, Morris. He serves Crystie. Why do you concern yourselves with us?"

"We came to pay our respects to the McCormicks," Jeremiah said. "We knew Button."

"But you know Wayne and Crystie better. Your loyalties are to them."

"I speak for myself," Jeremiah said. "I'm a soldier of the Line. So is David. I think I speak for him when I say we owe our lives to the soldiers who took us in, who enlisted us so we could have homes. I'll not betray anybody."

"Nor I," said David.

Bowzar nodded. "Well spoken. But there's

nothing to betray. All we're about is writing down our grievances."

I didn't believe that, and I don't think Jeremiah or David did, either. I don't think half the people in the room believed it. But one of the camp women who was tending the bacon put a plate of it on the table then, and another took a pot of coffee that had been bubbling on the hearth, coffee made of grain, no doubt, and poured it. The men passed around the jug of rum. Someone sliced the bread.

The talk turned to the 8th Regiment of the Line, which was at Pittsburgh, guarding the frontier against Indian attacks; then to the weather, which was mild; then to the rumor that extra rum would be issued for New Year's Day. Someone brought up the fact that five companies of German soldiers were expected here on January first.

"We're mostly Scots-Irish in the Line," Bowzar said. "From what I've gathered about the 11th, seven of its sergeants were born in Ireland, seven in England, one in Scotland, four in America, and six in other countries."

It was then that a terrible thought seized me, a realization so bold and so chilling that I wondered where my mind had been up until now that I hadn't noticed it before. And I stood, dumbstruck, staring at Bowzar.

His accent was British!

And suddenly the candles on the table in front of me flickered and cast shadows on everyone's face, and I felt as if I were in the middle of a bad dream.

9

All I could think of was what Henry had said in the barn this morning. Was it only this morning? It seemed like days ago. Poor old addled Henry, not right in the head, they all said, yet right enough to know that Tempe was in danger from the British in camp.

Bowzar! I recollected then a piece of information, a piece out of the whole cloth of my experience here at Morristown. A fragment, torn loose, almost discarded.

I recollected hearing once that Bowzar had defected from the British!

I became chilled then, and I untied my tin mug from its piece of rawhide around my waist and held it out for coffee. Someone filled it. I drank the concoction, wishing for the sweetness of sugar, yet at the same time savoring the bitterness of the drink, hot and raw in my throat. Like the truth I had just discovered.

Bowzar was the *British* that Henry had spoken of.

The conversation had died out, and a silence

settled over the room. And then another thought seized me with such clarity that it was like a revelation.

The small talk had been labored. They were waiting to speak of things more important.

Bowzar spoke then. "We've other matters to discuss," he said. "But they're not for all ears. I think I speak for the McCormicks when I thank all for coming. I speak for myself when I ask certain of you to leave now so we can go about our business."

He mentioned no names. But in turn Tempe and I and Jeremiah and David embraced Molly McCormick, and then Adam, and left. The cold outside hit me in the face, steadying me. We walked a few feet from the hut. Jeremiah had a lantern. I can't, to save my soul, recall what he and David and Tempe were talking about. I just kept staring at my cousin's profile and thinking of her friendship with Bowzar.

Then from behind us the door of the hut opened again, framing Bowzar in the yellow candlelight from within. "Tempe!"

We halted. He strode toward us. *He's an arrogant little man*, I thought, for I perceived that what he lacked in height, he made up for with a sense of his own superiority.

"A word with you, Tempe," he said softly.

She hesitated, her profile unyielding.

"Just a word." He held out his hand. She looked to me, and I said I'd wait with Jeremiah and David, and so she allowed Bowzar to lead her to the darkness by the side of the hut.

"I was proud of you in there, Jeremiah," I said.

He shrugged. The three of us looked at one another above the scant light from Jeremiah's lantern.

"Do you think they're planning mutiny?" I said it plain.

Jeremiah lowered his eyes, and David did not answer.

"They'll not mutiny," Jeremiah said finally. "They like and respect Wayne."

I looked at David. "Do you say the same?"

He scowled. "They're just letting out their anger," he said.

"No." Jeremiah disagreed. "It's more than that this time. But I don't put it down to mutiny. I don't think they do, either."

"I don't think they know yet where today's actions will take them," David said. I was surprised at the wisdom of his statement, and I made a note not to discount his opinions in the future.

"True," Jeremiah agreed. "But not mutiny."

We both asked why.

"You heard them say they founded a Committee of Sergeants. Committees are for sane men, not for the madness of mutiny. It's all we've done in these colonies since the beginning of the revolution, set up committees. Committees of Correspondence, Committees of Safety, committees for this and for that. Men who write down their grievances and form committees don't mutiny."

"Such men formed a revolution," David reminded him.

"No," Jeremiah insisted, "I wouldn't worry about that."

"What will you tell Wayne about tonight?" I asked him.

"That I paid my respects to the McCormicks. There's naught else to tell. It isn't for me to inform Wayne that they're writing down their grievances. He'll find out soon enough."

I glanced in the direction of Tempe and Bowzar. They seemed to be arguing. Or at least having a rousing discussion. "You two had better get back to camp," I suggested. "Standing about in this cold will make you sick."

"We thought to walk you home," Jeremiah said. "You and your cousin."

I smiled at them, so shabbily dressed and freezing, yet acting the gentlemen. "We'll be all right," I said. "Everyone in camp knows us. Go, before you both catch your death."

They seemed glad enough to be excused and take their leave. I inched my way toward my cousin and Bowzar, close enough to the hut to hear anyway.

"We've pledged," he whispered to her.

"Well, I haven't," she answered. "It isn't my fight."

"Sooner or later, Tempe Wick, you're going to have to make something your fight."

"When the time comes, I'll pick my own, thank you."

"I'm not asking for you, just for the loan of the horse."

"No."

"Would you spit in the face of little Button McCormick, then, as he lies cold in that hut?"

"It has nothing to do with him."

"Lass, haven't you been listening to me all along? That's exactly what it has to do with. He represents the ills we want remedied."

"I want no part of your mutiny, Billy."

"It's no mutiny. I won't allow the word. The men know it. All we want is to gather on the parade and form up to present our list of grievances, proper-like, to the officers. We want them to see us as men and not like the dogs we've been made to feel."

"You said Wayne can't do for you what needs to be done."

"Out of courtesy, we mean to present them to him first and get his permission to take them on to Philadelphia."

"On Colonel? You want to take Colonel to Philadelphia?"

"No. Would you listen, woman? I just want the use of him for when we form up to approach Wayne."

Silence. I held my breath, trembling.

"No," Tempe said.

I let out my breath, not realizing I'd been holding it.

"So, all along then you've spoken one thing to me and meant another," he sneered.

"I've made you no promises, Billy Bowzar. I've said over and over that I'm tired of all this and I want it done with."

"We're all tired of it, lass—the war, the cold, the famine, the coughing our guts out, the dying. But it'll never be over if someone doesn't take action. There will be more Button McCormicks dead. Do you want them on your conscience?"

"Don't put it on my conscience, Billy. I'll not have it."

"Your conscience is clear, I suppose?"

"Yes. I've done my best through all of this. When the army was here last year, and now. My father gave his land. What more . . ."

"And your brother Henry?" he interrupted.

I could almost feel Tempe's stunned silence. "What?"

"Your brother Henry. Running in British rum. Is he doing his best, also?"

"Leave Henry out of this."

"Ah, but he's in it. As is your brother-in-law, the good doctor. Your own sister's husband."

"You threaten me?" my cousin asked.

"I hear the talk in camp that you won't allow Henry in the house to see his own mother. That she thinks he's dead."

"That's my business."

"It's the business of the local authorities if they find out he and your brother-in-law are running in British rum."

"You . . ." I heard Tempe gasp. "You poltroon!"

He laughed. "Such language from a sweet young woman."

"I'll not stand for your threats, Billy. I'll tell Wayne."

Now his laugh was low and cunning. "Tell him what? That your brother and brother-in-law have a cozy little arrangement going, selling rum for the British? You forget how Wayne feels about his own wife for dealing with the enemy. You wouldn't want your brother arrested, would you?"

I heard a strangled cry from Tempe, then Bowzar's voice, low, soothing, and all too familiar for my liking. "What am I asking that's so terrible, lass? I'm driven to it. We're desperate men, half naked, shivering, without food. Our children are dying. You and I have been friends right along. And you hate Wayne as much as I do. You hate this war as much as I do. You hate what it's done to me, to you, and to everyone. At least I've the courage, and others like me have it, to draw a halt to what we've suffered. All I want is the horse for one day, Tempe. You can tell everyone I stole him. I don't care. I'll not connect you with it."

She was sniffing.

"Think about it. I'll ask nothing of you tonight. Will you just think about lending me Colonel?"

"And what of the revolution?"

"What of it?" he asked.

"Is this the end of it, then?"

"No! Don't you understand? This will save it. Bringing our petition to Congress will get food and clothing for the men."

"If this Line goes, the revolution goes with it," she said.

"This Line won't go if they're fed and clothed and paid, Tempe. And that's what we're after. *All* we're after. I swear it."

"I have to go home," she said.

"Go, lass. We do what we do whether you give us Colonel or not, you know. All I wanted was to have the horse, to ride up to Wayne and do it with dignity."

"I have to leave now, Billy."

I saw her pulling away, saw him holding on to her wrist.

"You'll think on it?" he asked.

"I'll think on it."

I moved quickly back to where she'd left me on the path and pretended to be preoccupied with my shoe buckle as she came up.

"Come along," she said briskly. "Mama will worry, and Ebenezer Drake will have to be on his way home. Come on, Mary, stop lollygagging. I'm cold."

We walked home in silence. She never said a word, but she walked so fast I could scarcely keep up with her. And her profile, when I could see it etched against the harsh outline of the camp, was rigid and carved out of this new worry she had, which I knew she would never share with me.

10

Needless to say, I did not sleep well that night. My dreams were torn, tormented things in which I saw poor addled Henry and little Button McCormick. Once during the night Oliver Cromwell growled and gave a low and menacing bark, which roused me enough to think I heard footsteps outside.

Henry! I thought. *He was creeping around out there.* The idea terrified me, although I don't know why. I knew old Henry was harmless. I reached out to pat Oliver's head, and he moved closer to me, and all was quiet again. Perhaps Oliver had had a dream, too. Then I heard some branches scratching against the house, and I determined it was the wind picking up. I could not sleep. And my thoughts became strange, lying there. Ideas that would seem ridiculous in the light of day always appear to be most respectable at night, of course.

Consider, for instance, the thoughts I conjured up in the dark.

Everyone, I pondered, *myself included, is just*

part and parcel of the whole of their life experiences.
Everything we do in life, every transaction we
have with another human being, is overshad-
owed by the events that make us what we are.
We carry with us always the burdens and joys of
the past, like so much baggage. Oh, if only we
could perceive what baggage the other person
brings into the room, how much easier it would
be to figure people out!

My cousin Tempe, for instance, is the sum
total of all her experiences. She is the youngest
of the family and spoiled, yes, as Aunt Mary says,
the child of her parents' old age. Because she
watched her two sisters marry and bear and lose
children and settle into proper, if dull, lives, she
rebels against all that. Yet she wants marriage
with her Will, I know that.

Left to care for her elderly parents while others went about their business so freely, she both
languishes in and despises her role, I think. And
now that her father is no longer around and she
takes the place of a man around here, she flaunts
her newfound independence, riding all over,
with no one's by-your-leave, on Colonel.

She has said she refused to marry Will because of the war. Yet I think she knew she
couldn't leave her mother. So she blames the
war. For everything. If she did not have the war
to blame, I don't know what she'd do.

That's Tempe's baggage. Mine is of another bolt of cloth, which I've yet to smooth out someday. It's always much easier, I think, to ponder someone else's problems, rather than your own.

I fell asleep finally as the first light grayness of dawn appeared in the window. I slept late, and Tempe never woke me. I got up to find her and Aunt Mary already in the kitchen having breakfast.

The talk was of the new hired man Ebenezer Drake had secured for us.

"His name is Sprout," Tempe said. "That's all I know of him, that and the fact that he's too old to be in the army. He'll be here around noon. After which I have to go to Button McCormick's funeral. I've asked Ebenezer Drake to come sit with you again, Mama. I hope you don't mind. I want Mary to accompany me to the funeral. Will you, Mary?"

I saw her steady, unblinking gaze and knew she didn't want to go alone because she didn't want to be alone with Bowzar. Which meant she hadn't yet formed her mind about loaning him the horse.

"I'd be happy to go with you," I said.

"Perhaps you'd make one of your pies to bring. It would be a proper gesture," she said.

I agreed. And during the rest of the breakfast, she chatted with Aunt Mary.

"You look tired, Tempe," Aunt Mary observed.

Truth to tell, there were dark circles under Tempe's eyes, and her face was pinched and drawn.

"Something woke me in the middle of the night," she said. "I heard a sound outside the house. And I distinctly heard Oliver bark."

I knew then, in one of those unswerving moments of revelation that come upon a body so unexpectedly, that Henry had been lurking outside the house. She had heard someone, too.

"The wind was scraping branches against the shingles," I said.

"There was no wind," she said shortly. And she got up to put more wood on the fire. "That was Bowzar. And if he comes round again, I'll use Father's fowling piece and give him a round of grapeshot for his trouble."

She would, too. Only it wouldn't be Bowzar she'd shoot. It would be her own brother. I had to get to Henry and warn him to stop skulking around the house. Or we'd have a tragedy on our hands out of all proportion.

"Bowzar?" Aunt Mary asked. "Who's this Bowzar fellow? You walking out with someone else now, Tempe? What about Will Tuttle?"

"I'm not walking out with anyone, Mama."

"Do you want me to milk Daisy this morning?" I interrupted. I had to get Aunt Mary's mind on another subject.

"She's milked," my cousin said. "I was up at first light. But I'd be gratified if you'd feed the other livestock and put the horses in the paddock. I'll be working here in the kitchen and want to be able to look out and see Colonel whenever I wish."

So then, she was afraid Bowzar was out to steal Colonel! It was worse than I'd thought. I finished breakfast quickly, sneaked some biscuits into my haversack with some apples, and left. I needed to speak to Henry as much as he needed to speak to me.

I knew he was in the barn as soon as I got there. The livestock were spooked, and the barn swallows wouldn't light on the rafters the way they usually did. But I went about my business, Oliver Cromwell tagging along.

It's of no consequence to me, I told myself, *if Tempe goes and shoots her own brother. Or if she wants to give her horse to Bowzar.* I was weary of it all. *She treats me so shabbily*, I thought. *Why should I care?* But I knew that was as big an untruth as I dared tell myself in one day and still consider myself a Christian. It would just undo me to know she was handing Colonel over to that weasel, Bowzar. And if she shot Henry, it would be my fault. I resolved to say nothing to her this day about her horse, however. Not until I could speak with Henry. For I had determined by now that he knew more than he was disclosing. No, that's wrong, I decided. Henry had tried to tell. I just hadn't listened.

Abraham always said that if people listened as much as they talked out of turn, the world would be a better place.

I fed the horses and let them into the paddock. When I finished, I stood in front of the empty barn. Through the cracks in the walls bars of sunlight shone in, filled with dust and straw bits.

"Henry Wick, I know you're here." I said it plain. "So why don't you just come out and make your presence known. Because I want to talk to you."

I heard a rustling of hay from the loft. And within moments Henry was making his way down the ladder. He stood there, all six feet of him, careful to hold his battered old hat in his hands, the hay clinging to his disreputable clothing.

"Mary," he said in wonderment. *Well, good heavens*, I thought, *who else did he expect to see here?*

I was brisk with him. "There's a hired man

coming this afternoon. So you can't hide out here anymore. And unless you want a round of grapeshot in your pants, you'd better not lurk around the house anymore at night, either. Tempe heard you. She thinks you're Billy Bowzar creeping around out there. And she's about to use your father's fowling piece on you. I need to talk to you, Henry. And I haven't all day."

His jaw was slack, but his eyes were alert. *Plenty of sense in those eyes,* I told myself. And I recollected what David had said about Henry not really being lunatic. Again I reminded myself to put more store in what David thought. He made an awful lot of sense sometimes.

"Was that you making scratching noises against the house last night, Henry?"

He looked at the floor.

"What were you after?"

"Talk to you," he said.

"Well, I'm here now, Henry, so talk."

It took him a while to compose himself, and I waited. I could almost see him forming his words in his head. "Ask Tempe for me," he said.

"Ask her what?"

"Henry wants to see Mama."

Well, I had to give him credit for getting right to the point and not beating around the bush, all right. Still, couldn't he have come up with an easier request? I eyed him warily. "You know Tempe won't allow that. Why do you persist? Is it because you want to know if your father left you anything in his will? That's what they say about you in camp."

He shook his head violently. "Henry don't need his daddy's money. Henry has the king's shillings." And he reached into his haversack and retrieved a fistful. "See?"

I saw. "Is that from selling rum?"

He nodded. "Henry just wants to see his mama."

It tore into me the way he said it. And it gave me a new worriment. He was not only running rum, he was boasting about it. All kinds of people probably knew of his activities by now. I decided to settle something once and for all in my mind. "Are you rum-running with Dr. Leddell, your brother-in-law?" I asked.

He nodded yes, grinning at me, and his eyes lit up. "William," he said.

So it was true. Well, I couldn't worry about that, too. If Dr. Leddell persisted in such a pastime, he could just abide the consequences. I had more immediate concerns. "I'll speak to Tempe about letting you see your mother," I said. "I can't promise you anything, but I will broach the subject to her. Now we must talk of other things, Henry. But first things first. Are you hungry?"

He gave me such a soulful look I couldn't bear it. So I immediately took the biscuits and apples out of my haversack, and he sat down unceremoniously and commenced to eat.

That was a mistake, I decided immediately. *He doesn't have all his faculties. He won't hold with anything I say while he's concentrating on food.* But I was wrong.

"How can Henry help little Mary?" he said.

I sat down on the straw next to him. "You can tell me what I need to know, Henry. Bowzar is British, isn't he?"

"Bowzar." He nodded. "Yes."

"Is he the one you were speaking of when you said Tempe was in danger of the British in camp?"

"Bowzar," and the nodding became vigorous.

"Is he a spy, Henry?"

"No. No spy." He said it with such conviction that I could not help believing him.

"What do you know of him, Henry?"

"Was with British. Came to Americans."

"I've heard tell he defected. That he's a turn-coat."

He devoured the remains of a biscuit. "Ummm."

"Then why were you worried about him and Tempe? What trouble could he bring her?"

He wiped his mouth and considered an apple solemnly, polishing it with his sleeve. "Henry," I said, "please tell me what you know."

"Bowzar is bad man," he said. "Casts dark shadow."

"Why?"

"Planning bad things."

"What?"

He bit into the apple. "Mutiny," he said.

The sun seemed to go behind a cloud then, and the barn darkened. All the sound in the world was some twittering of barn swallows and Henry crunching his apple. We stared at each other, he and I. And I fancied that in his eyes I saw the truth and not the babbling of some idiot.

"How do you know?" I asked weakly.

"Henry is in and out of camp. They think Henry is lunatic. They say things in front of Henry."

I saw the hurt in his eyes and understood.

"And what do you say of yourself, Henry?"

He lowered his eyes. "Henry is coward. Not lunatic."

It was as if I heard the beating of drums inside my head. But it was only my own heart. *Why*, I asked myself, *am I privy to this revelation when no one else is, not even his family?* But I could not ponder on that now.

"Why are you a coward, Henry?"

"Long time ago," he said, "Henry was soldier. With British."

"With Washington in the French War," I said. "They told me."

"Henry ran under fire," he said dismally.

"Lots of men did, Henry."

"Other men not Henry's concern," he said quietly. "Only Henry."

Tears came to my eyes at this profound answer.

"Many men were killed because Henry ran. Braddock. Almost Washington."

"But Washington wasn't killed. He lived. They even thought him a hero afterward. His name was known for his actions by the king in England! And he's our commander now, and it's a different time, Henry. A better time. Because we fight for ourselves now. Not for the British. Don't hate yourself, please."

"Henry don't hate himself," he said. "Henry hates the king's men."

That stunned me. He smiled blissfully.

"But you're running rum for them," I said.

"Running rum for Henry. Give rum to Americans at good price. Sell king's men short."

Good heavens! I could scarcely believe my ears. "You cheat the British?"

He nodded yes. I asked him why. And his face clouded over with pain.

" 'Tis no profit to remember," he said.

He said it with a lilting sadness, speaking now as a normal man.

So David Hamilton Morris was right all along, I thought. "Sometimes it helps to air old ills in the sunlight, Henry," I said. "Take them out of dank places. You'd be surprised at how they don't look so bad then."

He sighed. I waited.

"They laughed at us provincial soldiers, the British. They jeered at us, called us names, made us do their bidding, kicked us when it pleased them to do so. They gave us slops to eat. On the day of the battle I didn't move fast enough to do an officer's bidding, and he hit me with the flat of his sword. When the enemy came at us, so many hundreds, with men and horses screaming all around, my face still hurt from where I'd been hit with the sword. I thought, why die for people who treat you worse than a dog? So I ran."

I gazed at him in wonderment.

"Washington fought. Had two horses shot from under him. I ran."

"Washington was an officer," I said. "They never hit him with a sword."

"They wouldn't listen to him, either. He told that man Braddock how to fight. Not to march in sunlight, but to hide behind trees. Washington told him this was the wilderness. He wouldn't listen. I saw no reason to die for someone who would hit me with a sword and wouldn't listen."

"So why do you allow it to burden you so, Henry?"

"We can't help what burdens us."

"So now you cheat the British and sell rum to the Americans at a good price."

"Henry gets back at the British," he said, lapsing back into his accustomed manner of speaking.

"And you hear things in camp. Because they all think you're lunatic. And you've heard now of the mutiny."

"Henry heard, yes."

"And that's what you really wanted to tell me last night, isn't it?"

He said it was.

"Why don't you go to Wayne and tell him of the mutiny?"

"Wayne thinks Henry is lunatic. Couldn't get near Wayne. Bowzar knows Henry runs rum for British. Henry don't want Wayne to know."

I pondered all this, seeking the sense in it. It all seemed so logical, and I was gratified Henry had confided in me. I was enlightened. Yet saddened at the same time. And I knew that precious little good would come of everything he had told me. Who would believe me if I said Henry wasn't really lunatic, that he was just pretending because it was the only way he could face life?

It only concerned Tempe and Aunt Mary. And Aunt Mary's mind was more addled than Henry's was supposed to be. And I sensed there was never any love lost anyway between Tempe and her older brother. Would she want to hear now that he was in command of his own senses and welcome him back as head of the family? And give up her place to him? I thought not.

I also realized that I had more pressing matters to consider at this time. "What do you expect me to do about the mutiny, Henry? Tell Wayne? They say he already expects it. Do you know when it's to be?"

"No," he said dismally.

"Then what can I do?"

"Tell Tempe. Stay away from Bowzar."

"Heavens, we've all been telling her, Henry. Even Wayne. She doesn't hold with what we say."

He gripped my wrist. "Tempe don't know of mutiny. Henry heard Bowzar say he has Wick girl fooled. Boasting. That she's with him!"

So that was it. What I'd witnessed myself last night when Bowzar lied to my cousin and swore

137

there was no mutiny. That was it. The humiliation I saw in Henry's eyes of having to overhear Bowzar boast that he had the heart and the loyalty of the Wick girl. Right in front of Henry. Because the only Wick man on the place was lunatic.

I patted his hand. "I'll speak to her, Henry."

"Don't let her give horse," he begged.

"I won't." I got up. He stood up with me. I smiled up at him weakly, wondering how I purposed to deliver on my promise. "And I'll mention to her, before this is over, that you want to see your mother," I said.

He took my hand then and raised it to his lips and kissed it.

I felt chilled all over, witnessing this display of displaced gallantry from a past he said it did not profit to remember. And I dared not ponder on the anguish that was in this man's mind to make him turn his back on that past and choose, instead, to be called a lunatic.

11

It's a terrible thing to see a child put into the ground. It's a violation of all that is decent and right amongst good people. And I think it demeans the rest of humanity to realize we could not protect and care for such a little one. I know most folk think it's the will of the Almighty, but I'm disinclined to believe that way. I don't hold with such thinking. Although it does give comfort to the mother and father. I truly believe, if I allow myself to consider the matter, that the Almighty has better things on His mind than to take little children. And I think it's incumbent upon the rest of us, when it happens, to ask why.

We knew why it happened with little Button McCormick, of course. He died from the cold, from the lack of food, and because his parents didn't have the remedies to make him well. And, as I stood at the gravesite with the others that afternoon and looked around me at the gathering of faces, I saw that the knowledge of why it had happened was very much in everyone's mind.

There was no weeping. At least not until Molly McCormick handed a book to Billy Bowzar, and he stood at the head of the grave to read from it.

I saw from the engraving on the cover that it was *The Book of Common Prayer*.

And, in his clear voice with his British accent, Bowzar read.

But first he spoke.

"I think it fitting, as do the parents of Button McCormick, that I read the burial service for a soldier."

There was no emotion on any of the faces as we listened, but I sensed the effect of this announcement. It was both disturbing and gratifying.

As it was getting on to dusk now, someone lighted a pine torch and handed it to Bowzar. *It could have been a lantern*, I thought. But the torch added so much more flavor to the reading.

"Forasmuch," Bowzar read, "as it hath pleased Almighty God of His great mercy to take unto Himself the soul of our dear brother here departed . . ."

We wept in silence.

We dallied at the gravesite as people do, held there by some spell, loathe to leave and yet hating the sight of it. I stayed close to Tempe as she'd asked me to. Several times during the service Billy Bowzar had cast her significant glances, but she kept her head bowed.

As we were leaving, it was not Billy who came over to us, but Molly McCormick.

"I thank you so much for coming." Her cap was white and starched as was her neck kerchief. Her shawl was middling worn. Tempe nodded to me, and I handed her the chicken pie.

"Would you come back to the hut for some refreshment?"

"No, thank you," Tempe said. "I've left my mother and must needs be getting back. I offer you my condolences."

The eyes of Molly McCormick were dry. "A word with you then, Miss Wick, before you go."

"Yes," Tempe said.

"He was my only child, Miss Wick."

"Call me Tempe, do."

"Very well then, Tempe. We'll not stand on formality. You've been kind to us, and I am most grateful for all you've done."

"I've not done anything," Tempe said. "And if the truth be known, Molly McCormick, I feel guilty. Though I hate the feeling. And have resolved not to allow myself to feel this way. But I still do."

"Then do something about it," Molly McCormick said.

Whatever Tempe expected, she hadn't expected that. Nor had I. She stood stone quiet and stared at the plain, round face of the sorrowing woman before her.

"And what can I do? Can I, or any of us, bring your child back? What are you asking? Say it plain."

"What I ask is not for myself or my man. There's naught anyone can do for us now, Tempe Wick. What I ask is for other children like Button in camp. So the same fate won't be theirs."

Tempe nodded, giving her permission to go on. Molly continued.

"Give Billy Bowzar the use of your horse," Molly McCormick said.

I could scarcely believe my ears! Here was this woman supposedly overcome with grief, just having buried her child, and she was speaking for Billy Bowzar, who stood this very minute huddled with the men in the distance. I looked quickly at my cousin. Her head was bowed.

Then she raised it and looked directly into Molly McCormick's eyes. "I think less of you this minute than I have thought of any woman," she said.

"And why is that, Tempe Wick?"

"Because you have allowed the burial of your child to become a rallying point for Bowzar."

I could have thrown my arms around my

cousin at that moment. Oh, how I loved her! But I kept my face straight and showed no emotion.

Neither did Molly McCormick, but her voice, when she spoke, quavered. "Who are you to say how I should behave as I bury my child, Tempe Wick? You haven't a babe of your own. Not even a man to worry over. You go prancing around the countryside on that white horse of yours like a fairy-tale princess, waiting for her knight in shining armor. This war has not touched you."

"It's touched us all," said Tempe.

"Your brother goes about camp selling British rum. In league with your brother-in-law. Oh yes, we know. As we know that you've been friends with Billy Bowzar. Until he asked for your horse. And then, when this war touched you, you drew in that fine red cape of yours and all you owned with it. You were only playing in your friendship with Bowzar. And now when he needs you, you want to take your chessmen and go home."

It took a while for Tempe to reply. "I was not playing chess with Billy Bowzar. I offered my friendship in earnest."

"Then withdrew," the older woman said.

"No." Tempe drew in her breath. "He asks too much. My horse is . . . all I really have left of my father."

"I have nothing left of my Button," Molly

said. "Which is why I allowed his burial service to be a rallying point for Bowzar, yes. If, in doing so, I can rally anyone to pledge with us, then Button's death was not for naught. Don't you see . . ." She reached out a reddened hand and grasped Tempe's forearm.

" . . . If I don't make some sense out of Button's death, I'll die myself! If I can use his death for some good, then perhaps I'll be able to sleep again at night. Don't wrinkle your fancy nose at that thought, Tempe Wick, until you've had a babe of your own someday. Then you'll be fit to remark on it."

To my surprise, Tempe took this rebuke in silence. Then spoke. "And my loaning my horse to Billy Bowzar will justify your child's death?"

"Nothing will ever justify it! But your loaning your horse, so he can ride proper-like to present our appeals to General Wayne, will lend dignity to our cause."

"And what cause is that?"

"That our grievances are settled! That no other child in this Line will have to die for lack of food or warmth, as Button did!"

"If it's mutiny," Tempe said, "there will be more death. Have you thought of that?"

"It's not mutiny," Molly McCormick said. "We have Bowzar's word on that."

And why God did not reach out from his leaden skies and strike me dead at that moment for not speaking out, I shall never know. For I knew it was mutiny. Yet I kept mum, perhaps out of the knowledge that I could never be as eloquent as Molly McCormick. Perhaps because I was afraid to speak. And perhaps because I sensed they would never believe me, since the only argument I had, the only weapon I could use to call Billy Bowzar a liar, was the word of a man they all knew to be a lunatic.

And how could I prove that Henry Wick was anything else? He would never admit it to anyone. Never would he show any face but that of an idiot to anyone in camp.

"I told Bowzar I would think on it," Tempe said then.

Molly McCormick nodded. "Thank you, Tempe Wick. Now I'll be getting on home." And with that she turned, with all the dignity and grace of a woman at a town social, and joined her women friends who were waiting for her.

Tempe put on her hood, set her shoulders straight, sighed, and looked at me. "Well, come along, Mary. Ebenezer Drake can't stay all afternoon with Mama."

I walked with her, keeping stride, determined to remain silent. *If she wants to give her horse* to Bowzar, *I'll not interfere*, I told myself again. *My thinking on the subject is done.*

"I'll thank you not to mention any of this in front of Mama," she said.

"Of course not, Tempe."

"Go ahead. You might as well say what's on your mind before we get back to the house."

"I have nothing on my mind, Tempe."

"That would be a rarity, when a Cooper has nothing on her mind. I live with one, you seem to forget. Well, go ahead, out with it."

"Are you going to lend him Colonel?"

"I said I'd think on it."

"And in what way would your thoughts be going, then, Tempe?"

"To lend the horse and be done with it. These people have always wanted something more of me than I've been able to give. I thought it was bad last year with the Connecticut and Maryland men. But these Pennsylvania people are all blockheads. Once they get their heads set in a direction, they're like Ebenezer Drake's mule. Stubborn! I've given them food, clothing—d'you think they're happy? No, that's not enough. Nothing is! They want something more from me, always. And that *more*, that *something*, is all bound up, for some queer reason, in my horse. It isn't just any horse they want. Do you see them asking for Buckwheat? They've seen him in the paddock. No. It's Colonel they want. They see him as some kind of a symbol."

"Of what?" I asked.

"I wish I knew."

"Did you ever think . . ." I hesitated.

She cast me a sidelong glance as we trudged along. "Go ahead, out with it."

"Could it be they see him as a symbol of freedom?"

She didn't laugh at that as I thought she would. She had too much respect for Colonel. "That's very pretty, Mary," she said. "And just what I would expect from you. But I don't think they see him as a symbol of freedom so much as they see my giving him up as a symbol of their victory."

"Why?"

She stopped short, and I with her. She stood staring out over the winter landscape, and I saw it reflected in her blue eyes, making them gray and sad. "Because they see me as gentry," she said.

"But that's foolish."

"Of course it is. My father was a farmer. I have no pretensions. But so many of the men in the Line don't even own land. They can't read or write. They hate the gentry. And I'm afraid that when I ride about on Colonel, that's what they see."

We walked in silence for a moment or two. "Do you think," I asked carefully, "that's what General Wayne thought, too?"

"I'm sure General Wayne has more important things on his mind these days. Or will, shortly."

"Will you give Colonel to Bowzar, then?"

"I've a mind to," she said. "I'm sick to the teeth of all of this. Then, perhaps for once and for all, they'll leave me be."

Now I stopped dead in my tracks. "You can't, Tempe."

"Oh? And pray, why can't I?"

"I didn't want to tell you this."

She looked back at me, weary resignation on her face. "Don't then. I've had enough to plague me this day."

"But I must."

She waited.

"Billy Bowzar is lying," I said. I don't know what gave me the strength to say the words, to go against her cold stare. But I went on.

"They're planning mutiny, Tempe."

She stiffened. "Who told you? David and Jeremiah?"

"No."

"Who then?"

"Your brother," I said, barely able to get the words out. "Henry."

Her eyes narrowed. "You want me to believe that you've had conversations with Henry? And that he knows about a mutiny?"

"It's true, Tempe." And my voice got small and sounded as if it were coming from someplace far inside me. I nodded my head. "Henry has been sleeping in the barn at night. It was he, not Bowzar, who was lurking around the house last night. I spoke with him this morning when I fed the horses."

"And he told you about a mutiny," she said dully.

"Yes. He's heard talk. In camp. And he wanted to warn you. He's worried about your friendship with Billy Bowzar."

"Oh." And she looked up at the sky and shook her head back and forth. She sighed in resignation. "Oh, Mary, you honestly expect me to believe this? That after all these years my brother Henry has been given back his reasoning? And is worried about his little sister? Henry is a lunatic, Mary! Don't you know? He is akin to a slobbering idiot!"

"He doesn't slobber," I said. I must say I uttered it with considerable dignity.

"All right! So he doesn't slobber! Neither does he have the sense of Ebenezer Drake's blind mule! Honestly, Mary, I gave you credit for more sense than that."

"I don't care what you give me credit for, Tempe. I've spoken with Henry, and he utters lots of sense. You ought to talk with him sometime."

She continued walking. "No, thank you. I can do without the honor."

"But why, Tempe? Did you never ponder that he may not be addled in the brain at all? That something else may be ailing with him?"

Again she stopped. This time she closed her eyes. "The next time you have a conversation with my wonderful brother Henry, ask him about his wife, Elizabeth. And his two children, Mary and Chloe."

Well, I had no reply for that, since it shocked me near out of my senses. Henry married? No one had ever told me.

"He is such a lunatic, my dear cousin, that his wife forsook his bed and board, when indeed he did have any, and has had other children by someone else. Now, if you don't think all that upsets Mama . . ."

"I didn't realize that, Tempe," I said contritely.

"Well, it's a wonderment to me that there are some things you don't realize."

"You needn't be so mean."

"I'll be as mean as I like. You're a plague to me."

We continued on in silence for the rest of the walk. It occurred to me, of course, that a man's wife might leave his bed and board and that did not qualify him to be a lunatic. But I had just about run out of argument. There was no sense to it. Tempe's mind was set in one direction, and she was going to act on it.

When we reached the back door, the night was dark. Tempe paused before going in.

"None of this to Mama. Promise."

"I promise," I said. "You're going to lend the horse, then."

"Whether or not I lend Colonel will not stop them, whatever course they're on, Mary," she said. "Lending Colonel will only give dignity to their actions. At least this way, with a horse like Colonel to ride, perhaps Wayne will listen to Bowzar. Did you ever ponder on that? That if they present themselves properly and aren't thought of as dogs, Wayne might listen?"

"Wayne's done all he can do, Tempe."

"I would expect you to defend him. He's turned your head."

"He hasn't."

"Oh?" And she smiled. "Are you telling me he was less than delighted with your pie-making?"

"He was gratified that I brought the pie."

"And? How did he act then?"

"The perfect gentleman. He took time to speak with me. We had tea. But I'm afraid you were right about one thing, Tempe."

In the dark I could see her eyes focus sharply. "What's that?"

"He thinks of me as his daughter," I admitted miserably.

She stared at me for a moment. "And how think you of him?" she asked.

"I don't know." I shook my head. "I'm so confused. But I do know that I still consider him wonderful. And that he's done his best with his men. And if this is mutiny, Tempe, it will kill Wayne. It will just kill him!"

"It isn't mutiny, Mary," she said wearily. "I do wish you would get that out of your head. And grow up. And stop being so romantic."

12

Aunt Mary's parlor was full of people. From where I sat, I could see the day was bright but windy outside, with pieces of clouds pushed across the sky by a wind that seemed to want them out of the way. Stark tree branches were etched against the blue, and sun washed everything clean. *It is so simple*, I told myself, *to sit here with family all about and forget there is a war outside these walls*. And I wished I could push all thought of it away like the wind pushed the clouds.

Was there ever a time in my memory when the war was not part of the whole cloth of my life? Its rumblings, its unrest, reached way back to 1775. I was eight years old then. It seemed my childhood was formed of nothing else but talk of war, unfair taxes, and problems over imported tea.

The talk around me now was the catching-up talk of family who didn't see each other that often. At the center of it was Aunt Mary, bright as a magpie, with her teacup in her hands. On the floor at her feet, like flower petals, were her grandchildren on the hearth rug. Phoebe and Will Leddell's little ones, five-year-old Henry and two-year-old Temperance. Aunt Mary's other daughter, Mary, held another Temperance, a sleeping babe, on her lap. Her Absalom, Hannah, Jude, and Phoebe were on the rug, also.

I never did see such a family for names as this one, what with all the Henrys, Tempes, and Phoebes. Of course in my family we have our Nathans, Samuels, and Marys. My mother's name is Mehitable. And she had decreed it would stop right there with her. So I was named after Aunt Mary.

"What do you hear from Will?" Mary asked Tempe. Like any older sister, it was plain to see that she was pushing the marriage of Tempe and Will Tuttle.

"I had a letter two days ago," Tempe answered. I noticed she was different in her sisters' presence, amiable and placid and never revealing that boldness she displayed to the rest of us.

If Phoebe and Mary had known what she was about these days, they'd have taken her to task. How I wished I knew them well enough to confide in. For I was sore afraid that Tempe really was going to lend Billy Bowzar her horse. She'd refused to discuss it with me this morning as we'd prepared refreshments for today's reading of her father's will.

"Will fares well," she said. "But he writes that Washington is as near to discouragement as he ever has been, what with the fall of Charleston last May and the rout of the Americans at Camden in August. But what weighs on his mind and saddens him most is the treason and desertion of Benedict Arnold last September."

"Eb said that Arnold was one of Washington's best generals before he went to the British," Mary put in. "Whatever would make a man like Arnold become a turncoat and a traitor to his country?"

"I don't know," Tempe said in a very small voice.

"Eb says Washington is concerned for the temper of the troops at New Windsor. There is a shortage of flour, clothing, and medicines— no herbal remedies, no spirits even."

Mary's husband, Ebenezer Blachley, was the finest of surgeons with the army. What he didn't report from there, Will Tuttle did. *I must tell Abraham to seek them out*, I thought. *They are kin, after all*.

We sipped tea, British tea, brought by the Leddells for Aunt Mary and shared, by her decree, for the occasion. A ham was on the spit for supper. In a corner, talking, were Leddell and two of Aunt Mary's lawyers from Mendham, Nathan Burt and James Furgerson.

"Well, let's get started, gentlemen." Aunt Mary handed her teacup to me and got to her feet with the aid of her cane. "That ham is smelling better to me by the minute. Mary, are the turnips cooking? Is the cornbread in the oven?"

"Yes, Aunt Mary." She may have been old and palsied, but she had a better appetite than any of us.

"I intend to open my best wine for supper. Thought you could keep from me that my Henry was dead, did you? Because I'm an old lady, you didn't think I could take it." And she surveyed her relatives, bright-eyed. "Well, I'll show you how I can take it. You men stop jawing over there and let's read the will."

There was a movement for seats. This all had been Ebenezer Drake's idea and a brilliant one at that. Have a reading of Henry Wick's will, he'd advised Tempe, and your mother will accept the fact of her husband's death. Tempe had conferred with her sisters, and they'd agreed. And it was working. Except that Aunt Mary thought we had all conspired to keep her husband's demise from her, when indeed it was her own mind that had refused to accept it at first, and Tempe had simply gone along with the charade.

I settled by the fire with baby Temperance in my lap. This was, after all, not my affair, but I could keep the children quiet for them, at least.

" 'In the name of God, amen, on this twenty-sixth day of January in the year of our Lord, one thousand seven hundred and seventy-one,' " Furgerson read. " 'I, Henry Wick of Morristown and County, in the province of New Jersey, be-ing well in body and of sound and disposed mind, blessed be God for it, and calling to mind the mortality of my body and knowing that it is appointed for all men once to die, do make and ordain this my last will and testament in manner and form following.' "

He gave to his daughters five shillings each, all three of them. All the rest of his estate he left to his wife. His son James was not mentioned.

His son Henry was.

He gave to his son Henry the sum of five shillings, also.

Outside the windows the sky was turning streaks of purple and red as the afternoon waned. The little ones slept on the rug at my feet. In the entranceway Oliver Cromwell lay snoozing. I could hear the ham sizzling on the spit. Baby Temperance was warm in my arms. James Furgerson's voice droned on, and I nes-tled in the bosom of this family, feeling secure and safe.

Within the hour we were all seated around the kitchen table, eating ham and cornbread and greens and turnips. Will Leddell had been named joint executor of Uncle Henry's will, along with Aunt Mary. He sat now at the head of the table in Uncle Henry's place, opening a choice bottle of wine.

"I'm so gratified that Mama has finally accepted Daddy's death," Phoebe murmured to Tempe as she passed the bowl of turnips.

"I must invite Ebenezer Drake to supper some night," Tempe said. "He is invaluable to me."

Phoebe leaned closer to her sister's ear. "What has Mama said about Daddy's leaving Henry five shillings? Has she put it together in her head and concluded this means Henry is still alive?"

Tempe shrugged. "The will was written in 1771. So it means naught to her."

Phoebe sighed. "I daresay I haven't put it together in *my* head yet. You know how fond I am of Henry. Still, I wonder what Daddy could have been thinking of. Poor Henry has been addled in his mind for years now. He isn't responsible. He can't even add to five."

"Yes he can," I put in quietly.

From across the table Phoebe stared at me, her gray eyes two pools of concern in her plump face. She was a kind, generous woman with

never a malignant thought in her head for anyone.

"You've seen Henry?" she asked.

"He's been around," Tempe said vaguely.
"Lollygagging about the barn. Now that we have
the new hired man, however, he doesn't come
anymore."

But Phoebe's gaze was fixed on me. "You've
spoken to him?"

"Enough to know he can add to five," I said.

"And where has he gone, then?" she asked.

"Oh, he's in and out of camp," Tempe said.
"The soldiers feed him and make sport with
him."

So, I thought, *Phoebe is innocent of her husband's
dealings with Henry, of the rum-running, all of it.
Phoebe didn't even know Henry's back in the area.
And Tempe is too considerate of her sister's tender
feelings to inform her of what her man has been up
to.* It was starting to make sense.

"Poor dear Henry." Phoebe sighed. "And
what of James? Do you ever think of James, sister? And what's become of him?"

"Probably dead by the hand of some Indian
by now," Tempe said bitterly.

At that moment Will Leddell popped the cork
from the bottle of Aunt Mary's choice wine and
startled us all. Everyone looked in his direction.

And for a moment, just a moment, his eyes

held mine across the table as he began to pour the wine into pewter goblets. And it was then that I realized that Will Leddell knew that Henry was not lunatic. And that he was aware of the fact that I knew it, too. For there was a warning in his eyes. And his round, usually cheerful face was set in determined lines.

I raised my chin and returned his steady stare. *I will have those five shillings, Will Leddell,* I said to myself, *for Henry. If I have to pick them up and deliver them to Henry myself.*

When they had all departed and Aunt Mary, overexcited, was made comfortable and put to bed, I followed Tempe around as she banked the fires for the night.

"How will they get the five shillings to Henry?" I asked.

"I haven't thought on it."

"Are you of a mind that he should have them?"

"It's in Father's will."

"Henry should have been here today for the reading."

She sighed and swept the hearth clean, then set down the broom. "Don't badger me, Mary. Wasn't it enough for Mama this day to finally accept that her husband is dead?"

"Yes," I said sorrowfully. "I didn't think."

"Well, think once in a while, do."

"What of Leddell? Will he give the money to Henry?"

"I don't know about Leddell. He'll try to cheat Henry out of it, I suppose. I shall have to speak to him of it. And I don't like speaking to that man at all. Do you see how he doesn't tell Phoebe anything that goes on? How he keeps her in the dark? She doesn't even know Henry's been seen in these parts again, and all the while her husband's been using him for his evil purposes. I tell you, when I see that part of marriage, I've a mind to tell my Will no-thank-you, I think I'll remain a spinster."

"Will loves you," I reminded her. "You told me yourself."

"Love." And she sat down by the hearth. "I wish I knew what it meant. I recollect when Phoebe and Leddell were courting. I was all of ten. And it seemed so wonderful to me. I thought he was quite dashing. He'd boast about being the illegitimate son of his father, who was a surgeon in the French Naval Service. I fancied him myself, in my own childish way. Now I realize that Leddell, for all the good he does as a doctor, never earned a thing on his own. His father left them that farm. And if not for Mary's husband, who took him under his wing and taught him medicine, I daresay he'd be a wastrel."

I let her talk. She was coming around to my way of thinking about Leddell, and without realizing it she was laying the groundwork for what I wanted to ask her.

"He doesn't need to run rum. That's what angers me. His practice supports them, and his father left considerable money. But that's not the worst of it. I hear tell that he's seeing another woman, a Hannah Sturgis. If Phoebe finds out, either about the rum-running or his loose morals, no good will come of it. Especially now that she's again with child."

"I'll ride over to Leddell's tomorrow, if you want, and ask for Henry's five shillings," I proposed. It was what I intended to ask for permission to do in the first place. For I wanted to see Henry again. And I needed an excuse to seek him out in camp, now that he no longer came around our property. I needed to keep abreast of the mutiny talk.

"You would do that for me, Mary?"

"I'll even get the shillings to Henry. Jeremiah and David will tell me where he is. Leddell doesn't worry me, Tempe. He reminds me of Nathan. I've had plenty of doings with his species."

"I'd be most grateful, Mary. But mind you, watch your tongue with him. I've no heart to make him an enemy. He's opinionated and quick

162

to anger. I need no rift between this house and Phoebe's, especially now that she's to have another child."

"You want me to coddle him, Tempe?"

"I want you to remember that he is my dear sister's husband. And she needs us. And, for all his provoking ways, he does care for Mama. He's the only doctor within riding distance I can depend on for that."

"I wouldn't care if he were the only doctor in this colony," I said. "If I felt about him as you do, if I knew about him what you know, I'd put him on notice."

"Well, you're not me, Mary Cooper. So you'll kindly do my bidding. And keep a civil tongue in your head. And take Buckwheat tomorrow. The new hired man finally shoed him. And don't wander about in camp."

13

It came to me, as I set about on my mission the next morning on Buckwheat, riding the mile or so to the Leddell farm on the road to Mendham, northwest of camp, that my cousin Tempe was resorting to compromise again in her dealings with her brother-in-law.

It was her way. And I might as well learn to accept it. Yet I knew compromise was not the way I chose to live my life. And not the way a fiery and energetic person like Tempe could live for long without something fairly bursting inside her.

Why, even Billy Bowzar had told her that sooner or later she was going to have to make something her fight. Which was by way of saying that she couldn't back off from life forever.

I wondered, with a cold stab of fear, whether she would make the decision to lend Colonel to Bowzar her way of committing herself to something, finally, after a long history of staying clear of the turmoil around her.

I found Leddell in his surgery. Phoebe was

busy with the children, so I told her I'd just wait in the little parlor where he received patients.

After about twenty minutes the door opened and a striking young woman came out. She looked to me to be a bit older than Tempe, and she was dressed in a lovely blue woolen cape with a silk lining and good leather boots. Her petticoats were of fabric more likely to be seen in my brother Nathan's neighborhood than around these parts.

In her hands she held a jar of herbs. "My mother will be most grateful, Will. How can I ever thank you?"

"It's thanks enough to see your cheerful face, Hannah."

My blood fairly froze in my veins when he said that. The woman gave a saucy laugh, and as she passed me to go out the door, my nose caught the scent of her. She smelled like lilacs. On the thirtieth day of December.

Will Leddell stood there like Ebenezer Drake's mule, staring after her for a full minute before he noticed me sitting there.

"Well, Mary Cooper. What ails you today?"

"Nothing." I stood up. "I've come on a mission for Tempe."

He motioned me into his surgery.

"Who was that woman?" I asked.

"Hannah Sturgis. From Mendham."

"She looks like a very fine lady."

"She is." He lowered his eyes. "One of the finest ladies hereabouts. Now what can I do for you, Mary?"

"I've come for Henry's five shillings."

His whole surgery smelled of lilacs, I noticed. The fragrance almost made me ill.

"And why would I have Henry's five shillings, pray?"

"You're the executor of Uncle Henry's will."

"I haven't the money yet. The will's only been read yesterday."

"You can give it to me from your own pocket for now."

"Why the urgency? Has Tempe suddenly discovered she has a conscience about her brother?"

Oh, the familiarity of the way he said that, daring me to reply! I kept my head, remembering Tempe's words of warning.

"Tempe has many concerns, Dr. Leddell, not the least of which is her brother Henry. But her main concern these days is her mother. She's your patient. I'd think you would be of the same mind. I know what you've heard about Tempe. That she won't allow Henry in the house. It's only her mother's delicate health that forces her to act so."

He nodded. "Has it never occurred to Tempe

166

that her mother's health might improve considerably if she told her Henry was alive?"

"It isn't for me to interfere, Dr. Leddell. I'm only visiting."

"You've already interfered, Mary."

"Now, what is that to mean?"

He smiled languidly, stretching his long legs out in front of him, relaxing in the chair. It was his superior manner I hated, I decided. As if he were gentry and we were all peasants to be dealt with at his will.

"You've made a friend of Henry," he accused.

"What business is that of yours?"

"It is my business. I've tried to keep Henry in line, tried to keep him behaving so he doesn't cause trouble to the family. He keeps sneaking back to the Wick place to talk to you. And every time you let him, it undoes all the good I'm able to do for him."

"All the good!" I got to my feet then, my blood boiling, my promise to Tempe forgotten. "I ought to warn you, Dr. Leddell, I'm not a wishy-washy young woman. Thanks to my brother Abraham, my mind is sharp and my thinking processes are unsullied. You can't fool me. You know the truth about Henry."

He laughed, low and cunning. "Yes, I know

the truth. He's caused his family nothing but expense and heartbreak for years. They can't be rid of him. That's the truth."

I stared at him stonily. "The truth I refer to is that he is not lunatic," I said quietly. "That it's a veneer for the fact that he cannot face the world except on his own terms. You know this. And you've been using him to run in British rum for you from New York. You're making money on the scheme. And you're using Henry as the scapegoat. Because people believe he's lunatic and won't hold him responsible!"

The smile faded from his face. "You're a brazen little piece. No wonder your family packed you off from Long Island."

"I speak the truth and you know it. You're using Henry."

"But you're wrong on two counts. One, if Henry is caught, they *will* hold him responsible. And two, he, too, is making money on the scheme. If, as you say, he isn't lunatic, then he fully knows what he's doing. So don't blame me."

"I do blame you. You could have been a good influence on him. He may not be lunatic, but his mind is sick in another way. And you've made no attempt to help him."

He leaned forward, smiling again. "What is your stake in this?"

"Henry's been a friend to me. I don't like to see him used for ill."

"And so now you're going to tell the world that he has the mental capacities of Dr. Benjamin Franklin, I suppose."

"No." I hesitated. "Henry doesn't want that. He couldn't bear it if he was made to face the world on its terms."

"Then what do you want of me, Mary Cooper?"

"I want Henry's five shillings."

"Is that all?" His eyes narrowed.

I looked at him. And I saw a real concern. For he knew I was on to him, not only for what he was doing with Henry but for Hannah Sturgis as well.

"You allow your wife to think that Henry can't count to five," I said. "He's her brother. Yet you'd cheat him and tell her he's too addled for money. And you haven't told her he's been coming around here again."

He said nothing, waiting.

"No," I went on. "That's not all I want. What I want, I know you won't do."

"And what is that, pray?" His voice was raspy.

"For you to treat Henry as a doctor would treat a patient. I've spoken at length with him. And it's as plain as the nose on your face that he suffers because he can't forgive himself for running from battle years ago. And that if he could be persuaded, now, to do something worthwhile, it might add to his self-esteem."

"So you fancy yourself a healer then, telling a doctor what to do."

"I fancy myself nothing. Just a human being. And a Christian. Which is what you're supposed to be, as well as a doctor."

"You're impertinent as well as brazen. Your family is well rid of you."

"I'm sure you're right, Dr. Leddell. They think so, too."

"And what is this something worthwhile you think I should persuade Henry to do?"

"I don't know. But I do know he's attracted to the encampment and the soldiers and the idea of the war."

"He's attracted to the encampment because he makes money there selling rum."

"You are a man without heart, Dr. Leddell."

"And you, Mary Cooper, are a meddler. A woman can be forgiven for many transgressions but not that."

"I have been called worse. And by people I hold in more esteem than you."

"Ha!" And he threw his head back and laughed. He got to his feet and began pacing, his arms folded in front of him. "I pity the poor man unfortunate enough to marry you some-day. He writes his own ticket to hell."

"If he does, then I'll make that hell as pleasant a place for him as I know how. But I won't deceive him and tell him it's heaven, then stoke the fires behind his back and cover it all with the scent of lilacs."

A dreadful silence followed. He stopped pacing and gazed out the window to the garden in back. For an awful moment he said nothing, and all that could be heard was the ticking of the clock in the corner. Then, quietly and without turning around, he spoke.

"We're getting into dangerous territory here, Mary Cooper. I suggest we end this conversation." And with that he turned and crossed the room, opened a drawer in a cupboard, and took out some money. Then he came toward me and held it out. I took it and counted.

Five shillings.

"Thank you. I'll see that Henry gets it."

He nodded. His face was ashen.

I looked at the shillings in my palm. "You won't try to help Henry, then?" I prodded.

"One thing I have learned in my years as a physician, young woman," he said solemnly. "You do grant that I am a fair-to-middling doctor. When I apply myself to the task."

I looked up at him. "I have heard that you are an excellent doctor," I said.

He nodded. "Very well, then. One thing I have learned is that most of the time the patient has to want to help himself."

I sensed now that he spoke from the heart. So I listened.

"And when the patient decides to help himself, he is three-quarters of the way to the cure."

"Thank you for the advice. I must go now."

He saw me to the door and held it open while I stood in the sunlight that spilled onto the threshold. I drew my cloak around me. "Do you think Henry would be likely to help himself in the near future?"

"There is no predicting what Henry will do. Especially when he is around the encampment. As you said before, it excites him. It reminds him of many things."

"Thank you again, Dr. Leddell."

"A moment before you go, please."

"Yes?"

"Would you be telling Tempe that her brother is not really lunatic?"

"I think not. He's asked me not to. I can keep secrets."

"Can you now?"

"I pride myself on not being a silly girl with a loose tongue."

"Would you be telling Tempe, then, the whole of our transaction here today?"

His eyes held mine. And I knew he was referring to Hannah Sturgis. I sighed. I am not so far above silliness that I wouldn't love to tell Tempe I'd seen her here today. But my mind quickened, and I saw the larger profit to be gained. If I earned his trust, or even if I had him in my debt, he might be more inclined in the future to help Henry.

"Tempe has enough on her mind these days," I said. "I'll not burden her with any more."

He inclined his head. I left him a more solemn and thoughtful man than I'd found him. I'd managed not to alienate him, yet I'd earned his respect. I had Henry's five shillings. And Leddell could still hold up his head if he had to come to doctor Aunt Mary.

Also, I'd given him much to ponder. Perhaps the next time he saw Henry, he'd see the patient, not the fool. He did take his doctoring seriously, after all.

As for Hannah Sturgis, well, there wasn't much I could do on that score. But I'd be willing to wager that in the future he'd be more careful about prancing her in and out of his surgery, where poor Phoebe was likely to bump into her.

How easy it seemed, I pondered, solving

everyone else's problems! Especially in this family. As an outsider I could see them for what they were, clear cut, and knew what to do about them.

It was another matter entirely, of course, to face my own.

14

But while I was riding along under a bright noonday sun feeling proud of the morning's accomplishments, with Henry's five shillings jingling in my haversack, matters were worsening all around me. And my sense of serenity was short-lived.

No sooner was I near to approaching the encampment on the road down from Mendham than I saw David and Jeremiah running toward me.

"We've been looking all over for you," Jeremiah said. "Get down from the horse, quick. We must talk."

I slid from Buckwheat's back and held his reins as I walked the rutted road with them.

"What is it?" I asked.

"Things are coming to a head," said Jeremiah.

"What things?"

"We're not sure. But David and I both sense something is about to happen."

"What?"

"We don't know."

"Well, heavens, I'm so glad you almost killed yourselves to give me such a message."

They were both out of breath, for they'd broken into a run as soon as they sighted me coming down the road.

"We were to your house," Jeremiah said, "earlier this day. And guess who was there?"

"Are we playing games? You must tell me the rules, if we are."

"Bowzar!" David said. He wagged his head in satisfaction as he said it.

I stopped dead in the frozen, rutted road. "Bowzar? In our house?"

"Well, he wasn't exactly *in*," David amended. "He was outside. By the well. Talking to Tempe."

"About what?"

"We don't know," Jeremiah chimed in. "But when we came up to ask for you, they looked like a couple of bears with their paws caught in the honey pot."

"Were they arguing?" I asked.

"They were talking," David said. "In a most amiable manner."

"Oh no!" I groaned. And all my satisfaction for the morning's work dwindled away. So that was it! Tempe had sent me off on a middling mission for her to get rid of me so she could confer with Bowzar! Most likely about giving him Colonel! And here I'd thought I'd accomplished something important this morning. My face stung with embarrassment. And a sense of betrayal. The errand I'd run for Tempe was of a trumped-up nature, the kind to be done by a silly little girl, while Tempe was plotting more important things.

"She's giving Bowzar her horse," I said dismally. "She's made her decision."

"If she has, it's because he told her something's about to happen," Jeremiah predicted. "The men in camp have been in a state of unrest all day."

"Why?"

"We don't know that, either," David said. "It's just something we sense. In the air. We did put it down, at first, to the fact that the day after tomorrow is New Year's Day. And preparations are being made to celebrate."

"What kind of preparations?"

"I don't know about the rest of the camp," Jeremiah said, "but I can tell you what's going on at Peter Kemble's plantation. He's brought musicians up from Philadelphia. He's holding a minuet at one of his manor houses. And rumor has it that three carriages of Philadelphia ladies are coming along, too."

I drew in my breath. "And General Wayne is to attend?"

"No. Kemble isn't holding his party at the main house, where Wayne is staying."

Peter Kemble, I'd learned since visiting Wayne's headquarters, had three manor houses on his four thousand acres. And over a dozen barns. Which is why he could afford to quarter Wayne and his officers in his main house and never suffer privation. Never even see them if he chose not to, but hunt with his hounds on his vast land holdings and entertain other gentry who held great parcels of land around Morristown.

"Kemble has two cows and several fat hogs hung up to cook for New Year's Day, too," Jeremiah said. "I saw them. And the men of the Line know about this. It doesn't hold well with them when they're so hungry."

"What of Wayne?" I asked. "What does he say?"

"He's been invited to dine on New Year's Day with Lucas Beverholt," Jeremiah said. "I heard him dictating a letter to Fishbourne in reply to the invitation."

Beverholt. I searched my mind for what Tempe had told me of the family. Dutch, she'd said. Owned over two hundred black slaves. And he lived untouched by the revolution, on good terms with both the British and the Americans. Once, in the early years of the war, one of his barns had been burned by Patriots, but because he knew the right people in Philadelphia and complained to them, he'd never been so bothered again.

"Is Wayne going to Beverholt's?" I asked.

"No," Jeremiah answered. "He turned the invitation down. Said in the note that he had to concern himself with the new arrangement of the Line. But I myself heard him tell Fishbourne that he can't be away from camp in this time of crisis."

"So Wayne senses something about to happen, too?"

"Yes," Jeremiah breathed. "He's invited some of his favorite officers to have dinner with him in his quarters. I heard him tell Fishbourne there's to be no spirits. They have to keep their heads clear. A little card playing, he said, but that's all."

"The men in camp have been promised a ration of rum for New Year's Day," David said. "But it hasn't come yet. Bowzar's Committee of Sergeants has someone at every checkpoint to keep watch for wagons with rum in them."

It was starting to fall into place. "So the men in camp are still hungry," I summarized. "And they know of preparations for New Year's Day being made by the officers and the gentry around camp. And they are angry."

"And getting angrier by the minute," David said.

"All morning they've been in the McCormicks' hut with their Committee of Sergeants, saying wild things and plotting," said Jeremiah.

"And how are you privy to this?"

"Men have been scurrying around camp and forming in little groups, and I heard the talk," he answered.

I nodded. "So the moment's come, and that's why Bowzar was at our house. To try again for the horse."

They nodded in unison.

"But there's more," Jeremiah said.

I sighed and looked up at the bright blue sky above, straight into the sun, which winked at me. My eyes teared, and I had to turn away. "I don't know if I can bear any more," I said.

"Henry wants to see you," Jeremiah told me. "He came seeking us out this morning. He's most agitated, and we couldn't make any sense out of the reason why. We told him we were on the way to meet you and asked him along. He said no. And in that strange way he has of speaking— do you know what he said?"

I dared not ask. They went on.

"That he wants to see you alone. And he'd wait by the magazine in your orchard. We promised him that after we met with you, we'd send you by. He was babbling more than ever, but perhaps you'd better see him, Mary. Just to calm him down."

I said nothing, but I walked along with my head down so they could not see my face. Henry. He knew something. More than what these two knew, I'd wager. And he wanted to tell me.

A strange sense of both excitement and dread permeated me. "Thank you both," I said. "I have to walk through the orchard to get home, so I'll see him."

"He gets crazier by the day," David said.

"Yes, he does," I agreed.

We continued walking. Henry's shillings jingled in my haversack. "To add to the unrest in camp," David said, "the men resent the newest order Wayne has posted. Anyone leaving camp after today must have a pass examined by the guard. Anyone entering will be subject to strict scrutiny. And the names of the occupants of each hut are posted outside. The officers will determine, at tattoo, if every man is accounted for."

"Why doesn't Wayne just put a stop to everything the men of the Line are planning and be done with it?" I asked.

"Because it isn't known yet that they are planning anything," Jeremiah answered. "Wayne can only suspect. And wait."

"What do you think will happen if they do try something?" I pushed.

"Wayne will prevail."

We'd been walking through camp, and now we came to the point where I had to cut across the field to walk through the Wick orchard. So we stopped, considering each other.

"If you have never seen Wayne angry," Jeremiah said, "you have missed a beautiful sight to behold."

It was clear to me that he worshiped Wayne as much as I did.

"I heard tell," he elaborated, lowering his voice, "that when he was at Fort Ticonderoga, from July '76 to May '77, he was quite capable of dealing with the men and became experienced in warding off the boredom that arises when men lose the veneer of civilization. At Fort Ti, for instance, a company arrived in the beginning of winter. Disease and homesickness and famine made desertions heavy that winter. And this particular company formed up in marching order to leave. Do you know what Wayne did?"

David and I waited, openmouthed.

"He put a pistol to the breast of the sergeant who led the revolt. The man backed down, cowed. Then Wayne gave an order to the company to lay down their arms. They did so. Then he talked them into going quietly to their quarters. One soldier refused to obey and was insolent. Wayne knocked him down and sent him to the guardhouse. And when one of his own captains came to the man's defense, Wayne sent him to the guardhouse, too!"

We fell silent, contemplating. Overhead a flock of crows cawed as they flew from tree to tree. The sound seemed ominous to me, even on this bright blue day. I shivered. Jeremiah's laugh rang out, carried on the clear air, frightening the crows into flight.

"Don't underestimate Bowzar," David said. "I think many of the men would follow him into hell. He's able to organize people. I hear that before the war he was a rope walker in a cordage house in Philadelphia. He organized his fellow workers to form a Committee of Safety."

We considered that. "It's true he casts an impressive shadow," Jeremiah agreed. "But Wayne's is larger. Wayne takes no sass from anyone, yet he has the devotion of the men."

I allowed that to be true, told them I must go, and thanked them both.

My friends grinned at me, and my heart went out to them, so ragged and so young—yet their lives were entwined in all of this. "You two be careful," I admonished. "If anything happens, stay clear. Come to our house if need be."

"If anything happens, I stay with Wayne,"

Jeremiah declared earnestly. "And David stays with Crystie. We've talked of it."

"You won't go with the men of the Line if they revolt?"

"No," Jeremiah said. "We serve our officers. We'll be safe with them. Although the soldiers took us in, they won't allow us to be part of whatever is going on. They've sealed us out. They know we sympathize with them, but they've drawn lines and put us on the side of our officers."

"It's because we work for Wayne and Crystie, and they don't trust us," David explained.

"It's also because they said we're too young to hang," Jeremiah said.

"Hang?" I gaped.

"Deserters and mutineers hang," David reminded me.

They laughed at their own words. Were they just being adventurous boys now, I wondered? No. While they were taking a certain devious pleasure in all this, I sensed that underneath their bravado they meant every word.

"You said it wasn't mutiny," I argued.

"That's right," Jeremiah agreed. "That's what we said, isn't it, David?"

"Yes," David murmured. "But only because the word has never actually been uttered. By anyone."

15

Within the next ten minutes the word was uttered. Plain. And in God's good sunlight. By Henry to me in the orchard.

He was sitting on the ground near the sentries, who did not take him into account as anything but an oversized half-wit. They nodded their hellos to me, and Henry and I walked away from them. He was fairly shivering with anticipation.

A distance from the magazine, I turned to look at him. "My friends said you wanted to talk to me, Henry."

He was almost jumping out of his skin, hopping from one foot to another as he stood there.

"Henry must tell you," he said. "Important."

"Talk to me, Henry, do. But talk to me as the real Henry. You know I'll listen."

He wagged his head steadily, compressed his lips. "Mutiny," he said. "They're planning mutiny."

"You already told me that, Henry. And others suspect it, even Wayne. But nothing's been done yet."

"There's more."

"Well?"

He sighed, took a moment to look to the heavens and compose himself, then recited carefully. "Bowzar's intending to take Tempe's horse, not borrow him. Take him away. And there's a good chance he's going to take the Line and go over to the British."

The sky seemed to whirl above me and come down on my head. "Defect to the British?"

He nodded vigorously, looking at his shoes as if ashamed to even utter such words to me. "It's not decided yet. Many of the men are indisposed to mutiny. Some may not fall in with the dissenters when the time comes. Many want to go to the British. Others say it is not their intention, and they will hang any man they suspect of such desires. But it is a possibility."

I nodded.

"At the crossroads out of camp," he went on, "it will be determined. If they take the road to the left, or go straight, they can march to Chatham and Elizabethtown, then on to the British if they wish. The other road goes to Princeton and then Philadelphia. No telling 'til they reach the crossroads which way they will go. And there is more."

I waited.

"With spies about, the British will hear of the

revolt. And do what they must to entice the Line to go to them."

I gazed in wonderment at him. He had figured out all the possibilities on his own. He was not stupid.

"Why do you care, Henry?" I asked. "When they all treat you so shabbily. The soldiers make sport of you. General Wayne wouldn't listen to you now, even if you could get through to his headquarters. He puts you down as a lunatic along with everyone else. Even Will Leddell treats you with disdain and uses you. Tempe won't let you in the house to see your mother. Why, after all these years, do you care?"

I was taking a chance, I knew, uttering such words. They might discourage him. And then again they might prod him to action.

"Because," he said, "I care about the army and what it's trying to do. I care about freedom. I hate the British, still. And because"—his voice quavered now—"because I failed to do my duty once before. And now I've been given another chance. They say things in front of me because they think me lunatic. I am privy to information. And now that I have that information I must come forth. Or loathe myself for the rest of my life. It isn't often, little Mary, that a man is given a second chance to make up for when he failed the first time."

"And what will you do with that chance, Henry?"

"Tell you. No one else will believe me. You must tell Tempe. She must know this is mutiny and 2,500 men may go over to the British!"

"She won't believe me, Henry," I said dismally. "I tried telling her once before that it is mutiny. I told her of our conversation. She says terrible things about you and won't hold with anything you say."

He nodded, sighing, knowing this to be true, and we both stood there in the middle of the orchard, commiserating with each other.

"If this is mutiny and they go to the British, they'll do it whether Tempe gives Colonel to Bowzar or not, Henry," I reminded him softly.

"I know. But she shouldn't be connected with it. She shouldn't lend her support. It would do to her what my running did to me years ago. She'd never forgive herself."

"You care that much about Tempe," I said.

"She's my sister. Yes."

The poignancy of this almost moved me to tears. I wanted so to help this troubled man, more than I cared now about Tempe.

"We can't go to Wayne," I said, examining the issue. "He knows something is afoot. He suspects. And since we haven't anything more to tell him than he knows, that would be a waste of time. And a humiliation to us both."

He agreed. "What do we do then, Mary?"

"There's only one thing to do, Henry. And you know it as well as I."

He shook his head, denying what I implied.

I moved a step closer to him. And there, within sight of his home, in the Wick orchard, I told him what he must do. He listened respectfully as I spoke. And I even saw tears come to his eyes as my words penetrated the years of defenses he had built up around himself.

"I will bring Tempe to you," I murmured softly, letting my words fall on him like a warm, soothing rain, to wash away all his fears. "And you will speak to her as you speak to me. As Henry Wick, who is intelligent and caring and hurting and concerned. You will tell her your lunacy is only a charade. You must tell her why you act so. Then she will believe you about Bowzar. And the mutiny. And the possibility of the Line going to the British."

He compressed his lips, set his face in a determined mask, and looked past me to his old home. Tears were coming down his face.

"I can't do this. She will never forgive me."

"You must do it, Henry. It's the only way."

"She'll think I want to come back home and take her place."

"You must assure her you don't want to return home. That all you want is to make peace with yourself. And make up for the past. And having done so, you'll go away again."

"She'll think I'm doing it to get my daddy's money."

The money! I'd forgotten it. I reached into my haversack now and took it out. "I have your daddy's money, Henry. He left you five shillings. Tempe is quite content that you should have it."

I held the shillings out to him. He took them and fingered them in his hands. I saw the features of his face contort as he absorbed all this. I waited, praying inwardly that he would be strong enough to come to the right conclusion. And then another thought came to me.

"Bowzar was at our house this morning," I said. "My friends told me he was there. Talking to Tempe. She must have promised him the horse, for they were getting on most amiably."

He seemed to draw in his breath in a gulp and make a tremendous effort to control himself, brooding on it still.

"I'll do it," he said. "It's the only way."

"Oh, Henry, I'm so glad. I'll bring her to you. Tonight. In the barn. After the hired man leaves. Wait there. At the hour of eight."

He nodded, agreeing, but his mind was set on another line of thought. "My daddy never forgave me when he heard I ran from battle," he said. "Do you think Tempe will?"

"Tempe's only concern is that you're rum-running for Will Leddell. She lives in fear you'll be apprehended and arrested, and it will break your mother's heart."

"I'm not disposed to argue with her on that count," he said. "Bring her tonight to the barn. I'll be there."

I turned to go, feeling warm and good all over.

"Mary?"

Something in the way he said my name made me glance back quickly. He was holding out his hand. In it was the money I'd given him.

"Give this back to Tempe. Tell her Henry doesn't want his daddy's money. Tell her Henry doesn't want anything from her. Just to talk."

I felt the blood rushing in my ears. Something soared inside me. Now I was the one with tears in my eyes.

"Are you sure, Henry?"

"She'll be more likely to believe you if I give back the shillings," he said.

He was right. The gesture was exactly what it would take to get Tempe's attention.

"You're brilliant, Henry," I said. "Anyone

who calls you addled deserves to choke on their words."

I accepted the money and smiled up at him. "Do you think," he asked, "that after all this is done with, she'll allow me to see Mama? Just once?"

My spirits fell then, to the floor of my soul, wretched now at this new realization. He did not know his mother thought he was dead. *Well,* I thought, *that has to be Tempe's worry, not mine. I can't concern myself with everything.*

"You can ask her, Henry," I said. *And I wouldn't want to be in Tempe's shoes*, I thought, walking away, *when he does.*

16

"And what right did you have to promise him I'd come out and speak with him! I don't wish to speak with him! If I had any such wish, I'd have gone to Leddell myself and gotten the shillings and delivered them over to him! You had no right to make him such a promise!"

My cousin's face was white with rage, though she did her best to control her voice. Aunt Mary wasn't feeling well. Too much excitement yesterday. And Tempe had already put her to bed and closed the kitchen door. Aunt Mary was feverish, her mind off somewhere, talking about her childhood and her brother Nathan in the well. This was never a good sign.

The table was set for our supper, and Tempe was slicing bread, emphasizing each word as she spoke.

"I want no part of him, do you understand? I want him off our land!"

"He must needs talk with you, Tempe."

"About what? The five shillings isn't enough? Well you can just tell him our father left the same amount to the rest of us. And he can take it and go and consider himself lucky. I'll accept no whining from him."

"He doesn't want the shillings." And I took them out of my haversack and placed them on the table. They made a clunking noise as I set them down, and I stepped back.

This got her attention, all right. She set the knife down and eyed the shillings as if they had tails. "Doesn't *want* them?"

"That's right. He said, 'Tell her Henry doesn't want his daddy's money. Tell her Henry doesn't want anything from her. Just to talk.'"

She wiped her hands on her apron, her lovely face all furrowed up, caught unawares now.

"Mama's sickly," she said. "Her mind is all confused and rambling. I can't leave her tonight."

"You must. What Henry has to tell you can't wait."

"Oh?" And she started to spoon some soup into bowls for us. "And what's so important, after eleven years of being away and not concerning himself with us, that he can't wait?"

"He has to tell you himself. You won't want it from my lips."

"Something tells me I won't want it from his, either. Well, sit down and eat your supper."

I sat and watched her eat. "You'll go then, with me? To the barn at eight?"

"I haven't said I will."

She maddened me, sipping her soup so calmly now. "Tempe, please!"

"Why should I?"

I stared at her, unable to comprehend her coldness, seeing her for what she was, an unyielding, selfish, and ungiving woman and not at all the wonderful older cousin I had always thought her to be.

It was a revelation all right, this vision of her I had while sitting across the table with Henry's shillings between us. Revelations are not always pleasant. I didn't want to know what I was finding out now. I didn't want to lose the sense of hope she always held out to me, that I would someday be different from as I was now.

That I would someday be bold, as she was. And admired. And pretty. And slimmer and more graceful. And in charge of my life and all around me. Always I have looked up to her, and now I was finding there was nothing to look up to anymore. That there perhaps never had been.

And if this is what growing up means, I told myself sitting there, *then I don't like it*. Not if growing up means that you see the faults of those around you and can no longer hold them above you, unattainable and worshiped from afar.

For then what is there? But one's self? And in my case, I was not enough to sustain myself. I knew that, too, sitting there.

"You should go to the barn because he's your brother," I said in answer to her question.

"We've had this out, Mary," she said. "He's lunatic. Did you ask him, as I reminded you once before, about his wife Elizabeth and his two children, Mary and Chloe?"

"No. We spoke of other things."

"Ah, yes. You communicate with him. I forgot. What did you speak of then?"

So I told her, God forgive me. "He said that Bowzar, and the Line, when they mutiny, will go over to the British."

Her pewter spoon made a dull noise on the wooden table as she set it down. She stared at me, her fine features carved out of disbelief now. It made me sorry I had to be the one to tell her. But it was the only way I could get her to listen to me.

"He's more daft than I thought."

"No, Tempe." I broke off a piece of bread and crumbled it in my fingers. "He's saner than either of us thought. Which is another reason why you should go to the barn tonight. I've known for a long time. And so does Will Leddell. I wanted Henry himself to tell you tonight in the barn. But it's plain I'm going to have to tell you just to get you there. He's not lunatic. He only pretends to be. He's as intelligent as you or I. More so. And because everyone in camp believes him to be lunatic, they say things in front of him. So he has information. And he wants to give it to you."

I had never before in my life made such a long or imploring speech. And never before in my life had I spoken so quickly and fit so much into so few sentences, it seemed.

She blinked, staring at me. "Why does he pretend to be lunatic?"

"I don't know. I don't understand, leastways. But it has something to do with the fact that he can't bear his life as it is. And it's easier for him this way."

"Well, isn't that courageous of him! Who can bear life as it is these days?"

"He never claimed to be courageous, Tempe. That's part of his trouble. And he's the first to say it plain."

"And has he decided now that he's had enough of playing the slobbering lunatic and wants to be Henry Wick again and come home?"

"He doesn't want to come home, Tempe.

That's the last thing he wants. He doesn't want anything of you. And that's why those five shillings are there on the table between us and not in his pocket."

"I suppose you think I'm terrible, speaking this way of my own brother."

"I mind that I have a brother of my own that I speak of in kind," I said.

She nodded, sighed, and tightened her lips. "You've meddled, Mary," she said.

"I know." It was the second time this day I had been accused of doing so.

"I'd just about made up my mind what I'm going to do about Colonel. It wasn't an easy thing to do. I had it all straight in my head. And now it's all muddled. If what you say proves to be true."

"I couldn't *not* tell you, Tempe."

"You've meddled," she said again. "I wish you hadn't come to stay with us, Mary. Then I would have just done what I had to do, right or wrong, and been done with it. Now I'm all confused again, which is worse than anything. I wish you hadn't come! And in a few days, when this is all over, I'm going to send you home."

My heart stopped beating, I know it did. Hearts do that sometimes, for just a beat or two. Then they start up again. But they never regain those missed beats, and nothing is ever the same afterward. Life proceeds to a different cadence, and never again as harmonious as before.

But I knew she was going to the barn with me this night to see Henry. What else, after all, could she do?

17

We spoke no more to each other as we finished supper and cleared up the dishes. I took up some knitting by the fire while Tempe attended to Aunt Mary. I was making a Liberty cap and some new stockings to send to Abraham in New Windsor. I heard Tempe in there with Aunt Mary, talking in a low and soothing tone, then she was moving about the rest of the house, securing the front door and checking the fires for the night.

At seven-thirty she came back into the kitchen and went to the pantry and brought out the makings for bread. I stared as she started mixing flour and lard in a bowl. Her arms were white with flour when, at quarter of eight, she looked up at me.

"You might as well go and fetch him now," she said.

"What?"

She was mixing her dough. "Are you dim-witted? I said you can fetch him up from the barn."

"You'd have him here? In the house?"

"And what am I to do? It's clear you have to be in on this, since it's only when you're around that he speaks in tongues. Fetch him here. I'll close the kitchen door. He's to speak in low tones and not wake Mama. Be sure to tell him she's ill and can't be disturbed. And we can't leave her. And that if this is a trick to get himself inside the house, he'll soon have some grapeshot in his pants."

"It isn't a trick, Tempe. Why won't you believe me?"

"I believe no one anymore." And she was as sour as bad milk when she said it.

It was no mean feat to convince Henry that it wasn't a trick, either, his being invited up to the house. As much as he wanted to see his mama, he shook like a wet kitten when I told him I was to fetch him up to where he used to live.

"It's the only way, Henry," I said. "Tempe can't come down here because your mama is feeling poorly and in bed and can't be left alone."

"Will she listen to me?"

"She'll hear you out."

"Why?"

Why, indeed? "Because I told her, Henry. I told her that you're not lunatic but as bright as the rest of us. That you've only pretended all these years because it's pleased you to pretend.

I had to tell her. It's the only thing that would make her mind. So when we get there, Henry, you just be yourself, the real Henry Wick. No more pretending. The time for that is over. We've other matters to attend to now. And we haven't time for anything but the truth."

"She isn't going to like the truth I have to tell her," he said.

"We none of us do when the time comes to hear it," I said to him. And we walked up the path from the barn to the house in the dark.

"She isn't going to like Henry's truth," he kept saying over and over. And I prayed that he wouldn't take refuge in his old addled self as one takes refuge in an old shawl or flannel nightdress when one needs comforting.

It was eight now, dark and with that dampness that seems to seep up from the very ground in this colony in midwinter, no matter how mild the daytime is. Tempe had a candle in the window.

I knocked on the back door, something I never did. But I knew she'd have it latched from the inside. In a moment she released the latch, but when I opened it and stood there with Henry, she was clear across the kitchen by the fireplace, her back to us.

"Don't stand there like fools. Come in and close the door. It's cold," she said.

We stepped across the threshold, and I led Henry in and motioned him to sit down. But he wouldn't sit. He just stood there in his old home, his battered hat in his hands, gazing around, his eyes lingering on things I took for granted every day—the hutch in the corner with the pewter dishes, the long table, the overhead beams hung with dried herbs, and, I supposed, the very smell of home, which one thinks forgotten until one goes back. And which I supposed I had forgotten about my home, but would smell again when I returned, also.

"When you speak, it is to be softly," Tempe said, still not turning around. "I'll not have Mama even know you're here. Or you go. Is that plain?"

"It's plain, Tempe," he said.

She turned around then and raised her eyes to look him over. And I saw, in the lovely contours of her face, the struggle for memory as she tried to find the brother she remembered in this large rumpled being.

For a moment or two they just stared at each other.

Henry held his old, worn hat in his hands. "Tempe," he said. "You've grown."

She gave a little laugh. "I should certainly hope so. I was eleven years old the last time you made a proper visit."

"You're so pretty!" Henry said.

"I don't feel pretty." She turned back to the hearth and made a pretense of doing something. "I've too many responsibilities to be pretty these days, Henry."

He nodded in agreement. "You're still fine-looking, Tempe," he said.

"Well, you aren't." She turned to face him again. "You're not even respectable-looking, Henry. Look at you!"

He gazed down at his own clothing, which was as nondescript as clothing can be, as well as tattered and soiled. He shrugged and smiled. "I'm like all the soldiers."

"But you're not a soldier, Henry! So there's no excuse for the way you are! It was quite one thing when we thought you were lunatic, as you had us fooled into believing all these years. But now Mary tells me you aren't. Why, Henry, why did you allow this to happen to yourself?"

"I like my life, Tempe," he answered simply. "I come and go as I please. I answer to no one."

"And this makes you happy?"

He shrugged.

"I don't suppose it profits me to ask why?"

"I don't know myself sometimes, Tempe," he said. "I mind only that it's easier."

"Well, I'll wager it would be. For a man. My life is lived mostly inside this house, taking care of Mama. I go out only to ride Colonel and do a few errands or pay some calls or go to church. I don't much like the world out there myself these days. The choices one has to make are too difficult. Even for a woman."

I felt myself taking a breath for the first time since I'd brought Henry into the room. Tempe was going to be kindly toward him, anyway. She wanted this to proceed smoothly, I decided, to hear him out and get rid of him, I supposed. He was an embarrassment to her. So she was being as amiable as possible to get the whole thing over with quickly.

"Well"—and she covered her bread dough with a cloth and wiped her hands on her apron—"it's your business if you want the world to think you're a half-wit. We all live with the choices we make. Although I would think you'd feel guilty for deserting your family. Daddy always spoke about you, Henry. And he sure could have used you around here these last few years before he died."

Henry bowed his head. *Dear God*, I thought, *I was wrong*. She was going to be cruel to him. Oh, how I hated her this moment!

"I am guilty, Tempe," he said. "For many things. I don't need you to remind me of my sins. I didn't come here for that."

"What did you come for, then?"

"You know," he said softly. "Mary told you."

"I know, Henry, yes. But I want to hear you say it. I want to hear what Mary told me, from your lips. So tell me. Why do you want to speak to me?"

"To beg you not to give your horse to Bowzar. To tell you there's going to be a mutiny. And that the Line may well go over to the British." And he looked up at her again as he said this, meeting her eye to eye.

"How come you by this information?" she asked.

"When one is taken for a half-wit, anything is said in one's presence."

His looking her in the eye and direct response befuddled her. She sighed, wiped her hands on her apron, and looked around.

"Mary, put up some coffee."

I did so. And she sat down on her side of the table. "Would you have some bread and meat?"

"I wouldn't refuse if it was offered me."

"Mary, get some bread and meat from the pantry."

I moved quickly.

"Are you sure of what you heard?" she asked him.

"As sure as I am that my name is Henry Wick."

"Then why haven't you gone to Wayne with

it? You're in and about camp all the time selling rum. British rum, I might add. Which you run for our brother-in-law. Am I right?"

"I don't go to Wayne because I can't bear for anyone to know I'm not lunatic. Wayne has wind that something is about to happen, and he's prepared. He just doesn't know when."

"So you come to me."

"Yes."

"Why?"

"Because Bowzar's been bragging that he has your heart and your loyalty. As well as your horse. You can't do that, Tempe. You can't give him Colonel. Don't aid their mutiny. Don't be part of it."

"Bowzar swore it isn't mutiny. They only want to present their grievances to Wayne."

"Bowzar lies. It would be the feather in his cap he needs if he gets this horse that all the officers in camp envy. It would make him more powerful than he is now with the men. You don't understand, Tempe."

Her face was hard in the candlelight. And Abraham once said to me that if a woman's face is sharp in candlelight, by daylight you wouldn't want to know her.

"Then why don't you explain to me?" she said sarcastically.

Henry hesitated. I saw him groping for

words. "This horse you have. The men in camp see you flying through the woods and over the roads on him. And he means something." He halted, then went on. "Don't mock me."

"Why should I mock you? What does Colonel mean to them?"

"Freedom." Henry breathed the word. "The freedom we all hear about and hope for."

Silence fell on the room. The fire spit and the coffee bubbled. Tempe sliced some meat and bread, put it all on a plate, and shoved it across the table. Gingerly, Henry moved his chair forward and began to eat.

"Fetch the coffee, Mary," she ordered.

I did so. I poured three cups.

"It's all very pretty to hear about freedom," Tempe said dully, "but the men of the Line are hungry and starving. Their children are dying. For most of them, freedom will never come if they don't take action now."

"They may go to the British," Henry said again. "If they do—all 2,500 of them—the revolution is finished. Give Bowzar your horse, and you go to the British with them."

"How dare you?" Her eyes flashed.

Henry did not answer. Calmly, he kept eating.

"Who are you to concern yourself with what I do or do not do, Henry Wick? Where were you when our father was sick? Where were you all these years when we needed you? You were always Mama's favorite. Her firstborn. And you broke her heart."

Henry chewed and swallowed. "I've not been the brother or son to this family that I should have been, Tempe. There's a demon lives inside me. And I answer his call before that of those I love. But now I pay no mind to him. My thoughts are for you. Heed what I say."

"Why should I?"

"Because we both love the Cause."

"Love it?" She sneered. "I'm sick of it. Sick of what I've seen all around this farm for two years now. Sick of seeing people suffer and die."

"You don't mean that, Tempe. Our daddy was a Patriot. He served with the Morris County militia."

"Our daddy was a fool. He never should have allowed the army on our land."

"Mayhap I was wrong," Henry said. "Mayhap we both just hate the king's men more than we love the Cause. It all comes out the same in the end."

"Sometimes I think I hate the Continentals more than I hate the king's men," she said.

"You hate the war, Tempe. But surely the answer can't be in the Line going to the British."

"I never said it was. Whatever the Line does, my refusing to lend Colonel won't stop them."

"It won't help them, either. Don't give the horse, Tempe. You'll end up like me."

She just stared at him.

"I ran in battle. Daddy never forgave me when he found out. Worse, I can't forgive myself. I live with this, every day."

No reply was forthcoming from Tempe. I saw that she believed him. But believing, to her, was a matter of no importance these days. She got to her feet wearily and turned to prod some wood in the hearth. The firelight played across her face. "What would you have me do?" she asked. "It's too late now. I've promised Bowzar the horse."

And there was in her voice a kind of pleading that I had never heard before.

"Break your promise," Henry advised. "Tell him you've pondered on it and decided that lending him Colonel isn't seemly."

"I can't."

"There is no virtue in such a promise. And no sin in breaking it."

"I care little for the virtue or the sin of the matter, Henry," she said. "There's nothing can be done anymore about it. It's settled with Bowzar. I've put things in motion. I won't be talking with him until the moment comes when I'm to deliver Colonel."

"And when is that, pray?"

"I don't rightly know. No one does. I think not even Bowzar. All I do know is that there will be a white rag tied on a fence post out there, nearest the barn. And when I see it, I'm to leave, forthwith, and meet Bowzar or some of his men at an assigned place with Colonel. Now what have you to say of that, Henry Wick?"

"Don't go."

Her laugh was short and bitter. "Then he'll come here and demand Colonel. And upset Mama. Or worse."

"Of what are you speaking?" he asked.

She looked at us quickly, one to the other. "He knows about your rum-running, Henry. And Dr. Leddell's part in it. He says he'll tell Wayne if I don't lend him Colonel. And Wayne deems dealing with the British contemptible. He never sees his own wife because she engages in such activities. He'd have you and Phoebe's husband turned over to the authorities. It would kill Phoebe and break Mama's heart. What say you now, Henry Wick?"

He gulped the remainder of his coffee and stared into the fire. There was an edge in Tempe's voice like a knife. And it cut through me, and my breath came out in spurts. Like blood.

"This is a nice fellow you have dealings with, this Bowzar," Henry said.

"You're not my keeper. I need no chiding from you. Before I realized what Bowzar was about, it was too late."

Henry thought for a moment, then spoke. "Would you heed what I say?"

"I haven't heard you say anything yet."

He got to his feet and walked across the room, looking around, up and down, as if he'd never seen the place before. He went to the door and took the breadth and height of it, measured it with his hands.

"Not all the rooms in the house are occupied now, are they?" he asked.

"No," Tempe answered. "The bedroom off the parlor is empty."

He nodded, thinking. Then spoke again. "Meet with Bowzar or his men, on Colonel, when the time comes to do so. They will not be on horses, will they?"

"They have none. Unless they intend to steal some. And that is quite possible."

"But your Colonel would be faster than any horse they could get or steal around here? Even from one of the officers?"

"I can fly on Colonel," Tempe said.

"Good. You may have to."

"What are you saying?"

"I am saying you should meet with them. Feign consent. Let them think you are about to hand Colonel over to them. Talk with them. When they are relaxed and off guard, take the moment to dash away. To fly away. On your horse."

I saw a light come into Tempe's eyes, saw her interest quicken. "And where should we run to?"

"Here. Back to the house."

"With them in pursuit? What then? They'll only find Colonel in the barn and take him."

"They will look in the barn," Henry said. "And the paddock. And perhaps even the woods. He won't be there."

"And where will he be, Henry Wick? Are you lunatic, after all?"

A benign smile crept over Henry's face. "The horse will be in the house," he said quietly.

"In the *house*? You *are* mad," Tempe said. "You're . . ." And then she stopped. For the quiet smile was still on Henry's face. But the look in his eyes was one of patience. He was waiting for her to understand.

And she did. Swifter than I, she understood. For I saw the same slow smile of understanding spread over her face then. And I saw something else, a light of recognition, of mutual appreciation transpire between this brother and sister that I thought only happened between Abraham and me.

Tempe put her hands over her mouth and stifled a little cry of delight. "Which room?" she said.

"The bedroom no one is using. He can fit through this door and that door leading to the parlor. The bedroom you speak of is just to the left of that door, as I recall."

Tempe's hands were still over her mouth, but she was fairly dancing with the delight of the plan. "They'll never think to look in the house," she said.

"You must keep him quiet," Henry admonished. "Put padding on the floor and around his hoofs."

"I can do that," she whispered. "Mary can help."

"Cover the window."

"Yes. Yes. I can do that, too."

"In the heat of the moment Bowzar and his men won't have much time to spend looking for a horse. Things will be happening too fast. But everything depends on your approaching them in an amiable manner and allowing them to think you are going along with their plans."

"Yes," she breathed.

"And on how fast Colonel can get you back here, even if they have horses."

"We'll fly," Tempe promised. "Like a hooty owl in the night, we'll ride into morning."

The three of us just stood in that kitchen for a few moments, looking at each other, caught in the wonderment of this plan of Henry's. It was so plain. And so wonderful.

"But what of you?" Tempe said. "What if he carries out his threat to tell Wayne of your rum-running? And Will's?"

"When he comes face to face with Wayne—if, he does," Henry said, "they'll have much to discuss, once the wheels of this plan are put into motion. The least of which will be my rum-running."

She nodded.

Henry picked up his rumpled hat, which he'd set down on a chair. "I must go now." And he moved toward the door.

With his hand on the latch, he turned. "Be careful, Tempe," he said.

"I will. And thank you, Henry."

He nodded, smiled at me, and lifted the latch.

Tempe took a step forward. "Henry?"

"Yes."

"You have saved me, Henry. From I know not what."

I thought I saw tears in his eyes just before he turned to go, but I could not swear to it. I mind that he turned away quickly and that the door thudded behind him as he went back into the night. To where I did not know, for we never did know where he slept. And if it was under some old tree someplace like a dog, burrowed half in the ground, well, we never found that out, either.

When he was gone, Tempe looked at me. "He was fighting with Washington in the French War three years before I was born," she said dully.

I could think of no words to say.

"If Mama knew that I had him here in this room tonight! He was her favorite. Her first-born. If Mama knew."

Still I said nothing. *But will you tell her,* I pondered silently. *Will you do the right thing and tell her?* But I could not say the words out. For she had agreed to speak with Henry this night. And I knew that for now, at least, I must be content.

18

We didn't go to church the next day, though it was Sunday, because of Aunt Mary. "I'd just as soon not take her down to Mendham on a day like this," Tempe said. "I don't think even the Lord would abide that. Mary, the Leddells are stopping by in their carriage to pick us up. You may go if you wish."

I didn't wish. For two reasons, the foremost being that if anything happened, I didn't want to be in church in Mendham. I was conjuring up visions of that white rag tied around the fence post, of course. The second and no less important reason was that I did not want to ride in a carriage with Dr. Leddell. For though we had parted amicably enough, I could see no profit in being in his presence.

Tempe didn't push it, for which I was thankful. And when the Leddells, Phoebe and Will, stopped in so he could see to Aunt Mary for a moment, I managed to be in the henhouse fetching some fresh eggs.

When the carriage pulled away and I returned to the house, I found Tempe in a fit of anger. "That man! He acts like a damned Tory!"

"Tempe!" I was no prude. Heaven knows, I'd heard curses enough out of the mouth of my brother Abraham when the occasion warranted them. But it was one thing to avoid church on the Sabbath and use one's own mother as an excuse, when indeed Aunt Mary looked fit enough to me to go. And quite another to further provoke the Lord with language of a French seaman.

"What's happened?" I asked.

"Leddell. Always poking his nose in where it doesn't belong. 'Why don't you invite that nice Lieutenant Reeves to sup on New Year's Day? It would cheer your mother considerably, especially since her friend Ebenezer Drake can't accept the invitation.' " She so succeeded in mimicking Leddell that I could scarcely keep from laughing.

"I don't need company tomorrow," she said. "I don't want people about. Of course, he went and said it right in front of Mama. So now I've got to invite Reeves. He's put the thought in her head!"

"It wouldn't bother me if Lieutenant Reeves were to come to supper tomorrow night," I said.

"Oh, it wouldn't bother you, of course not. All I need is him making cow eyes at me across the table. I'm in no mood for it, I tell you. And what, may I ask, do we do if there's a white rag tied around the fence post when Reeves is here? Have you thought on that?"

I hadn't. But now I did. And saw her point. "Perhaps Reeves won't be able to come," I said. "I heard that the German soldiers are marching in tomorrow, down from Suffern in New York colony. Perhaps Wayne will need his officers to help settle things."

She'd been about to make a sharp retort, but her face softened.

She pushed some hair from her face, considering me. "Mama's got her heart set on it now," she said wearily.

"If you see the white rag tied on the fence post when he's here, you'll just need to make an excuse that Phoebe's with child and feeling poorly and wants you," I said brightly.

"With her husband a doctor? Of course, I know Phoebe might prefer to have me about, but Reeves wouldn't know that. No, there's nothing for it but to pray I don't get the signal tomorrow. Go tell the hired man to kill a large chicken. Reeves likes chestnut stuffing, doesn't he? And we'll have ham with raisin sauce."

She set me to the baking. All afternoon I baked. There was enough pearl ash on hand to make the most stubborn dough rise, so I made a cider cake and two fine pies. Doing so, I minded how Abraham would hunt for pheasant and we'd roast them on New Year's Day. With oyster stuffing.

Then I commenced thinking about Abraham. I hoped he'd gotten my letter by now and would soon write. And that he had enough to eat. Tempe's sister Mary had said her Eb wrote from New Windsor that they hadn't enough flour up there. Would they have rum, I wondered? I'd heard our men were to be issued half a pint each tomorrow.

From where I stood in the kitchen, I could see Tempe racing Colonel up and down the path from the barn to the house and back again. I stood watching, my arms white with flour. *Oh, he is so beautiful*, I thought. *He prances and tosses his head so proudly!* He was in a fine fettle, doing all sorts of tricks. And the whiteness of him made him stand out so! For several moments I stood by the kitchen window watching her and thinking, yes, she can fly on him. Just like a hooty owl in the night. But I noticed she did not take him off the path that led from the house to the barn. *She's afraid*, I told myself. And as I watched her racing up and down, her red cape billowing out around her, making a spot of brightness against the drab landscape, I thought, *It's a long ride into morning, Tempe. I hope you can reach it in time.*

I turned from the window thinking how tomorrow was General Wayne's birthday. *I'll make hot buttered rum tomorrow,* I told myself. *And perhaps we will toast him.*

New Year's Day dawned bright and clear and not very cold. The first thing Tempe told me when I came into the kitchen was that she had given the hired man the day off, so I had to make the breakfast while she went to the barn to tend the livestock and milk Daisy.

She was cutting an old blanket into long strips.

"What's that for?" I asked. But I knew. With a solid sense of dread inside me, I knew. Just like I knew when Nathan locked me in my room in his house that there was no turning back from what I'd done, and I would pay for it.

"What do you think?" she said. And she ripped some more. "To wrap Colonel's hooves in. I've gotten a discarded quilt down from the loft. It's on the floor in the spare bedroom."

"So you're going to do it. Bring him into the house."

"I said I was the other night, didn't I?"

"I thought I dreamed that night."

"Well, you didn't. And neither did I. Take these strips of blanket and put them in the spare bedroom."

"Is that why you gave the hired man the day off? Because you expect it will happen today and you don't want him around?"

"You should stop asking so many questions, Mary Cooper. It isn't good for your well-being."

"Are you still going to send me home after it's all over?"

"After it's all over, I may go home with you. If it doesn't turn out the way I've planned, I may have to."

"Do you think bad things are going to happen this day, Tempe?" I asked. There must have been a quality of terror in my voice to soften her heart. For she stopped what she was doing and looked at me.

"I don't know what will happen, Mary. But I know that after this day it will never be the same. For our army or for the revolution."

"I wish we could tell General Wayne," I said.

"Wayne knows." She reached for her cloak. "I'll wager he's always known. He just never knew when. Or how many will take part."

"Today's his birthday."

"Well, he'll remember it always, then, won't he?"

"Are you sorry I brought Henry home, then, Tempe?"

She paused at the door, tying her cloak in front. Her profile was etched clearly against the grained wood in a way that I shall never forget. For there seemed to be a more regal posture about her this morning and a determination that I had never seen in her before. Not even when she was being her most brash self.

"In a way I am, yes," she answered. "Because before that things were simple for me. And plain."

"And now?"

"I don't think anything will ever be simple and plain again."

"Do you blame me, then?"

"No. They were simple and plain because I refused to see them as they really were. I thought I was helping the soldiers of the Line. I thought they needed my help."

"And you don't think that now?"

"Yes, I still do. But it isn't my place to give that help. I needed to do something, Mary, in this fight. For two years now I've stayed apart from the doings around here, except for dispensing some soup. I hated what the war did to our farm. I hated all the trees cut down, though Father wanted the land cleared. I hated that army camped out there, hated that the war took my Will from me. And Mary's Eb from her. And that it killed my father. Oh yes, it did, in its own way. So I decided to hold myself above it all."

"And so you compromised," I said.

She smiled at me, wanly. "Yes. And everyone, from General Wayne to Bowzar to my own Will in his letters from up north, told me I couldn't stay removed from events forever. That soon I'd have to choose my own role in them."

She sighed. "Well, when Bowzar asked me for Colonel, I saw that as my part in all this. But it was the wrong choice."

I said nothing. She drew on her gloves. "I've pondered much on it. That's why I was so angry with you when you told me the truth about Henry. I didn't need to hear your truth. I'd finally decided to stop shilly-shallying and act and . . ."

"And Henry convinced you your actions were not seemly," I finished for her.

"Yes."

"Are you still angry with me, then?"

She chose to ignore that. "If the Line succeeds in this mutiny, the bones of the revolution will be crushed today. I want no part in that. Truth to tell, this fight doesn't make my blood pound anymore as it did at the start. Whose does? We've seen too much death, hunger, and destruction. But as Henry said, it's still a matter of hating the king's men more than our own Continentals."

"That's all the revolution means to you then, Tempe? Hating one body of soldiers more than another?"

"Yes."

"I don't believe that."

"As you wish."

"I mind that you lack vision. That's what I think."

"Vision, is it?" She laughed but not unkindly. "When you get older, you will understand that it matters not so much why a person does a thing as much as the fact that he does it. Don't look beyond the virtuous action for the motive in the heart, Mary. You'll not like, most times, what you see. Now, why don't you put up some coffee? I'll be back from the barn in twenty minutes. And I'll be wanting a good breakfast this New Year's Day."

Toward two in the afternoon, Aunt Mary started feeling poorly again. So we had to put her to bed.

"I won't go unless you promise me my supper," she said. "My infirmities are not such that I can't eat."

"We'll bring your supper in on a tray, Mama," Tempe said. "I promise."

"And that nice Lieutenant Reeves. He must come into my room and visit."

"I'm sure he'll want to pay his respects, Mama."

"Don't use such words. Pay respects, indeed! One would think I'd already gone on to join my husband!"

"I'm sorry, Mama. I didn't mean to sound so dreary."

"I will have my nightdress with the lace at the throat and the cuffs. And my best lace cap. The one with the blue ribbons."

We obliged her, fussing with her appearance so she felt dressed as if for a public occasion.

"I'm a tough old bird," she said to me when Tempe had gone back into the kitchen to see to the food. "The only illness I ever had before this was the colic, which would come on me every fall. I never went near a doctor until my Phoebe married Will Leddell. All they can think to do is bleed you. It's their answer for every sort of ailment. Well, I never would have it, I tell you. Which is why I like Will Leddell so. He doesn't believe in bleeding a patient. For anything. Pull that screen away from the hearth so the room's nice and cozy, Mary. There's a dear child. Now get Tempe's cats. And tell that daughter of mine that some of that nice hot buttered rum will do better than anything to cure my disorder. Go now. I'm very comfortable."

So it was just the three of us at the table, which Tempe had laid in the kitchen rather than in the dining room.

"It's cozier," she said.

But I knew it was so she might keep an eye on that fence post through the kitchen windows.

We used the best pewter and candles and linen napkins. And Tempe even opened an old bottle of her father's Portuguese wine, which, in better days, he'd imported from Philadelphia. Lieutenant Reeves, his linen spotless, his boots polished, his regimental coat brushed clean, and his face eager and clean-shaven, was as gallant as could be.

No sooner was he in the door than he handed Tempe a small package done up in brown paper. Untying the string, she found an edition of *Sir Charles Grandison*, by Samuel Richardson.

"Oh!" I said. For back in Long Island several young women I knew had passed around this novel. But before I could explain this, Reeves produced another package, this one for me. I flushed and my fingers trembled, opening it. And there in the rough brown paper lay a copy of *Joseph Andrews*, by Henry Fielding. It was very handsomely bound in nice gilt. And there were flowers on the cover.

"Oh, where did you ever get them?" I demanded.

Reeves smiled. "A few of the officers sent to Philadelphia for a shipment of things to give to their women. I was brazen enough to order these. Where's Aunt Mary? I've something for her, too."

He'd brought her a silk handkerchief with a wreath of roses printed upon it. Tempe ushered him in to visit with her, and he stayed a while before coming back to the table.

Tempe was as jumpy as a toad all through supper, though she did behave most graciously to Lieutenant Reeves.

"What do you hear in camp?" she asked finally, after the small talk was dispensed with.

"It's been quiet all day. Most eerie," he said. "The German soldiers arrived, and we met with Wayne to make arrangements for them. The officers of the 10th are having an elegant regimental dinner tonight. Most of the officers are somehow engaged in celebration. A group of them went to the party at Kemble's."

The mutiny was on all our minds, I knew. Yet we never spoke of it. We tiptoed around it. There were long gaps in the conversation. And then, around eight o'clock, Tempe thought she heard a noise. So Reeves went to the door and stood looking out into the blackness.

Across the fields it came, carried on the night air. Reeves strained forward to listen.

"The men have begun to huzzah," he said.

The huzzah. A joyous word used in celebration. It is usually shouted three times, most often to the accompaniment of tricorns thrown in the air. But they did not stop after three huzzahs.

Reeves scowled, turned, and ushered us back inside. "I must needs be going," he said.

"What's happening?" Tempe asked.

He reached for his tricorn and pistol. "I can't be sure. It may only proceed from the men drinking. But the officers will be wanted to quiet them. I'll just ride over. And once they're quieted and accounted for, I'll be back."

His face was white and taut, but he attempted a smile. "I want some of that coffee and cider cake. I'll not be cheated out of it. And you both promised me a rousing game of chess. I'll be back by nine."

He disappeared out into the night. His horse was tethered to our apple tree by the well. He waved and rode off through the orchard to camp.

But he was not back by nine.

Tempe sent me out in the near vicinity of the house to examine all the fence posts, lest the white rag be tied on the wrong one. But no signal was in sight.

By nine the shouting in the distance had quieted down. By now, of course, Tempe was on pins and needles. She made me help her clean up the supper dishes and set out the coffee and cake for when Reeves came back. We even set up the chessboard. She made several trips out into the dark to look on the fence posts for her signal.

She made Aunt Mary a caudle of warm broth mixed with wine so she could sleep.

It was now nine-thirty. Tempe sent me out, once again, to check for the white rag. Halfway to the barn, on the fence along the path, I saw it.

It shone in the dark.

I ran back to the house, arriving breathless, and before I got the words out of my mouth she knew.

Quickly she grabbed her cloak. "Don't leave Mama. No matter what happens. Keep the latch on the door."

"Tempe!" I shouted her name.

"Hush. You'll wake Mama. In God's name, what?"

"What if Reeves comes back? What do I tell him?"

She hesitated not a fraction as she picked up her small riding whip and drew on her gloves.

"Play chess with him. Tell him I've ridden to Leddell's to fetch him because Mama is poorly. If he's here when I return, we'll simply say a soldier chased me and I brought Colonel back. No more! Do you understand? We tell him no more!"

"Can I come help you saddle Colonel?"

"He's saddled," she said. "He's been saddled all afternoon."

She went out into the blackness, and all I heard was the sound of her boots crunching on the cold ground as she ran down the path to the barn.

19

So I was alone then. And afraid. And I was thinking, *Well, Mary Cooper, what do you do now?*

And in the candlelight in the kitchen, with only the crackling of the fire and the occasional snoring of Oliver Cromwell for company, I answered myself.

"Now?"

Abraham always said that the person who could respond to such a question in a crisis had probably spent his whole life preparing for the moment.

Well, nothing I had done in my life had prepared me for any of this. I was alone with the remains of a New Year's Day supper. Aunt Mary was feeling poorly in the next room. A mutiny of a great part of the Continental Army was about to take place in the blackness outside, and Lieutenant Reeves might return at any moment for coffee and my cider cake.

Or never return at all.

Tempe had gone out into the night to meet the leaders of the mutiny and might, within the half hour, return to the house to hide her horse inside.

And I was responsible for a great part of all this.

I tried to ponder on what Abraham would have to say about the whole affair. But all that kept coming to my mind was the story he'd told me once about John Adams from Massachusetts, who, at the meeting of the Second Continental Congress in Philadelphia, had sat listening patiently while those around him were suggesting sending a concerned and polite petition to the King of England for redress of their problems.

"Oh, the imbeciles! The fools!" John Adams had roared. "The damned, damned fools with their talk of petitions!"

I know not how my brother Abraham came by that story, for he had never sat with the Continental Congress in Philadelphia. Yet the tale was one that rang true with Patriots right after the signing of the Declaration of Independence in 1776.

And those were the words that raced through my mind now as I walked about the kitchen, picking up objects and setting them down. "Oh, the imbeciles! The fools! The damned, damned fools with their talk of petitions!"

For I sensed in my bones that even if Bowzar had Tempe's horse, even if he marched up to

Wayne with Colonel prancing and dancing, no petition would save their necks now. And even if their Committee of Sergeants and the whole Pennsylvania Line got past Wayne and went on to wherever they planned on going and whatever they planned to do, they were doomed. All of them.

The word mutiny has a terrible ring, I minded as I sat there by the fire, waiting. *And I do not harken to the sound of it at all.*

I took up my knitting again by the fire. But I could not keep my thoughts to my work. All I could think of was Tempe racing through the night to meet Bowzar or his henchmen. And my friends, Jeremiah and David, out there in the blackness that was like the inside of the devil's ear tonight. And Lieutenant Reeves. If something happened, would he be shot? I could not abide the thought of that at all.

At ten o'clock I distinctly heard the sound of musket fire from the direction of camp. I jumped up, Oliver Cromwell with me, crossed the room, and opened the door.

Yes, it was musket fire. It crackled in the still night. Oliver Cromwell growled low and menacing, and I put my hand on his head to quiet him. I stood with the door open a crack, peering out past the kitchen garden and the Wick orchard in the direction of camp.

More musket fire—sporadic, to be sure—but it soon became a general noise, persistent in the night.

I slipped outside and walked to the side of the house nearest the garden, peering to the front to see if Tempe was coming from that direction. But there was nothing. The musket fire had stopped now.

And then I heard the sound of running footsteps coming at me through our garden. The latch gate to the garden opened.

"Are you all right?" came the voice of Lieutenant Reeves through his spent breath. "Are you all right? I came to see."

"What's happened?"

"Mary? Is it you? You shouldn't be out here. Let's go inside, and I'll tell you. I haven't but a few minutes. I came back to warn you."

Inside, he turned and leaned against the door for a moment, catching his breath. "The mutiny. It's started."

"When?"

I quickly poured some coffee into a mug. He took it, sat down, held the mug in his cold hands, and stared at me, not quite believing himself the words he was saying.

"The shouting we heard when I left here was from the 11th Regiment. We quieted them down. But whatever designs they have upon this night were not quieted. I stayed a while with the other officers, going from hut to hut. We kept finding numbers of men outside the huts, gathered in small groups. Whispering. No sooner did we get them back in their huts than another group appeared. And it seemed soldiers were everywhere, in spite of our efforts, busily running up and down between the huts and conferring."

"Drink your coffee," I urged. "You're trembling. Would you like some rum in it?"

"We exerted ourselves to keep the men from turning out." He pushed his mug toward me. I got up and fetched the jug of rum and poured some into his coffee, as I'd seen Tempe do for male visitors in the past. He drank a huge gulp, gave me a grateful smile, and looked around.

"Where's Tempe?"

"She's gone."

"Gone? Where, on this godforsaken night?"

I remembered to lie to him, though it pained me to do so to such a good friend.

"She's gone to fetch Doctor Leddell for Aunt Mary."

"She could have gotten Doctor Latimer, the camp physician and surgeon."

"Aunt Mary won't have anyone but her son-in-law attend her."

"Has she taken her horse, then?"

"Yes, but she said we were not to worry. She can ride him like the wind."

He shook his head and brooded on that for a moment, staring into his mug. "In spite of all we could do, the mutinous soldiers started forming up on the parade in front of their huts."

"How many?"

"Less than half the Line, I'd say. The 2nd, Stewart's regiment, seems to be holding aloof. The 4th is now responding to orders from one of its captains, Thomas Campbell. His men did advance a bit in the darkness but dropped off, one by one."

He gulped the remainder of his coffee, then stood up. "I must needs be getting back. I got permission to run over here and tell you folks to latch your doors and shutters and stay inside. They've already stolen my horse."

"Who?"

"The mutineers." He set his cup down and put on his tricorn. "Tempe should never have left," he said sternly. "When she returns, tell her to stay indoors, for heaven's sake. At least you'll have Doctor Leddell here. I feel better knowing a man will be on the property. Events threaten to turn ugly this night. Lieutenant Francis White of the 10th has already been shot through the thigh trying to control his men. Captain Sam Tolbert of the 2nd had an encounter with a soldier of his company. Someone named Absalom Evans, I'm told, and one of the first to revolt."

"Evans?"

He scowled. "Do you know him?"

"I know of him."

"Well, then you should know that Tolbert has run him into the thigh with his sword. Evans was loading his musket at the time and shot Captain Tolbert through the belly."

His quiet recitation of these nightmarish events horrified me. He moved reluctantly to the door.

"The only reason I managed to get away is because the firing of muskets became so general that we officers had to withdraw. We have no muskets, only pistols. We're no match for them. So we had to let them have their way. They've already broken open the magazine and are preparing to take off with the cannon."

"And Wayne?" I whispered. "Where is Wayne?"

He smiled grimly. He drew on his gloves. "It's a bit of a ride down from Kemble's at the fork in the road, as you know, Mary. Wayne is on his way. Fast. So I must needs be getting back."

Yet he paused at the door, wanting to say

more. He contemplated me with such a look of troubled intensity that I feared there was something terrible he wasn't telling me.

"What is it, Enos?"

He bit his lower lip, ruminating. "I worry about you, Mary, here alone."

I breathed a sigh of relief. Is that all it was? "I'll be fine," I said brightly.

But there was something else on his mind. "I may not be back this night, Mary. I'll be where I'm needed. Which is with Wayne."

I nodded. I searched his face, waiting to hear whatever it was that was troubling him. And he gazed back at me. There was uncertainty in his eyes. And he seemed tongue-tied suddenly.

"There isn't time to say what I want to say, Mary. Things have happened too fast. I needed more time here, and I don't have it."

So that was it, I decided. "Do you want me to give Tempe a message for you? Because you're leaving?"

The anguish deepened in his eyes. And then he did something for which I was completely unprepared.

He strode toward me, covering the distance between us in two purposeful steps. Then he put his hands on each of my shoulders, drew me toward him, and kissed me gently, on the forehead. "Your friendship means much to me,

Mary Cooper," he said. "And I'll not forget you. And I'll be back."

Then he was gone. Out into the blackness that was like the inside of the devil's ear this night. Leaving me to put my hand to the place on my forehead where he had kissed me.

He had kissed me chastely, as Abraham would have done. And yet, and yet, there had been a look in his eyes that had been like no look I had ever seen in Abraham's eyes at all.

I took up my knitting by the fire again. But I did more staring into the flames than knitting, for the softness of Enos's kiss lingered on my forehead, and it troubled me.

It was Tempe he was smitten with, Tempe he always came around to see, Tempe he'd done the chores for. Wasn't it? Then why had he looked at me so, with such anguish in his eyes?

I pushed the thought from my mind, determined to make light of it. Events were at a fevered pitch out there in the blackness of this night. No doubt, Enos's emotions were in such a state, also. The anguish had been in his eyes because he was leaving, not knowing when he would return, and Tempe hadn't been here to say good-bye.

Yes, that was it. And where *was* Tempe? Oh,

I could not tend to my knitting. Again, I heard musket fire, so I ran to the door, opened it, and peered out past the orchard.

Someone had sent up a rocket, a fireball into the night, shot out of one of the captured cannon, no doubt. I watched it pierce the darkness, then disintegrate. Was this a signal of some sort? Where was Tempe? Did Bowzar have her horse?

It was in that moment that I made my decision, with no pondering on it. I knew what I must do. And so, with Oliver Cromwell at my heels, I hurried into Aunt Mary's bedroom to check on her.

She was sleeping peacefully. So I spoke to Oliver and told him he must needs stay with Aunt Mary and not leave her. He whimpered at me anxiously. Then I patted the foot of her bed, and he jumped up and took his place there, next to the two cats.

"Good boy," I told him. Then I patted his head and crept out of the room, closing the door behind me.

Aunt Mary would be secure with Oliver by her side for twenty minutes or so. In that time I could be through our orchard and onto the Fort Hill Road. I had to see for myself if Bowzar had Tempe's horse. So I would know then if, indeed, something had happened to Tempe.

I was lying to myself, of course. We always do know when we are lying to ourselves in this life. My actions were prompted as much by curiosity about what was going on as by concern for Tempe.

But it was more convenient for me to lie to myself. Because I knew I was wrong leaving Aunt Mary. And, knowing all these things in the hurtful place that was now my heart, I did not heed them. But commenced upon my misadventure.

20

I suppose someday when I am old, my thoughts will slide back to this night and I will be able, if I close my eyes, to see it clearly as it was.

It was confusion. Whichever way I looked. I came through the Wick orchard in the dark, stumbling, though I was sure of my way. But fear put a different cast on things. Every step of the way, as I neared the camp, I told myself to go back, *Mary, you don't belong here*. But I couldn't go back. Not even if they hitched me to Ebenezer Drake's mule and he was doing the pulling.

To the left of me in the orchard was the brooding, hulking form of the magazine. I saw soldiers slashing about in the darkness, saw the winking of lanterns, heard low voices locked in argument. It was over the fieldpieces. It was a dispute over firing one of them.

"You oaf," came a loud whisper. "To what purpose, firing it now?"

"To arouse the timid soldiery," came the hissed reply. "We've only half the Line with us. The others are hiding out and skittering about like rabbits caught between a fire and a hunter's trap."

I ran by them. Up ahead I heard musket shots. As I ran, I almost stumbled over a body on the ground moaning, "Help me, help me."

He grabbed the hem of my petticoat, and as I peered down at him, I could see he'd been shot. I could smell the blood pouring down his face. And in that instant, while I pondered whether to run on and leave him or stay and assist, he loosed his grip, and his arm fell to the ground. He was dead.

I ran on. I leaped forward, wanting the darkness to swallow me up. But the night was lit by the belching musket fire, like fireflies all around. I beat my way through bushes and past tree branches, following the familiar path I'd taken to camp so many times.

My heart was a burning thing inside my chest. My breath came in spurts of pain. And then the path fell away, and I stopped and looked around.

I was in the middle of everything. But no one took notice of me.

Just ahead of me, like in some stage play— the likes of which Abraham had taken me to see in Boston one time—the soldiers of the Line were forming up in some kind of order. A few on the fringes had pine-knot torches. And within the ring of light cast by the torches, they were assembled. They stood straight and tall. Others ran up from out of the darkness with their arms, their accoutrements, and knapsacks. It was a rendezvous, to be sure. No uncertain thing, but something well planned.

I stood there like some petrified object, like a tree or a rock. Men brushed past me, running into the circle to join the formation, not seeing me or else caring little that I was there. For other women stood watching, also, many with children in their arms or held by the hand.

I recognized Billy Bowzar and the man they called Macaroni Jack in the middle of it all, consulting with others whom I supposed to be from their Committee of Sergeants. They were giving some sort of orders.

Bowzar was on foot. No horses were in sight. I breathed a sigh of relief, even while realizing, with an awful sense of foreboding, that this very moment Tempe might be racing Colonel back to the house.

I knew I should go. But I stood rooted and paralyzed by a dark sense of fascination and horror. The soldiers made a sizable force now, with more rushing up out of the darkness all the time to join in shuffling silence. Behind them some drummer lads were drumming. A fifer played a mournful tune.

The Line was forming up. The Line was getting ready to march! The mutiny was happening. Tears came unbidden to my eyes.

But the words do not do justice to the telling. For I mind that everything happened at once then. Footsteps scurried all around me in the dark. In the unfathomable distance a cannon fired. *So the one who wanted to fire won the argument,* I thought. A child behind me screamed as a roar of grapeshot was spewed over our heads with a terrible rushing noise.

Then, like some awful god of vengeance, Wayne appeared.

Horses' hooves announced him. He came into the torchlight, his cloak swirling about him, his horse prancing with its forelegs off the ground while he fought to control it. His two officers, Butler and Stewart, were astride their mounts next to him.

"Back to quarters! What in the devil's name do you think you're about here! What in hell is going on!" Wayne shouted.

Billy Bowzar stepped forward then and stood right before Wayne's horse.

"Who gave the men the order to form up like this?" Wayne demanded.

"The Committee of Sergeants gave it," Bowzar said in that British voice of his. And I marveled at the calm of him in the face of

Wayne's anger. For he stood there, a small man, and looked up at the general as Adam might have looked up at God in the Garden of Eden when he was being called to account for his sin.

"I know of no Committee of Sergeants," Wayne said loudly. "What is this Committee of Sergeants?"

"We formed it," Bowzar said.

"Oh, you formed it, did you?" Wayne said. And his voice was filled with a sarcasm born of his years of being a commander and unaccustomed to being disobeyed. His voice wore a mantle of authority as easily as he wore his buff-and-blue uniform.

"Well, I don't acknowledge your Committee of Sergeants, Billy Bowzar, so therefore it doesn't exist!"

And with that, still managing his restless horse whose prancing made him look like some god of war, he spoke over Bowzar's head to his men.

"Disband, I tell you! Back to your huts! This man is a malcontent, a troublemaker. If you follow him, you march into hell!"

They stood their ground in silence. And that silence was more terrible than the screaming of grapeshot.

"I've put down mutinies before," Wayne's voice crackled in the night air. "And I'll put this one down in the same manner. You're all good men. You don't realize the consequences of what you do here. Disband and report to your officers, and I'll forget you took an unauthorized walk on the parade this cold night."

Still, they did not move or reply.

"This is mutiny!" Wayne's voice was deep with warning, a live thing he hurled at them. "Do you mind what you're about here? You can all hang for this!"

And his voice broke then, almost a cry of pleading.

"We do not call it mutiny, General Wayne," Bowzar said. His men murmured their approval.

"And what name do you give to it, then?" Wayne flung down at him. "Is it not the same as I put down at Fort Ti? Think you that I do not recognize it? You men!" And he raised himself in his stirrups. "We've bled together on the field of battle! I was with you at Valley Forge when Baron von Steuben taught you to be soldiers! You've endured the fatigues of camp life! You're determined to be free! You've borne your sufferings with heroic patience! Don't throw it all away now!"

But they did not pay heed to him. My heart went out to his pleading, for that's what it was beneath the hoarseness of his voice.

Colonel Butler spoke up then. "If you don't

heed your commanding officer now, there's little we can do for you later," he said.

There was a ripple of amusement in the ranks at this. Then Bowzar spoke again. "And what's to come 'later,' Colonel Butler?"

"You know full well, Bowzar, you slime," Butler said crisply.

"And when is this 'later,' pray?" Bowzar prodded.

"When you feel the rope around your ungodly neck, Bowzar, that's when," Butler retorted. "You may not care for your own neck, but at least care for the welfare of the men!"

"And what of the welfare of the revolution?" Colonel Stewart's deep voice sounded like a death knell.

"We're as much for the revolution as any of you with the fancy lace at your throats," Bowzar said. "And more. For when the fighting's done, and if we're alive to tell the tale, we'll never know the feel of lace at our throats. Or fine leather boots on our feet. Or the softness of those doeskin breeches you wear. But we fight, just the same."

"Enough!" Wayne fairly roared the word. All fell silent. He dismounted and stood for a moment with one hand on the saddle, facing the men, his profile carved against the flickering torchlight like some Roman general come back to haunt us all. Then he threw the reins over his horse's neck and strode forward.

Truth to tell, I have never seen so terrible a sight as the way he looked coming toward his men. Terrible and beautiful he was, his dark blue cape outlining the flowing motion of his tall and supple form. His polished boots sounded on the frozen ground. His spurs gleamed. The lace at his wrists and throat stood out in the dark. His sword shone at his side. His gloves, like his breeches, were the buff color of doeskin.

But all this elegance was nothing compared to the power of his presence. We all watched him move, for he struck awe in the heart.

I felt a wild surge of breathlessness. For he was without fear. And in those few short moments when the moon slipped out from behind a shredded cloud and his boots sounded on the hardened ground, he not only marched up to face Billy Bowzar. He marched into my heart.

He drew his two brass-handled pistols and pulled back the hammers.

Immediately half a dozen men surrounded him with fixed bayonets.

"General Wayne," Billy Bowzar said gently and with great solicitude, "we love you and respect you. You have led us often on the field of battle, but you command us no longer. We warn you to be on your guard. If you fire, you are a dead man. If you attempt to enforce any commands, we will put you to death."

I stifled a cry, covering my mouth with my hands. For it was in that moment that the mutiny of the Pennsylvania Line of the Continental Army became a real throbbing and living thing. And Wayne knew it.

In an instant Colonel Butler made a movement to step forward and defend Wayne, but a soldier from the mob quickly attacked him. There was a short scuffle, and Butler was obliged to retreat to save his own life. Another soldier held a bayonet at Stewart's throat.

This all happened so fast that it took me days, afterward, to sort it out in my mind. Wayne never moved—except for his eyes, which took in everything around him.

"I exhort you all," he said once more, "to come to your senses. I will do my best to remedy your grievances. And there will be no punishment for tonight. On my word as an officer and a gentleman in the Continental Army of these United States, I swear that to you."

"You can do nothing for us," Bowzar said. "It's out of your hands, Wayne. We leave this night to remedy our own grievances."

"Where do you take these men?" Wayne's voice was raspy.

"Away from this godforsaken place where

our children have starved to death and our women have huddled in the cold," Bowzar said.

"You'll hang, Bowzar," Wayne roared. "And all with you! You may have the upper hand now, but I'll see you all in hell before I see you go to the British!"

At this last outburst, several muskets fired over his head. Some women behind me screamed. The children began to whimper and cry. Wayne went into a white rage then. He drew back from the bayonets that were fixed upon him and threw his pistols to the ground. Then he ripped open his coat, his waistcoat, and his shirt, baring his chest.

"If you mean to kill me, shoot me at once! Here is my breast!"

Again my hands flew to my mouth, and I commenced to cry silently.

"It is not our intent to hurt or disturb an officer of the Line," Bowzar recited quietly, "with the exception of two or three individuals who well deserve it for past actions."

"For many of us, General Wayne," a voice from the formation called out, "your life is almost as dear as our own."

Murmurs of approval rose from the soldiers.

"We revere you, we'll fight for you," the determined voice went on, "but we have more pressing business elsewhere."

More assent from the ranks.

"And now, General Wayne," Billy Bowzar said carefully, "with your permission, I'll just borrow your horse."

And he moved toward the powerful gray creature.

They had to hold Wayne back now, physically restrain him.

"Take your scrawny hands off my horse!" Wayne bellowed. "If hell is your path, walk in on your own feet!"

Laughter in the ranks. Billy Bowzar mounted the horse then, turning the animal to the left to lead them along the parade. The men started moving, following Bowzar.

Still physically restrained, Wayne shouted out as they began to move, his voice ringing with authority, "Listen to me! All of you! Don't desert your country's Cause!"

Half turned on the horse, Bowzar shouted back, "We are not deserting! Only demanding what our country long owes us. We'd fight with you fast enough, General Wayne, if the enemy were to come out right now! But until our wrongs are righted, we will not take further orders. Even from you. For there must be a settlement. And we must meet on equal terms with the officers. And for that we must first get away to someplace where we can be on our own ground. And be heard."

Silence now. Wayne said no more. For he knew he had lost this fight. The Line was marching! The Line was moving away!

I saw him shake off his captors, saw him stand there in the torchlight, his face ashen, tears streaming unashamedly from his eyes as he watched them go. He stood straight and tall, his firm strong jaw twitching, his hands clenching and unclenching at his sides.

And in that moment I think I would have run across the clearing to comfort him myself if I hadn't felt someone touch my shoulder. I looked around, and there were my friends, Jeremiah and David.

"They're going," David said.

"The cannon on the Fort Hill Road will protect them," Jeremiah noted.

"Can't somebody do something?" I whispered.

"It's done," David said. "It's all planned. Look around you. They're taking possession of horses, wagons, ammunition, provisions, tents, everything—all through camp."

I became conscious then of much movement in the background, of people scurrying about and gathering things and running like water rats to follow the formation of men as they proceeded down the parade.

"The 5th and the 9th don't want to go along with them," Jeremiah was whispering in my ear. "They've been made to fall out in front of their huts and were kept in order and threatened. The cannon up there are fixed right over their heads."

I saw this to be true. Saw the men of the 5th and the 9th mix in with the passing troops.

"Where will they go?" I asked.

"For now it looks as if they mean to cross Primrose Brook, which will take them in the direction of the fork in the road near Wayne's headquarters," Levering said.

So Henry had been right! The fork in the road, he had said. One way they go to Chatham and Elizabethtown. And the British. The other road, they go to Princeton and on to Philadelphia.

A movement just ahead of us caught my attention. The soldier who had held his bayonet to Colonel Stewart's throat backed away, joined by a few others who walked backward after the column of mutineers, keeping their muskets aimed at anyone who would follow.

My friends and I stood watching this incredible display in silence. Women and children mixed in with them, piling baggage and bundles of clothing and provisions onto the wagons. And so they marched off in regular platoons, under the command of their sergeants, their artillerymen with the fieldpieces, the wagons and the regiments in order, and the last two fieldpieces covered by the rear guard. Drums and fifes were piercing the shocked silence of the night. Tears streamed down my face. For I felt the end of something.

"I'd say they're going off very civilly," Jeremiah said, "considering they're such a mob."

"Look!" David pointed. And there ahead of us on the parade came old Fishbourne, leading a horse. Nothing like Wayne's horse, no. But a horse.

Another aide came up with one for Stewart. And Butler came bounding out of the blackness on a new mount—his horse, too, had been stolen. Other officers started appearing and gathering around Wayne, who was now remounted.

"The officers had no chance against the men with muskets," Jeremiah reminded us. "Remember, officers carry only pistols, swords, and spontoons."

At this moment Wayne and Stewart and Butler dashed away. "Where are they going?" I turned to my friends.

"Looks like they're going around the mutineers' flank, possibly to get ahead of them and take a stand at the fork in the road," David said.

"They'll kill Wayne!" I wailed.

My friends shook their heads. "They revere him too much," Jeremiah said.

We stood there a few more moments in the cold. And then Jeremiah spoke. "We must needs be off."

"Where?" I asked. So it *was* the end of something. I was right.

"With our officers," David said solemnly.

I nodded, bit my lower lip, and moved away from them. "You take care, now. Whatever happens."

They promised they would.

"Someday you'll be able to tell your children you were there the night Wayne's men held him captive with bayonets, and he still gave them no quarter," Jeremiah said.

I sensed he was saying this to comfort me. "But what will happen to Wayne now, Jeremiah?"

"He'll prevail," he told me. "You'll see. Goodbye now, Mary."

I ran, on impulse, to throw my arms around each of them, in turn. Jeremiah blushed, but David was pleasured by it.

"I'll miss you both so." Tears came from my eyes. "I haven't a friend left in the world when you leave here."

They cast sly glances at each other. "I'd say you had one," David ventured.

"Who?"

"Lieutenant Reeves. Or hadn't you noticed? He's taken quite a fancy to you."

"Go on with you, David! It isn't true." I looked at Jeremiah for confirmation, and he gave it, nodding his head.

And in that moment I felt myself go hot and cold all over, remembering Enos's kiss and the anguished look in his eyes. "He's sweet on Tempe," I countered weakly.

They hooted at that. "Tempe's too much for him. It's you he languishes over," David insisted. "Why do you think he started coming around to do chores at your house the minute you showed up from Long Island?"

I stared at them like some kind of half-wit. "Because it was just about then that Tempe's hired man quit."

"You can put any meaning on it you wish, Mary," David said solemnly, "but the man is smitten with you. If you want to be stupid about it, that's your privilege, I suppose."

I was about to argue, more out of embarrassment than anything, when Jeremiah pointed eastward to where beacons were beginning to flame up against the black horizon.

"Look!" he shouted.

And suddenly there was a whole line of beacons flaming brightly against the night sky. "What are they?" I asked.

"They're from the log pens that are filled with tar and dry fuel on hilltops all the way from Morristown to the Jersey shore," Jeremiah explained. "My guess is the militiamen all down the line heard the cannon and sent up their signals. The beacons are used to warn of the arrival of the British. The militiamen don't know yet this night what's happened, though. And they are ready for anything."

"Those beacons are an omen," David pronounced.

"Go on with you," Jeremiah hooted.

"A good omen," David elaborated. "That we'll all meet again. And soon."

No one disputed that. And we parted on this note, they going to join their officers and whatever fate awaited them.

And I going home. Where probably a worse fate awaited me. But whatever happened to me, it had been worth it, I decided. For this night I had been privy to things my eyes would recollect always. I had seen General Wayne give his troops no quarter when they held him captive. I had

259

seen the beacons flaring on the horizon, lighted by New Jersey militiamen who were ever watchful. And I had learned from my friends what I had been too blind to see myself, that Lieutenant Enos Reeves had taken a fancy to me.

What I would do with that knowledge, I did not yet know. For now it was only a warm and solid comfort inside me.

21

The night was still once again as I made my way home. The last strain of fifes and drums was gone from camp. The orchard was deserted, and the night came into its own again as I neared the house. I heard the hoot of an owl, and then another owl's answer. I saw the eyes of two raccoons peering at me as I approached the well, then they scampered away. In the distance I heard the bleating of Tempe's sheep in the barn.

It was a farm again. And I realized how glad I was to return. What time could it be? Near midnight? No candles shone in the windows. The house was deathly silent as I opened the back door.

Tempe had not yet returned. A stab of fear crept over me. No sooner was I in the kitchen than I heard another sound, to strike more fear into my heart.

Aunt Mary was moaning from behind her bedroom door. And Oliver Cromwell was whining.

Quickly I lit a candle and hurried to her room.

When I pushed open the bedroom door, the sight that I saw appalled me.

Aunt Mary was seated on the floor 'twixt her bed and the door, all rumpled in her nightgown and her bedclothes. Oliver Cromwell was seated next to her, licking her face.

"Aunt Mary! What's happened?" I set the candle down and went to assist her.

"Well, it's about time you came. I've been calling and calling! Where have you been? Where in tarnation *is* everybody?"

"Are you hurt, Aunt Mary? What are you doing out of bed?"

"What, indeed? I'm in need of some refreshment. After I called and no one came, I just decided to get up and help myself!"

Oh God, I prayed as I helped her to her feet, *don't let any bones be broken*. "Did you fall, Aunt Mary? Does anything feel as if it doesn't work?"

"I did *not* fall. And I'll thank you not to go telling my daughter I did. I simply found myself in the dark in the middle of the room, couldn't decide which way to go, and sat down to wait. *Now where is everybody?*"

"I'm here."

"The only one who was here when I needed somebody was that dog. Where have you and

Tempe been gallivanting? And where's that nice young lieutenant?"

Lieutenant? It took me a moment to realize she was talking about our New Year's Day supper, which now seemed like days ago, instead of hours.

"Lieutenant Reeves left. He was needed."

"He didn't come to say good night."

"You were sleeping." I helped her back to bed and propped her against a few pillows. No, thank heaven, nothing seemed broken. Or even sprained. She hadn't cried out when I'd moved her. "Would you like some nice cool water, Aunt Mary? Or some hot tea?"

"It's rum I'm wanting, and you know it. Wouldn't you think an old lady would be allowed a snippet of rum on New Year's Day?"

"It's not New Year's Day anymore, Aunt Mary. It's after midnight."

"After midnight, is it? And where have you two been off to, then?"

She peered at me from beneath her nightcap.

"Walking out with that nice Lieutenant Reeves. Is that where my daughter is? While her poor Will languishes away up in New York?"

"No, Aunt Mary." There was nothing for it but to tell her the truth, or as near to the truth as I could conjure without harming her sensibilities. If she was nothing else, she was persistent.

As well as shrewd. And she'd give me no peace until she had some answers. I knew that.

"Tempe's on an errand."

"At midnight?"

I sighed. Suddenly I was enormously tired and wanted nothing more than to put my head down on my own pillow and forget every terrible thing that had happened this day. My head had taken to spinning.

"She's gone to fetch Colonel," I said. Which wasn't a lie, exactly.

"What for?"

"To bring him into the house. Any moment now she'll be doing that, Aunt Mary. You're awake and you'll hear it, so you may as well be told."

For a moment she just stared at me, her gaze steady, unblinking. And it was as if I could see the years of wisdom in her eyes, rolling there like water, deep but undisturbed. Water beneath whose surface all sorts of turmoil and heartache were stored, the likes of which would probably make today's events seem calm.

She nodded, knowing something terrible was going on, needing only to be told the exact nature of it. "What's happened?"

"Mutiny, Aunt Mary. The Line mutinied this night. They assembled on the parade around ten, and no amount of threats or promises of General Wayne's could stop them."

Her gaze never wavered. "The rapscallions," she breathed. "They'll burn in hell. How is General Wayne?"

"He was wonderful, Aunt Mary. He stood right up to them. Why, he's gone, right now, to the crossroads with his men to head them off and keep them from going to the British."

"You were there, then."

I looked down at her fragile hand. "Yes."

"And you ran off against Tempe's wishes. You were left to watch me and you ran off. Is that it? Well, you might as well tell me."

"Yes, Aunt Mary, that's it."

"You both think I'm addled in the head. I'm not. My mind is as sharp as two flints. Where's Tempe, then? Tell me."

"I can't, Aunt Mary."

She made a motion of impatience and peered at me in the flickering candlelight. "Look here, Mary. I like you. I like your spirit. It's after my own. I hear the way you speak out, the way you won't be put down. It's the only way to be in this life, girl, if you're to survive. It's what kept me alive times when I wanted to die."

"My father always said I was just like you, Aunt Mary. He said I have your sharp tongue."

"It's more than a sharp tongue, only your father is too much of a ninny to know what it is. The only ones who do know are you and that brother Abraham of yours. The rest of them are a passel of fools. It's gumption, girl. It's wits. It's a hunger for truth, for knowing it and speaking it. It's an impatience with fools and a sense of fairness."

Tears came to my eyes as I listened. For never before had anyone defined for me what I was all about.

"But most of all," and she slapped the coverlet with her bony hand, "it's seeking out and speaking the truth! So now tell me and no more shilly-shallying. Where's Tempe? I can take it."

So I told her then. She listened, nodding wisely. I told her about everything except Henry. It was not my duty to tell her that. It was Tempe's duty, Tempe's job.

"That girl always did have the heart of a thoroughbred horse, the stubbornness of an ox, and the brains of a flea," she said resignedly. "Takes after those boys of mine. It comes from the Wicks. Half of them are crazy."

"I'm worried. She should be back by now, Aunt Mary."

She patted my arm. "Go outside and see if you can hear her coming. I'll be all right."

"I don't want to leave you again. I did wrong

leaving you. I know it was wrong. You could have fallen here in the dark all alone and broken your bones."

"Well, I didn't, did I?"

I said nothing for a moment. Then, "Tempe will never forgive me."

"Does she have to know?"

I looked at her in disbelief. She was grinning at me. "Tell you what," she whispered, though there was no one about but the two of us and Oliver Cromwell. "You go and get me a little bit of rum, and I'll never let beyond my lips the fact that you weren't here all night."

I stood up. "Oh, Aunt Mary, I couldn't!"

"Nonsense! Of course you could. So could I. And you will, too. It's another part of what we are that I forgot to mention before."

"What's that, Aunt Mary?"

She winked at me then. "We know how to conspire," she said.

"But you said always to speak the truth."

"When you get older, Mary, you'll learn the difference between speaking the truth and keeping your mouth shut when you aren't asked. It's something most people never learn. Now go quickly and get me some rum. Then go out and look for Tempe. But don't go far. I'll be right here with the dog. Fine fellow he is. He's no Wick, I can tell. He's a Cooper."

I started for the door. "Mary," she called out.

"Yes?"

"You say General Wayne was wonderful through all of this."

"Yes, Aunt Mary, he was wonderful."

She nodded her head sagaciously. "He would be wonderful," she murmured to herself. "Yes, he would be."

22

I put on my cloak to go out again, but first I went into the small spare bedroom off the parlor.

All was in readiness. I shivered, closed the door, and went outside.

It was that hour in which the night comes into its own and a person is an intruder. I am not given to fear of the dark. I never was. When I was a child, Abraham told me things about the night to help me appreciate it. He explained the stars and how they are fixed in the heavens. He told me about the pull of the moon on the earth's waters. I must confess I have been more frightened, sometimes, in God's good sunlight, facing some people who considered themselves upstanding Christians but turned out to be worse than creatures of the night.

Nevertheless, I trod cautiously, lantern in hand, outside the back door. I took the path on the side of the house that led to the front, where the old black locust tree stood. It was at least two and a half feet in diameter. And it loomed with its bleak branches reaching into the sky. At the east end of the grassy hill in front was the largest red cedar I have ever seen. These trees seemed to guard the house and protect it. And I felt very comforted by them.

I don't recollect how long I stood there waiting, peering into the darkness at the road that leads westward to Mendham and eastward to Morristown. I do mind that my hands and feet got cold. The night was so peaceful now. *Was it possible that just an hour or so before it had been shattered by gunfire? Where was General Wayne now? Where were my friends, David and Jeremiah? And what about Enos?* Oh, I did not want to think of Enos. Yet, at the same time, the thought of him warmed me.

And what of the mutiny? Only then did it come to me that it could mean the end of this revolution that had been playing itself out in the background of my life for six years now. *Was it possible that tonight's events could mean the end of this freedom I'd heard about from Abraham and others at home since I was eight years old?*

Freedom. I recollect how simple and direct the word had sounded to me at one time. I know now, of course, that it is anything but simple and direct, that nothing about it is clear anymore. For I had not only seen the mutineers and their families, but I had come to know some of them.

And truth to tell, with a little prodding, I could have taken their side.

Tempe had said things were plain and simple to her before I came here. She had blamed my meddling for changing all that. *Had I changed anything? And was it for the better or for the worse?* Perhaps everyone would have been better off if I had let them be, if I had not forced the meeting between Tempe and Henry that led her to this insane plan she was carrying through tonight.

What if the plan did not work? What if, as I stood here, she lay dead somewhere in the woods? The fault would be mine, surely. I began to walk up and down the stone path, worrying the matter to the bone. My shoes on the stones were the only sound now. And then I paused. In that moment I heard what I had been listening for.

I heard the steady tempo of a horse's hooves in the black distance on the road out front. I strained my eyes, raising my lantern. To no avail.

And then the moon came out again from behind some clouds.

And I saw what I wanted to see. I saw a vision on a horse, galloping down the road from the west. And for a moment it was like a dream.

The girl was part of the horse, surely. The horse's feet scarcely touched the ground as it strained forward with an effort that made every muscle in its powerful body stand out. And something magical there was in the sight of them. For it did seem as if they were flying in the night.

They were parting the night and pushing it back in rolling waves as they winged through it.

The very whiteness of Colonel was a shock to the sensibilities as he dove through the waters of the night, the girl leaning forward on his neck. Her long hair streamed out, all mixed in with his mane.

And I knew what she was doing as she leaned forward, close to his neck. She was whispering in his ears. She was telling him how wonderful he was. Stones scattered around him as he flew along. And my heart lurched when they turned off the road and headed up the hill to the house. *Would he trip and fall? Would the darkness come tumbling around them both, claiming them for its own? Or would they, indeed, ride into morning?*

They made the turn with perfection, and now they were coming at me fast. I could hear the snorting of this great creature. And then I felt the night pushed aside, *felt* the power of him passing me.

"Tempe!"

"Hush! Get to the back door! Open it!"

I ran, but they got there first. She slid off Colonel and held the reins in front of him.

"I was so worried. I . . ."

"Quiet! I'm being followed. *Open the door!*"

I did so, fumbling in the dark, clumsy as I always was in her presence. I pushed the door open but forgot to pick up my tin lantern, which I'd set on the ground. Colonel kicked it. It made a clattering sound on the stones that would wake the dead. The candle went out, but there was no time to retrieve it, for Tempe was right behind me, leading that great creature into the kitchen.

"Close the door! And latch it! Douse the candles!"

I did so. I stumbled, dropped things, and tripped over myself while Tempe glided that great mass of whiteness through the kitchen. She was murmuring to him, caressing him and calming him.

"There's my love. There's my sweet Colonel."

She led him through the kitchen door to the parlor, off of which was the spare bedroom. He hesitated at first, his eyes shining and afraid. But Tempe's loving words of endearment never ceased, and gradually she got him to follow her into the spare bedroom.

I stood in wonderment as she reached into her haversack and pulled out a piece of sugar cone, and he nibbled on it fastidiously.

"Get those blanket strips and come here and

hold these reins while I wrap his hooves," she ordered.

Except for a slanting bit of moonlight that favored us, coming in through the window, the room was dark. But I remembered where I'd set down the blanket strips and fetched them.

"We'll have to work in what scant light we have," she whispered. "As soon as I'm finished, I want you to close the shutters."

I held Colonel while she worked, kneeling to wrap his hooves. She talked to him the whole time, while she bade me to keep feeding him bits of sugar.

Colonel, of course, was quite agreeable to the whole arrangement. He was a spoiled baby, truth to tell. And mentally I thanked the Lord for that. I knew he would stay in this room a week, if need be. As long as Tempe spoke to him in loving tones and fed him bits of sugar cone.

When she finally finished wrapping his feet, she took the reins from me, and I closed the shutters. She was taking deep breaths, and when I accidentally touched her hand, I realized it was icy cold.

"Who's after you?" I whispered.

"Two of Bowzar's lackeys. I waited at the assigned spot. I thought they would never come. I heard muskets and cannon fire from camp.

Then, just when I decided they weren't coming, they showed up."

"And what happened? Tell me."

"I pretended I was delivering Colonel to them. They commanded me to dismount, but I wouldn't abide that. I think they were in their cups. I smelled rum on them. I spoke to them gently. I entreated them to care for my pet. They said they would. Then I made them promise to return him to me when they were finished with the use of him. They promised that, too. Then, just when I had them nicely relaxed and perfectly off guard, I touched the whip to him and we shot away."

I waited.

She leaned against her horse's side. Her breath was still labored. "He shot home like an arrow drawn from a bow by a strong arm. They had muskets. They fired after us."

"Oh, Tempe!"

She gave a short laugh. "They'd been drinking. Their aim was bad. But they followed me, running, and for all I know they still are."

"Do you think they'll come here?"

She draped her arm over Colonel, who turned to nuzzle her. "I hear them still. I think I shall always hear them."

The sound of my own breathing mingled

with hers. *What could I say that would comfort her?* Nothing. I felt so useless in her presence.

"How is Mama?"

"She's resting. I gave her some rum to help her sleep. Would you like something, Tempe? There's coffee left from supper."

"When I met those men, I saw what poltroons they were. So uncivilized. And I knew how wrong I was to ever have agreed to hand Colonel over to them. What could I have been thinking? How could I have been so stupid?"

"But you didn't hand him over. You tricked them."

"I came near to doing it. And I'll never forgive myself."

There was real anguish in her voice. And she was trembling.

"Don't go on so about it. It's over," I said. "We all come near to doing foolish things. But we don't carry them out."

"How can you say that to me?" She pulled herself away from the horse, and in the ragged dark I made out the harsh outline of her face. "What have you ever come near to doing that was foolish?"

I was shocked by this assault. There was considerable hatred in her voice. It was like a gauntlet thrown down at me. But I did not know why.

"Why do you speak to me so, Tempe?"

"You're so self-righteous. I'm sick to the teeth of it!"

"Tempe!" I drew in my breath. "How can you speak to me so?" I could scarcely keep my voice from trembling.

"After tonight I can say anything to anyone," she said bitterly. "So now I'll tell you. Since you came here, you've been a plague to me. I tried with you. But I could never succeed. Oh, what's the profit in this?"

"I think you should say what's on your mind, Tempe."

She hesitated, then spoke. "I've hated you, Mary. That's what's on my mind. In you I saw everything I would not allow myself to be. I held myself close. I've tempered my wild nature. I've had to, with this war all around and my father dying. Then you came and started running around here, never heeding my advice, doing what you wanted at will. There were times you did things no respectable young woman should. Oh, I'm no prude, Mary. You see me riding about on Colonel. But that's the only freedom I allow myself. You take your freedom wherever you find it. And you have such an impudent manner that—oh," and her voice faltered and trailed off.

"I think you should finish what you started, Tempe," I said softly.

"I waited for you to suffer for your actions," she said. "But it never happened."

"You wanted me to suffer?" I stared at her in the dark.

"That business with General Wayne and the pie. I swore they'd mock you when you brought it there. You were so *pushy*, Mary, with your adoration of him."

"It was admiration, Tempe," I said quietly. "But not the kind you thought."

"What was it then? What *is* it? Have you finally decided?"

"Yes, I've decided. I simply will always admire him as a wonderful leader. And be proud that I can someday tell my children I met him. And watched him stand firm the night his troops mutinied."

"You are so fortunate, Mary," she said sadly. "Even your infatuation with Wayne turned out well for you. That's just what I mean. Things always do. As for me, things are never simple. I had to struggle with my feelings, to *compromise* to keep from going mad around here once the army came. You never would compromise, either. That drove me wild. And look at what you accomplished with Henry. All these years we all thought he was lunatic. Henry's *my* brother, but he revealed his true self to *you!*"

"I listened to him, Tempe."

"As for Mama," she went on unheedingly. "Well, one would think *you* were her daughter instead of me. I'm the one who's done everything for her since my father died. But it's Mary this and darling Mary that, all day long. She's *my* mother, Mary, not yours. But she loves you because you're so much like her. You have her spirit, she says. Where does that leave *me?*"

"I think you need some rum, Tempe," I said. "Not coffee."

"You're not one to lecture me about how we all come near to doing foolish things, Mary. You've never done a foolish thing in your life, I'll wager. Have you?"

I stared at her in the darkness. "There may be drunken soldiers searching outside for Colonel this minute," I said.

"Let them search. They'll not find him."

"If they come to the door . . ."

"They'll go away. Stop changing the subject and answer me!"

"Heavens, Tempe, I've forgotten the question!"

"*Don't* be impertinent! I won't have it! Answer me!"

She was hysterical, I was sure of it. As sure as I was that it was my job to calm her. "Must you have your answer this minute?" I asked.

"Yes!" Her whisper was fierce.

"You're shivering. Please let me get you some rum."

"Talk to me," she entreated. "I need you to talk to me now more than I need rum. I need to know if you have ever done anything foolish."

"Yes, I have."

"What was it? Tell me. And don't give me that nonsense about dancing around the Liberty Pole back home, or I'm liable to slap you."

I stifled a giggle, and she shushed me. And it was in that moment that it came to me. She had been frightened out of her wits this night. She had faced drunken soldiers, yes. They had fired upon her, chased her. But it was something more.

What more? I searched my own mind. And then I realized.

For the first time in these two winters that the army had been encamped on their farm, she had violated her own commandment of compromise.

That compromise that had been so dear to her and that she'd told me provoked less wear and tear on a body she had thrown to the winds tonight. And she was a different Tempe now than the one who had gone out to meet Bowzar's men earlier this evening.

That long ride on the road from Mendham had brought her into a new understanding of herself. She had done something she had sworn she would never do. She had stood up for something in this war she hated so.

And she did not know if she could live with the new Tempe, as she was now. For she was hiding no more from what she was. She saw herself in a harsh new light.

She had, indeed, taken a ride into morning.

She was waiting for my answer. So I gave it to her. For it was all I had to give. And she needed something from me now.

"I've done something foolish this very night, Tempe."

"What? Tell me?"

"I left your mama when you bade me stay here. I went into camp. I was there, and I saw the mutiny. And when I came back, Aunt Mary was on the floor in the middle of the room, calling out for someone."

Only her labored breathing came at me in the dark. But it was becoming less labored now and more calm. I could feel her calming.

"You left Mama alone?"

"Yes."

"She could have fallen and hurt herself."

"I never gave thought to it, Tempe."

"I asked you to stay with her."

I did not answer.

She was silent for a while. "I was going to allow you to live with us," she said after a moment or two. "After this was over. I know I threatened to send you home. But after what you did with Henry well, I was going to allow you to stay. Now I can't Now I must send you away, Mary. I was right the first time."

Still I said nothing, only waited.

"Why did you tell me this?" she asked.

"So you wouldn't hate me, Tempe. So you'd know that I do foolish things, too. I don't want to go home. But I'd rather tell you and have you send me away and not hate me."

We were a long time there in the dark. How long, I cannot recollect. But whatever words could have passed between us were drowned in silence.

And then we heard shouting outside. Voices came from the direction of the barn. Closer they came, by the minute, to the house. And through the shutters we could see two men creeping around outside. They came to the back door. They knocked loudly.

"Come on, Tempe Wick! We know you're in there! Open up! Where's the horse?"

We scarcely breathed. Oliver Cromwell aroused himself from Aunt Mary's room and commenced to growl.

"Oh, I hope they don't wake Mama," Tempe said.

I said all the prayers I knew that Colonel wouldn't whinny. Tempe was stroking him, murmuring words of love to him, whispering for him to be still. And he understood.

The soldiers pounded a few more times on the door and shone their lanterns in the window, but they could see nothing.

Oliver Cromwell barked. I prayed Aunt Mary wouldn't wake up. Then we heard the soldiers go around the house, heard their voices receding.

"Tempe!" I whispered.

"Don't be afraid." She reassured me, forgetting her anger of a few moments ago. It comforted me.

"I'm not afraid," I said. "Will they go away?"

"They're in their cups," she said. "They have no real sense of purpose."

"What if they return?"

"We'll stay here all night if need be. And all day tomorrow."

"All night?" I asked in disbelief. I thought her daft.

"Yes," she said defiantly. "All night. We'll stand with Colonel and hush him. They'll not take my horse, Mary. I'll not give him over now. You may go to bed if you wish. I'll stay with Colonel."

"I'm not tired."

"Suit yourself."

The voices had gone away. We waited in silence for about ten minutes. Oliver Cromwell was padding about the house, going from room to room. I felt, rather than saw, his presence in the doorway. He whined a bit and came into the room, sniffing around the horse.

"Good boy, Oliver," Tempe said. She patted him. Then he came to me, and I patted him. "Now go back and take care of Mama," she said. "Go on. Go."

Oliver obliged her, obediently. Then I heard Tempe breathe a sigh of relief and move to fasten Colonel's reins to something.

"What are you doing?" I whispered.

"Fastening the reins to the ringbolt I put in the timber." Having done that, she undid her cloak and tossed it on the floor in the corner. "Go to bed, Mary."

"I'm staying with you."

"Won't you ever listen?"

"We could stay together, Tempe. We could take turns with Colonel, one talking to him and keeping him quiet while the other sleeps in the corner there where you threw your cloak. If you're sleeping and I hear something, I'll wake you. We can stand guard, like the soldiers do in camp."

"Why do you want to do that for me, after what I just said to you?"

"I don't know. I just want to help you. You want me to, don't you?"

She sighed. "To be honest, I don't want you. But I do need you. I'd be gratified if you stayed. But first go and check on Mama. Only, no candles. You'll have to make your way in the dark. Then you sleep first. I'll wake you in a little while, and then I'll sleep. That's the way of it. No arguments."

"I'm not about to argue with you, Tempe."

"Good."

"Just one thing."

"In heaven's name, what?"

"I only wish you'd want me as much as need me."

"Go, Mary. I mean it. Before I change my mind."

I went.

23

It was a night like no other in my life. I went to check on Aunt Mary, fumbling my way in the dark. Thank heavens I knew my way around the house by now. I peered down at her form in the bed and determined, by the steady sound of her breathing, that she was sleeping soundly. Oliver Cromwell was curled up at the foot of her bed again, and he sniffed at me and licked my hand as I patted him. Then I went back to Tempe and lay down on her cloak, which was in the corner. The floor beneath it was hard, but in no time at all, it seemed, I was sleeping. I was ever conscious of the muffled sounds of Colonel's hooves on the quilt Tempe had laid on the floor, ever conscious of his presence. And my dreams were tattered, fitful things rendering me more weary than if I'd stayed awake. Once I opened my eyes as if in a dream and saw the two of them, Tempe and the horse, outlined against the window.

Colonel was standing there, his whiteness a bulk of patience. And Tempe was leaning on him, one arm around his neck. His head was half-turned to peer at her. Her eyes were closed. *Was she asleep standing on her feet?*

I got up and went to her. "Tempe," I whispered.

"Ummm?"

"Tempe, I don't know what time it is, but all's quiet. Go and lie down on the cloak. I'll stay with him."

"No, I . . . I can't leave him," she said.

"Tempe, you're not leaving him. You'll be right over there on the floor. He can see you. Go lie down. Please. I want to help you."

She nodded and did so. I think she walked in her sleep to the corner. The fire was almost out on the hearth. I put another log on and went to take my place beside the horse.

"Wake me at seven," came the muffled sound from the floor.

"How will I know when it's seven? We've no clock in here."

"Wake me at first light then."

I took my place by the horse, who, thankfully, had the sense to know what was going on, or at the very least knew that something was going on that was not in the normal course of events. He nuzzled me, offering me his wide-eyed understanding and his warmth. I was grateful for both. And I found myself leaning against him as

Tempe had done and, even though I do not like to admit it, dozing.

It was Tempe who woke me at first light, coming to me even as I'd gone to her, gently, lest she frighten me. And I was aware of everything happening at once. Tempe's whisper in my ear, someone knocking on our back door, and Aunt Mary calling out from the other room.

"What is it?" I shook myself awake. The fire was out again. I was cold, my head was pounding, and there was a bad taste in my mouth. I ached all over, and I smelled of horse.

"I didn't mean to frighten you, but Mama needs the chamber pot. Get her back to bed afterward, and keep her warm until we can start the fires again and make breakfast."

"Who's at the door?"

"I don't know. Just stay here a moment until I see."

She left the room, and I peered out through the shutter and pushed aside the shawl, but I could see no one. In a few moments she was back.

"It's the hired man. He was to the barn and missed Colonel. I never thought about that. He's perfectly willing to stay the day and keep Colonel in the barn and sit there with that fowling piece he carries around with him all the time."

She went to the ringbolt and unfastened the reins.

"Don't you think we should keep Colonel a while longer?"

"No, I don't. The poor dear has been as quiet as a lamb, and it's all I can expect of him. He hasn't even used this place as a necessary. But I can't expect him to be good much longer."

So saying, she led Colonel from the room.

"Tempe?"

"Yes?" She paused in the doorway.

"If you want to walk him outside, then bring him back, I'll stay here with him. All day if need be."

"Thank you, Mary," she said politely. "But it's over. It's all over. We must go on with other things now that demand our attention."

I stood in the room for a moment after she left, looking at the rumpled quilt that Colonel had worn through in some places, leaving marks in the wooden floor.

I stared at those horseshoe marks, then at the red cloak shoved in the corner, then at the shuttered windows. I ached inside with an empty feeling that cannot be rightfully put into words, for it is more emptiness than feeling. But I was familiar with the likes of it; I recognized it well. It was loss.

It was over. Tempe was right. Everything was

over, and I must go on now to the things that demanded my attention.

The army was gone from this place. It was no longer an encampment. No more would I rush through the orchard and find my friends David and Jeremiah searching for me with delicious secrets. The camp would be deserted now, echoing with memories. Mayhap even the revolution itself was over.

What would I do? For this place and these people, all that had happened here, no matter how worrisome, had covered over that other loss inside me that I'd felt when I first arrived and missed my family so.

I walked from the room. Once more I looked back: Here my cousin and I had stayed all night. With a horse. Who would believe it, if I told them? In all the weeks I had been here, I had not come as close to understanding her as I had this past night. And what of her? Had she understood me as we huddled together in fear, with that quiet, gentle, and dignified animal between us?

What had we done here in this room? What had we stood for as we whispered our secrets to each other and resolved our differences even while those who would harm us lurked outside?

Had the real harm been lurking outside? Or

in ourselves? Oh, I did not know, I did not know. Was it all then for naught?

I closed the door to that room, not knowing. I took with me only the sharp bittersweetness of it, which cut at times more bitter than sweet over the day or two that followed. But which I clung to, nevertheless.

Aunt Mary was calling. I had to help her to the chamber pot. The time for mulling things over was past. Chores and responsibilities awaited. And anything that needed mulling over must needs wait. Stored away. Like good cider, it would keep, and be twice as sharp with the keeping.

24

One thing after another kept me busy that morning, so I had not a moment to sort out my feelings. After I helped Aunt Mary to use the chamber pot, then got her back to bed again with a warming cup of tea, I washed myself and somehow managed to look middling civilized. Halfway through washing over the bowl in my room, I heard a male voice from the kitchen. So I pressed my ear to the wall.

It was Lieutenant Reeves!

Oh, he was back, he was back! I found myself getting hot and cold all over again as I minded what David and Jeremiah had said about him.

Had he come back to see Tempe? I wondered. *Or me?*

The whole idea of this tall young lieutenant favoring me with his attentions was as unlikely to me as the notion of General Wayne suddenly inviting me to a frolic.

But thinking on it pleasured me. So I washed my face and arms and neck again, this time in a bit of scented soap I'd brought from home for special occasions. Then I brushed my hair and arranged it in a long braid, done high from the top of my head. But I allowed a few wisps of hair to escape about my face as my sister Martha had taught me to do. Then I put on a clean chemise and short gown over my petticoat, and I was ready.

I went into the kitchen.

He was standing there by the hearth, mug in hand. Tempe was bent over some cooking, and he had just assisted her in putting a heavy cast-iron pot on the crane in the hearth.

He saw me and bowed as if we were at a public occasion. I noticed how careful he was about his manners. More than usual, it seemed.

"Good morning! I see you are not much worse for your fright of last evening," he said.

I minded that I dropped a small curtsy, another result of childhood lessons from Martha. She would be pleased now to think her words had not fallen on deaf ears.

Tempe turned, saw me then, and pushed some hair from her face. In one glance her eyes took in my fresh clothes and arranged hair. Then she turned to Reeves and saw his eyes upon me, saw the steadfast look of admiration that one would have to be blind as Ebenezer Drake's mule not to see. And my heart near stopped.

For in this one moment was played out all the rivalry 'twixt me and my cousin. In Reeves's contemplation of me she saw my womanhood, now. Would she acknowledge it? Or would she chide me as a child?

Or, worse yet, would she say that this was one more instance in which things turned out so well for me? I know that even while she had no real interest in Reeves as a suitor, she had thought, as had I, that he was coming around because he was smitten with her.

My conscience was clear, however. I had done nothing to draw Reeves's attention away from Tempe. I had not bothered to sweet-talk him. Something fresh and sweet had simply grown between us. Would Tempe try to kill it now?

Her eyes met mine. And in them I saw her acknowledgment of my womanhood. In my own eyes was an appeal, and then, as the moment stretched into eternity, a determination that I hoped she saw and would respect.

"Mary," she said softly. Just my name. As if she were seeing me for the first time. And then, "You do look fresh and lovely this morning. Would you bring Mama in for breakfast? I must grind the coffee."

Her voice did not imply the usual curt dismissal.

"Of course," I said.

"Perhaps I can assist," Reeves offered. "I'll escort your mother to the table."

Tempe reached for the earthenware jar of coffee. "Mama would be gratified, Enos. Go along then, both of you."

Go along then, both of you. My cousin had given us permission then to form whatever alliance we would. I turned quickly, my heart soaring.

For the first time since I had come to this place, she acknowledged me as an adult!

In the next few moments, while I helped Aunt Mary into her robe and Reeves waited outside the bedroom door to escort her to the table, my heart traveled to places where I had, for so long, yearned to arrive.

"What of matters in camp?" Aunt Mary asked at breakfast.

Enos told us, never missing a beat in his eating. "General Wayne took his stand at the fork in the road last night with his colonels, Butler and Stewart. He told the mutineers they would go to the enemy over his dead body."

"What happened?" Tempe asked.

"They parleyed with him briefly and reassured him they were not interested in going to the British. Wayne then came back to camp and ordered some quartermaster wagons filled with provisions and sent them after the men."

"The rapscallions!" Aunt Mary rapped the table with her hand. "They don't deserve such consideration!"

"Wayne's first thought is still for his men," Reeves said. "This is far and away the best corn-bread I've ever had, ladies."

"What will General Wayne do now?" Tempe asked. "What chance has he now that he's lost most of his command?"

"His chance lies in getting them back. And he'll do that," Reeves assured her.

"How?" she insisted.

"Well, first, Wayne came back to camp last night to write a full account of events to General Washington, and he's sent Major Fishbourne along on the road to New Windsor to deliver it. Then, at four this morning, he wrote another letter. He's issued an order to the Continental brigade at Pompton to come to Chatham and meet with the militia. Those beacons we all saw on the hillsides last night might well be a warning that the British are on their way westward."

"The British now, that's all we need!" Tempe brought a fry pan to the table and dished out more eggs and ham.

"We all doubt the British are on the move, but Wayne has to be sure. At nine this morning Wayne and his colonels, Butler and Stewart, are to leave again after the mutineers. We've reports they camped about four miles away last night at Vealtown. During the night they kept sending sergeants back here to recruit stragglers."

"Are any other officers going?" I asked.

Reeves turned his full attention to me for the first time now. His large, sad gray eyes observed me, and I wanted to melt. *Good heavens,* I thought, *does anyone else see how he is looking at me?* I hoped not.

"We all want to go along, Mary," he said sadly. "But Wayne ordered us to stay here. The camp is still in turmoil. We officers must do our best to keep order. We wait, impatiently, to be ordered to take horse and arms and follow. Or to hear that Wayne has persuaded the mutineers to negotiate with civil authorities."

"Where are they headed?" Tempe asked.

"Wayne thought Philadelphia. So he's sent word also to the Continental Congress and the Pennsylvania Council, warning they might reach there in a destructive mood. Wayne hopes to catch them today, before they get to Pluckemin. He wants to meet with their sergeants and offer them redress for their grievances. Or exert his influence on them to stop at Princeton and negotiate."

"What if they kill him?" Tempe asked. I shivered at the words.

"He knows that is a possibility," Reeves said

calmly. "But the larger gains seem worth the risk to him. He's counting on the influence Butler and Stewart have. Because they're Irish."

"What?" Aunt Mary perked up now. "What's all this about the Irish? Rapscallions, the lot of them!"

"Wayne hopes the Irish soldiers in the Line, of whom there are many, will look favorably upon Butler and Stewart," Reeves explained.

"And why should they?" Aunt Mary demanded.

"Butler was born in Ireland, ma'am. He is very popular. His three younger brothers are officers in the Line. Another is commander of the 4th Regiment. Stewart is Irish, too, though not born there. And he's one of the youngest colonels in the army. And considered the most handsome."

"Bah!" Aunt Mary said. "*Bah* to the Irish. They can't hold a candle to the English! Wayne is the most handsome, far and away. And you're no slouch in that department yourself, Lieutenant. Is he, Mary?"

And she grinned at me across the table. I blushed to the roots of my hair.

"Wayne himself is a member of the Friendly Sons of St. Patrick because his English grandfather lived in Ireland for a while," Reeves reminded her. "That, too, will count for something with many of the men."

"My grandfather, John Cooper, came from Buckinghamshire, England," Aunt Mary said. "Came here in 1635 on the ship *Hopewell*. With four children. He was a voter in Boston and an elder in the Lynn Church. In 1639 he proposed the settlement of Southampton in Long Island! No finer man ever lived! And he was a signer of the Indian Deed. We English are no slouches, I'll have you know, young man."

"Mama, that has no bearing on this," Tempe said.

Reeves smiled kindly. "My own people are English, ma'am. And General Wayne's ancestry is English, also. Although his family tarried a while in Ireland. What we all must needs keep in mind, I think, is that now we are Americans. And we must stay together. And I, for one, will take horse and follow Wayne as soon as I'm ordered, to help him keep the Line."

We fell silent with this pronouncement. Reeves gulped the last of his coffee, stood up, and thanked us for the breakfast. "I came this morning to assure myself that you were all unharmed. There are still many stragglers in camp. And they're intoxicated from rum and applejack. I must warn you all to stay indoors this day.

The mutineers are still seeking horses. Are your animals in the barn? I saw none in the paddock."

Tempe and I sought each other's eyes across the table. I saw a warning in her glance and took it to mean I was not to divulge what had transpired here last night. It made scant sense to me at first. Reeves was our dear friend. And then I determined that what had happened in this house last night should stay between Tempe and myself. For to share it with another, even a friend, would take a piece out of the whole cloth and fragment it. And I did not want to do that.

"Our hired man has been asked to stay the day. He'll guard the horses in the barn," Tempe said.

"Good. Then I must needs be back to camp."

He brushed some crumbs from his regimental coat, and I felt, once more, the ending of something in my life.

Enos was leaving.

He went to Aunt Mary, bowed, and took her hand and thanked her. Then he awarded the same courtesy to Tempe.

"God speed you, Enos," she said. "You'll be missed."

They were the most kindly words she had ever said to him. And they were sincere.

"No one in the whole colony sets a better

table," he said to Tempe. "And I'll remember, always, the agreeable times I've spent here."

"Mary, why don't you accompany Enos to his horse?" Tempe suggested.

I could have kissed her. For I was standing there tongue-tied, wanting to speak, to say all sorts of things to Enos, yet rendered awkward by the moment. I ran for my cloak, hearing Enos tell them he had been commissioned to see to it that General Wayne's baggage was conveyed to a safe place. "The general suggested your brother-in-law, Doctor Blachley. Since he is an officer in the army."

"As Wayne wishes," Tempe said serenely. "But we'd be happy to receive his baggage and keep it safe for him here."

Enos again conveyed his thanks, and he and I went outside into the bright, fresh morning. We sauntered over to the well under the old cherry tree, where his new horse was tethered. I gathered my cloak around me, and we stood wrapped in silence for a few moments, each of us too shy to know what to say.

After all, the last time we had parted he had kissed me. Chastely, yes, but there had been no mistaking the anguished look of devotion in his eyes.

Enos cleared his throat. "It's a lovely morning."

"Yes," I agreed.

"It's been such a mild January. So different from last year."

"I know what a terrible winter they had here last year. Tempe told me."

Our eyes met, and for a moment I thought he would say what was on his mind. But he didn't. Instead he stepped forward, reached into his saddlebag, and pulled out a folded and sealed parchment.

"I have a note from General Wayne for Tempe. He wanted me to give it to you first."

"Does General Wayne wish me to read it?"

"No. He would have me tell you its contents. It concerns her brother Henry."

"Henry?" My heart quickened. "Is he in trouble? Or hurt?"

"No." Enos smiled. "It seems he's in the stockade."

"The stockade! Oh, Enos, he wasn't caught selling British rum! It's what Tempe's always feared! Why, Aunt Mary doesn't even know he's alive! If word got back here that he's not only alive but arrested, it could kill her!" I stopped then, clamping my hand over my mouth. "I've spilled family secrets," I admitted to him. "We aren't supposed to talk about how Aunt Mary doesn't know her son is alive."

"We all know that in camp, Mary. Wayne

knows it, though Tempe's reasoning confounds him. And Henry often let out that his mama thought him dead."

"General Wayne doesn't know Henry was selling British rum, does he?"

"No. The reason Henry is in the stockade is because last night he went to Peter Kemble's house and tried to appeal to Wayne to allow him to go along when Wayne and Butler and Stewart took horse and went after the Line."

"Oh, no!" I moaned.

"Well, of course the sentries wouldn't admit him. Wayne heard the commotion outside and went to see what it was about. He saw Henry and heard his babbling. Henry was saying something about not running from battle this time but doing his duty. Wayne sent him to the stockade more for his own protection than anything. Wayne's sentries are awfully short-tempered, as one would imagine. They came near to shooting Henry last night."

"Henry is harmless, Enos."

"Wayne knows that, Mary. But Henry had to be contained. He's been given food and blankets in the stockade. Then Wayne wrote a note to Tempe and asked that I deliver it on my visit here today."

"What does the note say?"

"It says that Henry is to be released after

Wayne and his men take their leave this morning. And only when Tempe comes to fetch him herself. I do believe the general is more annoyed with Tempe than her brother. His instructions to her, in the note, are rather firm."

I smiled. "All Wayne knew is that Tempe wouldn't allow her brother in the house. That's changed, Enos. Henry has been here for a visit."

"It seems your cousin has softened her stand about many things these days. Has it anything to do with the fact that she severed her relationship with Bowzar?"

I nodded yes.

"I noticed that she is kinder to you, now. It always pained me to see how sour she was to you."

"We all seem to have changed our way of thinking somewhat, Enos," I said. "Mayhap the mutiny has done it. All of us seem to have stopped straddling the fence and started knowing our own minds better these days, don't you think?"

He looked down at his worn boots. "Have *you*, Mary?" he asked softly. "Have you recovered from your recent infirmity concerning General Wayne? And decided that my friendship means as much to you as yours does to me?"

"Which question do you wish me to answer first, Enos?" I asked solemnly.

He contemplated that. "The one about Wayne, I think. For if you're still smitten with him, our friendship doesn't stand a chance."

"I've recovered nicely, Enos. My feelings for Wayne were childish fancies."

"Are you sure?" He peered at me intently. "There is no worse sickness than that of the heart, Mary."

"I'm sure. But what of you and your feelings for Tempe?"

He scowled. "Of what do you speak, Mary? Surely you don't think I felt about Tempe as I've felt about you!"

I stared at him, stared at his tall, solid silhouette that was outlined against the blue morning sky. "But you kept coming around to help with the chores. I saw the way you acted Christmas Day, languishing at the table."

"Over you, Mary. I languished over you."

"But Tempe sweet-talked you so. She fancied you in love with her."

"I can't be held to account for what Tempe thought. She is rather vain, Mary. She thinks all men in love with her."

"But you kept coming back to do the chores."

"To see you, Mary. To see *you*. I only started doing that when you came to visit."

I felt a great swelling of joy inside me, even while I felt a great subsiding of my fears. So, it

305

was as my friends Jeremiah and David had said. But I had needed to hear it from Enos's own lips.

He was watching me steadfastly. "I'm pleased you find my company so agreeable," I said.

"Most agreeable, Mary. Surely you know that." His voice, so soft now, healed all the hurting places inside me.

"I'm not as pretty as Tempe. Or proud."

"Mayhap she's too proud. And saucy. As for pretty, as your Aunt Mary would say, you're no slouch in that department, Mary."

"I've never been told such before. Except by Abraham."

"I say it then. But as no brother. Though I do regard you with respect in kind."

"Would that respect hinder us from saying a proper good-bye, then?"

He stepped forward and stood looking down at me. And in that moment, under the old cherry tree by the well, he kissed me.

This time he did not kiss my forehead as Abraham would have done. He kissed me properly. For a moment I was lost in the wonderment of it, and I clung to him. Then he released me and drew back, and I felt as if my heart would tear right out of me. For in the same moment I felt a sense of wholeness I had never known before, as if I had finally found my place in the world. And with it came a fear of losing what I had just found.

"How fare you now, Mary Cooper?" he said.

"Happy. And sad."

"Why sad?"

"Because of what you said before. And what I have just now learned."

"And what is that?"

"There is no sickness like that of the heart."

"Ah, Mary." And he touched the side of my face. " 'Tis a good sickness, most times."

"I'm afraid, Enos."

"Don't be."

"I'm afraid for you. That you'll fight and die. I never thought such before."

"Love does that, Mary." And he held me close.

"Why does everyone want love if it makes one feel so?"

"Because the feelings without it are worse."

"I mind they are, Enos. I've had such feelings."

"We weigh the profit against the loss in love. Accept the losses and hold on to what love leaves us, like misers. Yes, I'll go and fight, wherever I'm needed."

"I've come to hate the war."

"If not for the war, we would never have met, Mary Cooper." He stepped back and smiled at me.

"Does that make right all the hunger and starvation and sadness I've seen, then?"

"No. Nothing does. But it softens it, Mary."

"Before I came here I thought the war was wonderful. I thought there was something ailing in me that made me harken to the sound of the word freedom."

"It's ailing in us all, Mary. Even those mutineers who left. We'll none of us be contented until we have this freedom."

"But they left, Enos. And so the revolution may be over."

"No. They left because they must find their own personal dignity and be treated like free men. While in the army, it has not accorded them such. Wayne knows this, which is why he is so patient with them. No, Mary, the revolution will go on. And I with it. Until the end."

"I feel the ending of things now, Enos."

"No, we're at the beginning, Mary Cooper. It's only the beginning. For us all in this country. And for you and me. So be happy."

And so saying, he embraced me once again and turned to mount his horse.

"Are David and Jeremiah still in camp?" I asked.

"Yes. But they are kept busy. They'll go with us officers when we leave."

"Give them my best wishes. Good-bye, Enos."

He leaned down from his horse then as I'd seen men do on the village green at home in Long Island when they bade good-bye to their wives and their betrothed. I stood on tiptoe. And he brushed my face with a kiss even as his horse moved away.

I watched him go through the Wick orchard and up to camp. He made a fine figure on horseback, the white straps of his accoutrements crisscrossed on the blue back of his regimental coat. His tricorn hat was turned up in back, and there was fastened a white corncob pipe. His sword slapped his side as he rode. He looked like all the officers I had seen on this place. Yet I knew I would be able to pick him out of a crowd, if need be.

I turned and went back into the house to give Tempe the note from General Wayne. A warmth and happiness flooded my bones. *Events will conspire to a good end*, I told myself.

And then I told myself, *No*. Not a good end. A good beginning. As Enos had said.

25

What I had not told Enos was that Tempe might send me home. She had threatened to last night. I knew I had taken a risk in telling her I had left Aunt Mary unattended. But I had sensed in the telling that she needed to hear from my own lips that I was less than a perfect creation of the Lord. And I had admitted my failing to her in hopes that she would finally approve of me. It was that plain.

Truth to tell, I was still in danger of being sent back to Long Island. Oh, she had been most amiable to me at breakfast! But her moods were as changeable as the weather in this colony. She could be packing my bags this very moment, I pondered.

And now I had to hand her a note from General Wayne. A note in which, so Enos had said, Wayne was firm in his instructions to her about Henry.

What had Wayne written? Certainly he'd had enough to keep him busy last night. Why, he'd been more plagued than Job in the Bible. Yet, in the middle of all the commotion, when he came out of his quarters to see poor Henry, he must have recollected the way Tempe had sassed him. In this very house. That must have stuck in his craw. So he had taken the time, in the middle of all his troubles, to write to Tempe.

Of what? I had been told he was a proud man who sometimes flew into passions when he was not obeyed. And one had only to speak to him for a few minutes to understand he was a man of firm purpose and responsibility. He believed in doing one's duty by family.

He was, most likely, upbraiding Tempe about her brother in his note. But why make me a party to his action?

And then I recollected our conversation that day in his quarters when I'd brought him the pie. It comes back to me in bright patches of memory like the pieces of a quilt that I stitch up in my mind in quiet moments. We had discussed Henry that day. Wayne had asked me if I didn't see the wrong in Tempe not telling her mother that Henry was alive. I had said yes, it had seemed wrongful, but I minded that I was only a guest in the house.

"It is always ours to say when we see what we think is wrong, Mary," he had said to me. "That is what I instruct my own children."

I had so forgotten the conversation until this

very moment! Remembering, now, I felt a rush of warmth in my bones. General Wayne was counting on me to speak out when Tempe got his note!

Could I do so now? Knowing she might still send me away?

I thought of Wayne. And how he had faced the mutineers last night, daring them to shoot him. And I sighed and thought, *Well, Mary Cooper, you'll be finding yourself on a packet boat if you do that. But you know what you have to do.*

I waited until Tempe went into her own room, then followed and handed her the sealed parchment.

Her face went white when she read the contents.

"Henry's in the stockade!" She glanced up at me.

"I know. Enos told me."

"He made a commotion last night, wanting to follow Wayne and his officers after the mutineers. He babbled about not running when needed."

"Enos told me that, too."

"Wayne says I am to fetch Henry. Or he'll not be released."

I nodded.

"He also says . . ." And she sat down on the

bed she had been making. "He says it is incumbent upon me to welcome Henry into our home to see his mother. And that it is morally reprehensible for me to keep an elderly woman from seeing her son. Though the son be addle-brained."

I said nothing whatsoever. I do know when to keep a silent tongue in my head.

"And he further writes that while Henry's sickness would not be cured, it could be lessened if I brought him home for a proper visit. And that Henry would be likely to leave the vicinity if his wishes to see his mother were so granted."

I could see her anger and confusion, but still I kept silent.

"Do you know what else he writes here?"

"No."

"He says it will be on my Presbyterian soul forever if I do not take steps to remedy this outrage of keeping son from mother. He writes, 'Has the enemy not visited enough outrage upon us, that we constantly seek out ways to invite more?'"

"Oh!" She threw the letter on the bed. "Oh, that he would write in such a manner to me from his superior Episcopalian soul!"

For my part, I could not see that Wayne's being Episcopalian had anything to do with it. "He was in a fevered state last night, Tempe.

313

You should be gratified that he bothered to write at all."

"You are taking Wayne's part against me, again, I see."

"No, Tempe, I'm not."

"It's so easy for you, for everyone, to criticize what I've done, not allowing Henry to see Mama. But it was the right thing to do at the time. Can't anyone see that? Oh, why won't anyone realize what I've been through around here?"

She was highly agitated now. She began pacing up and down the room. "Do you think," she said, whirling on me, "that anyone even *tries* to understand what the last year has been like for me? No. All anyone can do is criticize! When the army was freezing and starving out there on our farm last winter, here we sat, right in the middle of it, trying to help! We had General St. Clair *living in this house,* not to mention all the people knocking at our door for food! Then I had my father ill, his spirit impoverished by seeing what was going on."

She stopped pacing and looked at me. "Does anyone consider that?"

I said nothing. She went on.

"Then the army came back again this winter. Oh, how I hated seeing the men come back! I vowed I wouldn't allow their presence to harm my father again. But there he was again, scurrying around and figuring out ways to share our food, worrying the matter to the bone. Then he got the pleurisy and died. And what did I have *then?*"

Did she expect me to answer? I did not. Her face was contorted with the pain of remembering.

"I had Mama addle-brained. And news that Henry was back, running around camp, scheming with Leddell! Oh, how I hated Henry! It wasn't bad enough that he'd never been the son to my parents that he should have been! Now he was back to make trouble! Well, I did the only thing I could. I told Mama he was dead. I'm only twenty-two years old, Mary. I did what I thought was right."

She was breathless, half-weeping. "I should be married," she said. "I should have married Will when he asked me. But I stayed here to take care of my parents. Phoebe and Mary are married, with children. And I stayed home to keep it all going. It isn't easy. You'll see someday, Mary. It's never easy for a woman. Did I make a mistake about Henry? I don't know."

She stopped pacing, stopped talking. She wiped some tears from her face and sat down on the bed. She took some deep breaths and brushed her hair from her eyes. "Now that I've met Henry again, and after what he did for me with the horse, I can't hate him anymore. I don't want to hate him. I'm not the pompous, indifferent person everyone thinks I am, Mary. I know you think I'm hard. Well, I had to be in order to survive. I know you think I'm unpatriotic, telling you to compromise. But it was the only way I knew to stay sane. I wanted to keep everyone happy, I suppose. I even tried to keep Billy Bowzar happy, and I almost gave him Colonel."

She gave me a beseeching, tear-stained look. "Well, I learned, almost too late, that compromise isn't the answer, either. But then, what is?"

"I don't know, Tempe," I whispered. "I'm not as sure of myself as I was when I first came here, either. Living in the middle of an encampment and seeing all the privation can make anyone addle-brained. All I do know is that I always looked up to you. And I always thought you had all the answers."

"Well, you know better now, don't you?" She gave a bitter laugh and wiped her sleeve across her eyes again. And in that moment my heart went out to her. In that moment I saw her for what she was, not the imperious, haughty cousin I'd known since I came to live here, but a confused and frightened young woman who had been trying to fill a man's shoes since her father died. And who was now as frightened and witless as a little girl.

316

"I don't have all the answers, Mary," she said, shaking her head woefully. "Sometimes I live in fear of what the next question will be. And now, it seems, the next question is Henry. And do I tell Mama that he's alive? Oh, Mary, what think you? Should I bring Henry home and tell Mama he's alive? Could Mama withstand it? Or would it kill her?"

She was asking for my opinions on the matter. *For the first time since I had come here, she was looking to me for answers!*

I knew I was still on precarious ground with her, that her mood could change again and she could still send me away if I offered my opinion and things went wrong.

But I also knew what was right. In my bones I knew it was right that she should tell Aunt Mary that Henry was alive. And I could no more hold back from telling her this than I could have held back from telling my brother Nathan that he was wrong dealing with the British. It is not in me to do so.

But more than this, I took pity on her, on her dilemma. Abraham always said that those closest to a problem cannot see the solution. That it takes one more removed to see it in proper perspective.

So I did not hesitate a moment longer. I walked to the bed, sat down, and said, "I think your mama is strong enough to withstand knowing Henry is alive, Tempe. I think you should allow him to see her."

We faced each other, appraising each other for a moment, equals now.

"Thank you," she said softly.

I nodded.

"I've been hard with you, Mary," she said. And so saying, she put her hand over mine on the bed coverlet.

I could not speak for a moment. I find it difficult speaking when I am at the point of tears. Finally I managed to utter something.

"You've had your troubles," I said.

"I've been vile to you, and I know it."

"I was hoping you didn't mean it."

She sighed. "Do you want to stay?"

My heart leapt inside me. I stared at her. She raised her lovely blue eyes, guileless now, and questioning. And in them I saw the warmth of real friendship.

"Do you want me to?" I asked.

She could have lowered her long dark lashes then, guarded the honesty in those eyes, shielded it from me and shut me out. She could have turned haughty and imperious again, but she did not.

"Of course I want you, Mary. As long as you wish to stay. Silly goose, I've gotten so accustomed to having you around, I couldn't bear your leaving."

I nodded yes, silently.

"And will you promise to come with me when I fetch Henry from the stockade? You know how he trusts you. Please?"

I nodded yes to that, too. But I could not speak, for my throat was filled with tears. She understood. She hugged me then for a brief moment. "I'm glad you came here, Mary," she said. "Now I must go and tell Mama that Henry is alive and will be coming home." She got up.

"Do you want me to come with you?"

"No, Mary," she said sadly. "There are some things we can only do alone." And she sighed wearily. "And I'm afraid this is one of them."

26

18 January, 1781

My dear Mary,

I was feeling very meager and entertaining some melancholy thoughts when I received your letter. I cannot tell you how delighted I was to hear from you. Your note brought me immediately to my senses.

Needless to say, I have not heard from home. I wrote to you often, there. And wondered and worried why my letters to you were not answered. I put it down to conditions of war. Now I find you have been with Aunt Mary and cousin Tempe this whole time. You sly little fox. Here I was worried about you, and you are right in the middle of everything that has gone on at Morristown.

Knowing you, Mary, you must have been happier than a raccoon with his paw in the cookie jar, in the middle of that encampment.

I am most saddened to hear of the death of Uncle Henry, for I was always fond of the old gent, although sometimes I thought him crazier than a coon. You know all the Wicks are. But here I am, the pot calling the kettle black. Our family hasn't too much sanity to recommend it, either, say you what?

I do not know what you have heard of our garrison, but in the several weeks we have been here, the winter's hardships have begun again. All new soldiers coming in have to be turned away because we lack provisions and clothing for them. Most of the army horses have been sent off for lack of forage. We have now barely enough horses for orderly duty and a few for express riders.

We have no wheat flour. All the breadstuff we get is Indian cornmeal, and most of the men here haven't the faintest notion of how to make it into bread. I'm sure you would know, Mary. I often think about your buckwheat slapjacks, flowing with butter and honey.

What we do is make it into hasty pudding. As for meat, it is as scarce as wheat flour. We are, however, making the best of a dolorous situation, which became more unhappy with the distressing news brought by Major Fishbourne on the third about the mutiny of the Pennsylvania men.

We could scarce believe this. And, in the week that followed, when we weren't busy figuring out what to eat, we pondered much on what was going on. At first Washington was worrisome about the New England soldiers near West Point. We heard they are resentful and restless for want of flour, clothing, and just about everything. He was afraid they would follow the calamitous lead of the Pennsylvania men and feared a revolt of the whole army.

All we pondered, Mary, was the end of the revolution. It sounded like a most ominous mutiny, what with eleven regiments with artillery running around the countryside and no one sure yet of their purposes. We heard they were desperate and organized.

Next we heard Washington was about to set out with a small escort of horses for Philadelphia, but changed his mind, determining he was more needed here to hold a part of the army together.

He decided, I suppose, to leave the mutiny to Wayne. And from what I hear, Wayne is most capable. Then, around the fourteenth of the month, we received word of what happened.

Wayne, Butler, and Stewart followed the mutineers to Princeton, where the men took over Nassau Hall at the College of New

Jersey, and Wayne and his men took other lodging.

It was like a garrison town, I hear. The mutineers kept everyone else out. The other officers from Morristown who followed were holed up in Penny Town, where they were stewing in the juices of their own impatience.

So there are Wayne and his officers in the Hudibras Tavern and the Committee of Sergeants in Nassau Hall. And messages going back and forth between them. And Joseph Reed of the Pennsylvania Council, waiting to speechify with them about taking their officers back and returning to the army.

Whilst all this is going on, Sir Henry Clinton in New York gets word of the mutiny and sends an agent to Princeton. The agent picks up a guide, and they get into town and try to get the mutineers to repair to the Chesapeake area, where old Benedict Arnold, the only one traitor this country has managed to produce so far, can take them in hand.

But to their eternal credit, the Committee of Sergeants took the spies, forthwith, to Wayne. They woke him at four in the morning, Mary! They turned the spies over to him, saying they never had any intention of going to the British!

Then Reed haggled with the sergeants to

water down their demands. But we hear the demands were met, not exactly as the mutineers wanted but with some compromise. Lordy, how I hate compromise, Mary. But I hear tell it's a necessary commodity in this old world. Anyway, the spies were hung, and the mutineers got most of what they wanted and were given a general pardon. This was in accordance with Wayne's promise to them.

Well, Washington is now satisfied that the troops around West Point will be faithful in any emergency, and so we are back to normal again, trying to figure out how to make bread out of Indian corn. Mayhap you will send along instructions in your next letter.

On a more intimate note, I have been inoculated for the smallpox. Have this done, Mary, at the first opportunity. In all my nineteen years I have never been more afraid of anything, but it turned out to be less onerous than I thought.

I am happy to report to you that I have met here with Sergeant Will Tuttle, who is Tempe's betrothed. He hears quite often from Tempe. He is a fine fellow. And he informed me that the British have opened a campaign in the South. They have largely conquered the lower colonies and are pressing a campaign against Virginia. Tuttle thinks Washington will soon dispatch one of his best generals to that part of the country.

Well, if there is to be a campaign in the South, Mary, I want to be there. Everyone is saying we can bring this war to a victorious conclusion, now that we have the French on our side.

I do miss you and all the fine times we had in the past. Though home was not always so agreeable, I choose to look at the past fondly and to the future with hope. This country can be nothing but a better place to live after we have won our freedom, Mary. For it is a fine land, a blessed land we will win for ourselves and our children.

Stay with Tempe as long as you can. And write to me. I shall continue to return your letters whenever I can. When the war is over, I hope to have a piece of land and set up a farm. If you do not marry by then (as I hope you won't, for you are still far too young), perhaps you will oversee the running of my household for me.

Until then I remain your most devoted brother,

Abraham

Afterword

What happened to the real-life characters I wrote about in this book? I searched through records, books, and papers from the National Historical Park at Morristown, the Local History and Genealogy Department at The Joint Free Public Library of Morristown and Morris Township, and the Suffolk County Historical Society in Long Island. Trying to find out what happened to someone who lived over two hundred years ago is not easy. But all these historians shared their books, papers, and genealogical charts with me. Sometimes I had to study them for hours to find pieces of information that, when pieced together with what I had, would make a more complete picture. Sometimes I was surprised and delighted to make a discovery such as the fact that Mary Blachley and Doctor Ebenezer Blachley's grandson married Tempe Wick's daughter Mary.

Many times, however, I ran into dead ends. I could not find the first names of Mary Cooper's (our narrator) two husbands or how long Mary lived. I made some connections from genealogical charts, such as the fact that Mary Cooper's second husband had the same last name as the family her brothers Abraham and Nathan married into. But I can only assume, given the limitations of the times, when people did not venture far from home and associated mostly with family and immediate friends, that she married into the same family.

So there are many empty spaces in my findings, many unanswered questions. But that is always the case when one chooses to pursue history. Yet I find it extremely satisfying and I never cease to be amazed at the fact that, if one bothers to go to libraries, historical societies, and historical shrines, one can learn a great deal. It is all there, waiting to be discovered. And the historians, curators, and librarians who keep and guard this material are always more than eager to share it.

So here, to the best of my knowledge, is what happened to the real-life characters.

Mary Cooper (1769–?), *our narrator:* Mary married twice. Her first husband's name was Sayre, the second's was Wills. No dates are given for the marriages and there are no first names of the husbands. But genealogy charts showed me that Mary's Aunt Elizabeth, who was her father's sister (and not a character in the book) married a man named Joshua Sayre, who was a descendant of Thomas Sayre, who was a founder of Southampton, New York. Thus Mary could have married her first cousin, for her Aunt Elizabeth and Uncle Joshua had twelve children— Sarah, Joshua, Edith, Paul, Silas, Caleb, Thomas, Eunice, William, Enoch, Rufas, and Ruth.

Although people seldom if ever divorced in those days, husbands and wives married quite soon after losing a mate to death. Mary's second husband's name was Wills. And I discovered that her beloved older brother Abraham married a woman named Anna Wills. Their brother Nathan was married to Elizabeth Wills, Anna's sister. Could Mary have married into the same Wills family for her second marriage?

No, Mary did not marry Lieutenant Enos Reeves. Although he wrote a "letter-book"— which was published in 1897 by a descendant— saying he had spent "many agreeable evenings at the Wicks'," his "romance" with Mary Cooper is of my own making.

Abraham Cooper (1762–1818), *Mary's older brother:* There were so many Abraham Coopers listed as serving in the Continental Army that I could not determine where he actually served. But I found an Abraham Cooper (Captain) who is listed as serving from 1777 to 1781 and who received a pension from the government in 1818 for fighting in the revolution.

Abraham's father, Nathan, left him land in Morris County. Nathan Cooper's will says, "To son, Abraham, land bought of Jabesh Mapes Swayzee at Black River, also one-half of land bought of Daniel Steward at Black River."

Abraham married Anna Wills, and they had eleven children—Beulah, Nathan, Lucetta, Jane, Nancy, Phoebe Ann, Lydia, David, William, Joseph, and Aaron.

Henry Wick (1737–1781), *Tempe's older brother, who, in my story, pretended to be lunatic:* In actuality, Henry was lunatic. His mother, Mary's, will, written in 1786, states that "our son Henry by unknown causes became lunatic and became exceedingly troublesome and expensive whilst in his lifetime."

The will of Henry Wick, his father, indicates that his father did indeed leave him five shillings. From this information I made up my story about Mary Cooper going after the five shillings from Doctor Leddell. In fact, by that time Henry had been lost to the family.

Church records indicate that Henry married an Elizabeth Cooper. Was she from the same Cooper family as his mother? I don't know. But

Henry and Elizabeth had two children—Mary and Chloe. Henry's mother, Mary, remembered these children in her will. And Chloe Wick married a Tuttle. (This is the name of the man whom Tempe Wick married.)

Henry Wick (1707–1781), *Tempe's father:* Although Henry Wick was born on Long Island, he moved to Morris County in 1748. He allowed General Washington's army to encamp on his land in the winter of 1779–1780 because he was a Patriot and because he knew the soldiers would clear his land of trees to make their huts. He also allowed part of his home to be used for Continental Army officers and allowed the army to return again for the winter of 1780–1781. He did, indeed, die of pleurisy just before the mutiny.

Henry married Mary Cooper in 1735. Since wealth in the eighteenth century was measured by land, farmer Henry Wick was "moderately rich," according to a handbook written by Morristown National Historical Park. The handbook tells us that Henry and his wife Mary "constructed and occupied this house in 1750. In the next three decades the Wick holdings expanded to 1,400 acres of mostly undeveloped land used for lumber. On the cleared land the Wicks grew corn, winter wheat, buckwheat, oats, and rye, and had orchards for apples. Cows, horses, swine, geese, chickens, and other livestock occupied the barnyard. By 1777 the house had become known as Wick Hall, which suggests it was considered to be a very substantial home and not just a farmhouse."

Mary Wick (1718–1787), *Tempe's mother and "Aunt Mary" to Mary Cooper:* After Mary Wick's husband died and willed her the farm, she and Tempe ran it and, in spite of hard times, increased the value of their estate. In her will of 1786, she left to her son Henry's daughter Mary a parcel of land "beginning at the white oak stump standing in the line of Peter Kemble's house near the great road ending from Mendham to Chatham, where the Pennsylvania Line of huts intersected the Kemble's line."

She gave to Henry's daughter Chloe twenty-five pounds. She wrote that since Henry's wife, Elizabeth, had "left his bed and board and has had children since, there is no apparent reason that they should be the children of our son's body. Nevertheless, I do give and bequeath them five shillings each, to make up for what I would choose to give Henry, who is now deceased."

She left to her daughter Mary Blachley another parcel of land and to Mary's children—Absalom, Hannah, Jude, Phoebe, and Temperance

—fifty pounds each. She gave to her daughter Phoebe Leddell a parcel of land and fifty pounds each to Phoebe's daughters, Temperance and Elizabeth.

To Tempe Wick she gave the house, cows, horses, sheep, hogs, farm utensils, furniture, wearing apparel, and her public securities. Among the many animals she willed to Tempe was "one white horse." I take this to be Colonel. In my story I had Colonel given to Tempe by her father to make him even more important to her because her father had just died. Mary Wick made her trusty friend Ebenezer Drake and Tempe joint executors of her estate.

Doctor William Leddell (1749–1827), *Tempe Wick's brother-in-law, to whom Mary Cooper went to get Henry's five shillings in my story:* It is written of William Leddell in Morristown National Historical Park research papers that "He frequently ran afoul of the law, ran an unauthorized mint in his house for a time, attempted to sell wholesale imported rum without a license in 1779, [was] charged twice with assault and battery in 1788 and 1789, and [was] charged with adultery with one Hannah Sturgis in July 1800." I built the character of Will Leddell on these facts.

Research also tells us: "He studied medicine with his brother-in-law, Dr. Ebenezer Blachley, and became a good doctor and skilled botanist and is considered an upstanding and distinguished man, despite his faults."

Leddell was a private in the American Revolution, a major in the Whiskey Rebellion of 1794, and a Captain of Cavalry in the War of 1812. He is also said to have been one of the first sheriffs of Morris County.

Will Tuttle (1760–1836), *betrothed to Tempe Wick in my story:* Indeed, Will Tuttle served at Morristown during the terrible winter of 1779–1780. And in the winter of 1780–1781 he was at New Windsor in New York State with General Washington. I like to think Will met Tempe that first winter and was corresponding with her as the book opens. Because they did, indeed, marry in 1788.

Tuttle enlisted in April 1777 and served honorably in the revolution. In the 3rd New Jersey Regiment he was in the battles of Brandywine and Germantown in Pennsylvania and in Elizabethtown, New Jersey, where he suffered a wound in his right arm. He was also in the battles of Monmouth and Springfield. After serving under Captain Joseph Anderson in the 1st New Jersey at Yorktown, Virginia, in the fall of 1781, where he acted as sergeant-major under General

Gilbert du Motier, Marquis de Lafayette, he was discharged with the rank of lieutenant.

In June 1828 Tuttle was given a pension by the United States government for his army service. An excerpt from the book *Washington in Morris County, New Jersey*, published in *The Historical Magazine*, June 1871, says this about Tuttle: "From the conclusion of the war until his death in 1836, he resided either on the Wick Farm or in the immediate vicinity. Very often he would go over the ground, especially with his young relatives, pointing out the precise spots occupied by different troops and filling up hours with thrilling anecdotes connected with that winter, but these conversations no one was at the pains to record and now they are hopelessly gone."

This was written by the Rev. Joseph F. Tuttle. It is not certain if he was a relative. He cannot be a direct descendant of Will Tuttle and Tempe Wick, because their two sons died at an early age.

Lieutenant Enos Reeves (?–1807) *of the Pennsylvania Line, who visited frequently at the Wick house and formed a friendship with Mary:* Reeves was mustered out of the service as a brevit captain (*brevit* means honorary and is a title given for meritorious service) after peace was declared in 1783.

He had fought in the Southern campaign and went back to South Carolina, where he had served, and, on December 21, 1784, married Amy Légaire, whose acquaintance he had made while in the army in that area.

There are many extracts from his notes in Morristown National Historical Park records. These little bits of information were very helpful to me when I formed my story. I only know he was serving at Morristown in 1781 and was often at the Wick house. His romance with Mary I made up. Reeves's notes, published in 1897 in the *Pennsylvania Magazine of History and Biography*, were contributed by a man named John B. Reeves, who was probably a descendant, from Charleston, South Carolina. I like to think Enos went back to the Wick household after the mutiny was over and visited again.

Jeremiah Levering and **David Hamilton Morris,** *friends of Mary Cooper's, in my story:* These two boys really served in the Continental Army, according to *Mutiny in January* by Carl Van Doren (Viking Press, New York, 1943). Many of the soldiers in camp that year were children. Jeremiah Levering was enlisted for three years in the artillery by the time this story opens. He was then only fourteen or fifteen. Since he was so undersized, the soldiers did not allow him or his friend David Hamilton Morris, who was only twelve, to carry muskets.

Levering had been homeless, a waif picked up by the soldiers and put through the process of enlistment so they could give him a home and feed and clothe him. Morris, at twelve, had already been in the army for a year, put there by his widowed mother, who lived near Morristown and probably could not afford to take care of him. She put him in the charge of Captain James Crystie, for whom Morris acted as waiter, or servant. Many other young boys who voluntarily enlisted as soldiers served officers in this same way.

I used these two boys as Mary's friends. After the mutiny, when the officers under Wayne were ordered to "Take horse and go to Penny Town"—today known as Pennington—I had Levering and Morris go with the officers, since they served them. Such being the case, they probably stayed with their officers for the rest of the war.

General Anthony Wayne (1745–1797), *commander of the Pennsylvania Line, who helped to put down the mutiny of American troops at Morristown:* Little more than a month after Wayne brought the mutiny of the Pennsylvania Line to a happy conclusion in Trenton, New Jersey, he was ordered to take what was left of the Line to Virginia to assist the Marquis de Lafayette in the Southern campaign, for the revolution had now moved to the south. On September 25, 1781, Wayne was summoned to Lafayette's headquarters in Williamsburg, Virginia, and was shot by overzealous sentries while entering the French camp. It was his fifth wound of the war, a leg wound that in later years he said turned to gout. But he was soon back on his feet, limping, in time for the Battle of Yorktown.

After the British surrendered to the Americans at Yorktown on October 19, 1781, Wayne stayed in the South for a while to help General Nathanael Greene in battles where the British held on. When the British finally left Charleston, South Carolina, in December 1782, Wayne went to Georgia to make peace with the Creek and Cherokee Indians.

He left the army in 1783, went home, and was elected to his old seat in the Pennsylvania Legislature, where one of his accomplishments was to establish the theater in Philadelphia, where it had always been prohibited by the Quakers.

But in April 1792 he accepted command of the United States Army. George Washington was now president and the current war was against the Indians who were disturbing farmers on the frontier. Serving in the Northwest (Ohio), Wayne brought peace to the frontier.

His wife, Polly, had died. His daughter was married; his son, studying law. He was a grandfather. He came home to Philadelphia in February 1796, to be greeted as a hero.

Mary Vining was waiting for him. He was now 51, she was 39, and they courted for six months. Then President Washington called again. The British were about to surrender the Northwest forts and he wanted Wayne to handle negotiations. In a handsome new uniform, Wayne left again to serve, completed his mission for President Washington, and was hurrying home to marry Mary Vining when illness struck. He was aboard the sloop *Detroit*, coming down Lake Erie, when his leg, which had continued to bother him, swelled and he became very weak. He said it was "the gout," probably trouble from an old leg wound. He died on the sloop, never seeing home again.

He was given many nicknames over the years, but the one that stuck in the history books is Mad Anthony Wayne. That name was given to him by Jemy the Rover, his old friend the spy.

Tempe Wick (1758–1822), *about whom legend grew because of the way she is alleged to have hidden her horse in her house to keep soldiers from stealing* *him:* Tempe lived with her mother until Mary Wick died in July of 1787. Records show that Tempe married Will Tuttle in 1788—the year after her mother's death—at thirty years of age. That is late for a young woman of that era, and she would have been considered an "old maid" already. But the war and the fact that Tempe cared for her mother may have influenced her decision to postpone marriage. National Park records—in this case from the Morristown Presbyterian Church—say that "she and William probably lived on the farm until 1798, when they bought property and built a house on South Street." I presume this is in Morristown also.

Tempe and Will had five children—William, who died at age 11 of dysentery; Mary Cooper, who married the grandson of Tempe's older sister Mary; Delia Johnston; Caroline Wickham, who died at age 21; and Henry Wick, who died at age one.

Morristown Presbyterian Church records also say: "Died in this town on the 26th of April, 1822, Mrs. Tempe, consort of Capt. Wm. Tuttle, at age 63 years. Will be sold at Public Vendue on Sat. Oct. 19th at 10 o'clock at the late residence of Mrs. Tempe Tuttle: A variety of articles of household and kitchen furniture, consisting of beds, tables, chairs, etc., one second-hand riding chair, one wagon, three cows, one hog, etc."

And so ends our beautiful and spirited Tempe, whom the public still ask about today when they visit Morristown National Historical Park. She was buried in the Tuttle vault of the first Presbyterian Church in Morristown. The remains of the vault were later removed to Evergreen Cemetery in Morristown.

The Wick Farm: Tempe's home stands to this day on the grounds of Morristown National Historical Park, and you may visit it if you wish.

When Tempe and Will moved from it in 1798, it was rented but remained in the family until 1871, when it was sold to Mason Loomis. After Morristown National Historical Park was established in 1933, the National Park Service researched the house in order to restore it to its eighteenth-century condition. The furnishings in the house today are based on inventories taken after the deaths of Henry and Mary Wick, who built it. The outbuildings have been reconstructed. The kitchen garden and orchard have also been researched and restored as near as possible to their original state.

Author's Note

Of all the historical novels I have written, I have enjoyed this one most of all. Perhaps because I had so much material to work with, and making the Wick and Cooper families come alive was a marvelous challenge.

Ironically, this is the one book I have written that was not born of my need to know. The idea of doing a book based on the mythical story of Tempe Wick was not mine. I had been to Morristown National Historical Park many times, mostly in the company of the Brigade of the American Revolution, with which my family and I did so many wonderful reenactments during and after the Bicentennial years. Many times I accompanied my son, Ron, to this park when he took part in the annual St. Patrick's Day celebrations and encampments when he was in high school. I was even in the Wick house (once in eighteenth-century dress).

But I never made the connection to writing a novel. Like everyone else who grew up in New Jersey, I knew the myth of Tempe Wick, the girl who hid her horse in the house to keep him from being stolen by soldiers. But I knew the story as just that: a tale told over the years that was now well established as a part of New Jersey folklore.

Perhaps because I saw it that way, I shied away even from thinking of doing such a book. When my literary agent, Joanna Cole of the Elaine Markson Literary Agency in New York, asked if I wanted to do such a book for Harcourt Brace Jovanovich as part of their Great Episodes series, I said no. I couldn't do that. For two reasons, first because the series was directed at a younger age group than I was accustomed to writing for and, second, because—"How am I going to make a whole book out of a myth about a girl who hid her horse in her house?"

Then Joanna Cole sent me one of the published books from the series, and I read it and decided it was not only well written and accurate, but it did not talk down to children. So I said yes.

But first I made a trip, again, to Morristown National Historical Park and started asking the very patient staff there questions about Tempe Wick.

Much to my surprise, they were ready for me. And for anybody else who asks about her. Because, they explained, that's what most people ask about when they come to the park. They ask about the girl who hid her horse in the house.

I am familiar enough with American history by now to know that it is the myths rather than the facts that remain in people's minds. They get the facts mixed up. The same people who may visit Valley Forge National Historical Park in Pennsylvania and ask a National Park staffer—"Isn't this the place where Martha told George to let them eat cake?"—those same people will get the place and era and names correct when it comes to myths.

So the staff at Morristown were ready for me, as they are ready for everyone who asks about Tempe Wick instead of asking how General George Washington's army survived that terrible winter of 1779–1780.

And since the National Park deals only in historical facts, they prepared papers on Tempe Wick—after doing as much research as they could on the family. They gave me those papers, as they give them out to others who ask about Tempe. It is their "position" on the myth. That position is that "as far as current scholarship can tell, the story of Tempe and her horse is merely a legend. The first written version did not appear until ninety-six years after the supposed event. When the version appeared in 1876, America was celebrating the centennial of the American Revolution. Many popular but inaccurate historical accounts appeared at this time.

"In 1876, Tempe Wick had been dead for 54 years. Her husband and children were all dead as well. Joseph F. Tuttle, the first author of the horse story *The Annals of Morris County, 1876*, gives no indication where he gets the story from. By the time Andrew M. Sherman introduces his mutiny version of the horse story, 124 years have passed since the mutiny. Like Tuttle, he also fails to give his sources."

And so the National Park paper reads. And goes on: "The only contemporary account that mentions Tempe and the mutiny is the letters of Lieutenant Enos Reeves of the Pennsylvania line. Reeves stays with Dr. Leddell and visits the Wicks socially on a number of occasions. After the mutiny, on January 6, 1781, Reeves wrote that the night before '. . . About one o'clock I returned from camp to the Doctor's, where I found the family up, with the addition of Mrs. Wick and her agreeable daughter, almost frightened out of their lives, as some of the mutineers made their appearance around their house and insisted on showing them where to find horses.'" (Although Reeves has Mrs. Wick and Tempe at Dr. Leddell's house, other accounts have Tempe riding to fetch Leddell when her horse is almost stolen.)

"Later," the paper goes on, "Reeves's horse is stolen. However, he makes no mention of Tempe hiding her horse. It would seem logical that Tempe would mention such an unusual occurrence to someone like Reeves who she was friendly with. Since Reeves is mentioning the Wicks and horses, one could safely assume if he heard the story he would have mentioned it in his letters, but he does not.

"Rangers in the Wick House hear many other variations on the story. The horse is being hidden from: the British, Hessians, Tories, hungry American soldiers, soldiers from Bucks County, or officers who want it for the army. The horse has been hidden: in the bedroom, in the bed or under it, in the attic or cellar, under the floorboards, and even in the well. The horse has spent from three hours to a year hidden in the house. Perhaps you have heard another version to add to our collection?"

Thus the Morristown National Historical Park staff give us their disclaimer, which is right and proper, as it should be from people concerned with dispensing historical facts. In another paper they give some historical facts about

Tempe—when she was born, facts about her family, whom she married, and when she died. They again give two versions of the horse story. One version has the event happening in the spring of 1780, the other in January of 1781.

I decided to go with the January 1, 1781, version of the myth. It was the more interesting since it involved the mutiny of the Pennsylvania Line and General Anthony Wayne and a period of our history we seldom hear about.

Once I got into the research, of course, I was delighted to find, in the will of Mary Wick, that her son Henry was "lunatic." Even more delighted to find, in unappealing old genealogical charts, that Tempe's brother-in-law Doctor Will Leddell was accused of "selling rum without a license and adultery." My plot began to take shape when I found out that Tempe's grandfather John Wick was a "local character" on Long Island suspected of murder and that local fishermen claimed to have seen "the devil carrying his black soul out to sea the night he died."

Here is the stuff of which real families are made, I told myself. Here are enough skeletons in the closet to satisfy any novelist.

Moreover, I found that Tempe eventually married Will Tuttle, who was stationed at New Windsor, New York, with General Washington in 1781—yet he served at Morristown the year before. Wonderful! She could be "betrothed" to Will yet still free to be a fetching and saucy and attractive and feisty young woman.

Most of the characters I used actually lived at one time. Only the camp followers were made up by me. And, indeed, there were so many camp followers at Morristown at the time, and they were so hungry, I feel I have not gone far astray. Molly and Adam and little Button McCormick are fictional, but then there were many like them at the time. Everyone else was taken from history.

In dealing with the real people who once lived, I studied them and tried to keep as much to their characters as I could. I admire them all very much, especially Anthony Wayne.

No, current scholarship cannot verify the myth of Tempe Wick. But there was, in January of 1781 at Morristown, a mutiny of the Pennsylvania Line. Soldiers were looking for horses. A young girl named Tempe rode her white horse about her father's farm in full view of the soldiers, who just might have cast envious eyes at him. She could have been very pretty. She did have a young cousin named Mary Cooper who could have been visiting. Henry Wick, who had owned the farm, had, indeed, just died. His wife, Mary, was getting on in years. Lieutenant Reeves did come visiting.

The soldiers were cold, freezing, underpaid, and resentful, and they did revolt. Peter Kemble did own the fine plantation where General Anthony Wayne (vain but accomplished, handsome and daring and capable, hot of temper yet calm under fire, wearing white lace at his throat and never forgetting his courtly manners) made his quarters.

There were boy-soldiers named Morris and Levering, hungry camp followers, a Doctor Will Leddell not far away who was a bit of a rogue. As well as Tempe's sisters, Mary and Phoebe.

I hope you like my story. But always remember—it is fiction. There are many books you can read to find out about the real encampments at Morristown and the mutiny of the Pennsylvania Line.

Ann Rinaldi
May 21, 1990

Bibliography

The books and papers I found indispensable when writing this novel are herein listed, with my heartfelt thanks to the authors, historians, and researchers who put them together and to the staff of Morristown National Historical Park for sharing their research with me.

Unpublished Papers

Genealogical charts of the families of Wick, Cooper, and Leddell from Morristown Presbyterian Church records and from research at the Morristown National Historical Park.

Morristown Encampment Chronology, courtesy of Morristown National Historical Park.

The wills of Henry and Mary Wick, courtesy of Morristown National Historical Park.

Published Papers

Observations on Mr. Wick's Reputation, from the Southampton Press, Long Island, September

19, 1985. Courtesy of Morristown National Historical Park.

Extracts from *The Letter-Books of Lieutenant Enos Reeves*, by John B. Reeves, Charleston, South Carolina, in *The Pennsylvania Magazine of History and Biography*, Vol. XXI, Philadelphia, 1897.

Extract from "The Wick House and Its Historical Environment," *American History Magazine*, Vol. 4, No. 3, May 1909.

Extract from Andrew M. Sherman's *Historic Morristown, N.J.: The Story of Its First Century*, Howard Publishing Company, Morristown, N.J.

Books

Fast, Howard. *The Call of Fife and Drum, Three Novels of the Revolution*. Secaucus, N.J.: Citadel Press, 1987.

Martin, J. P. *Private Yankee Doodle*, edited by George F. Scheer. Acorn Press, 1979.

Smith, Samuel Stelle. *Winter at Morristown, 1779–1780, The Darkest Hour*. Monmouth Beach, N.J.: Philip Freneau Press, 1979.

Sprigg, June. *Domestick Beings*. New York: Alfred A. Knopf, 1984.

Trussell, John B., Jr. *The Pennsylvania Line, Regimental Organization and Operations, 1776–1783*.

Harrisburg, Pa.: Pennsylvania Historical and Museum Commission, 1977.

Tucker, Glenn. *Mad Anthony Wayne and the New Nation.* Harrisburg, Pa.: Stackpole Books, 1973.

Van Doren, Carl. *Mutiny in January.* New York: Viking Press, 1943.

Pamphlets

Burt, Leah S. *The Farm & Garden of Henry Wick.* Morristown, N.J.: Morristown National Historical Park.

Morristown, A History and Guide. Washington, D.C.: Morristown National Historical Park, Division of Publications, U.S. Department of the Interior, 1983.

READER CHAT PAGE

1. Civil wars divide families. How has it divided the families in this story?

2. Abraham tells Mary that compromise is a necessary commodity, but not all the characters agree. How do Mary, Tempe, and General Wayne feel about compromise? How do you feel about it? When should you compromise, and when should you stand firm?

3. What does Mary mean when she says that everyone is part and parcel of the whole of their life experiences? In what ways have your life experiences determined who you are now?

4. Mary tells Henry, "Sometimes it helps to air old ills in the sunlight." What does she mean?

5. Tempe believes that a person's motives do not matter as much as their actions. Do you think one is more important than the other? Why?

6. In what ways might Henry's living as a lunatic make his life easier? Harder?

7. Abraham advises Mary that "those closest to the problem cannot see the solution." Do you think this is true? Who can you turn to when you have a problem?

8. In his letter to Mary, Abraham says, "I choose to look at the past fondly and to the future with hope." Why might he choose to see things this way? How should he handle his unhappy memories?

About the Author

Ann Rinaldi is an award-winning author best known for bringing history vividly to life. Among her books for Harcourt are *The Coffin Quilt: The Feud between the Hatfields and the McCoys*, an ABA's Pick of the Lists, and *The Staircase*, a New York Public Library Book for the Teen Age.

A self-made writer, Ms. Rinaldi never attended college but learned her craft through reading and writing. As a columnist for twenty-one years at *The Trentonian* in New Jersey, she learned the art of finding a good story, capturing it in words, and meeting a deadline.

Ms. Rinaldi attributes her interest in history to her son, who enlisted her to take part in historical reenactments up and down the East Coast, where she cooked the food, made the clothing, and learned about the dances, songs, and lifestyles that prevailed in eighteenth-century America.

Ann Rinaldi has two grown children and lives with her husband in central New Jersey.

Have you read these
Great Episodes paperbacks?

SHERRY GARLAND

Indio

KRISTIANA GREGORY

Earthquake at Dawn

Jenny of the Tetons

The Legend of Jimmy Spoon

LEN HILTS

Quanah Parker:
Warrior for Freedom,
Ambassador for Peace

DOROTHEA JENSEN

The Riddle of Penncroft Farm

JACKIE FRENCH KOLLER

The Primrose Way

CAROLYN MEYER

Where the Broken Heart
Still Beats: The Story
of Cynthia Ann Parker

SEYMOUR REIT

Behind Rebel Lines:
The Incredible Story of
Emma Edmonds, Civil War Spy

Guns for General Washington:
A Story of the American
Revolution

ANN RINALDI

An Acquaintance with Darkness

A Break with Charity: A Story
about the Salem Witch Trials

Cast Two Shadows:
The American Revolution
in the South

The Coffin Quilt:
The Feud between the
Hatfields and the McCoys

The Fifth of March:
A Story of the Boston Massacre

Finishing Becca:
A Story about Peggy Shippen
and Benedict Arnold

Hang a Thousand Trees with
Ribbons: The Story of
Phillis Wheatley

The Secret of Sarah Revere

The Staircase

ROLAND SMITH

The Captain's Dog: My Journey
with the Lewis and Clark Tribe

THEODORE TAYLOR

Air Raid—Pearl Harbor!:
The Story of December 7, 1941